sainted
in error

SUBPLOT
an imprint of Mascot Books

www.mascotbooks.com

sainted in error

Cover design by Luisa Fuentes

For more information, please contact:
Mascot Books
620 Herndon Parkway, Suite 320
Herndon, VA 20170
info@mascotbooks.com

Library of Congress Control Number: 2021907894

CPSIA Code: PRV0821A
ISBN-13: 978-1-64543-910-3

Printed in the United States

For the people I love whose lives have been touched

by mental illness.

sainted
in error
a novel

glenda winders

SUBPLOT
an imprint of Mascot Books

1

What do you wear when you testify against your best friend as she goes on trial for murder? It's ridiculous that I'm so anxious over such a minuscule and trivial part of this whole nightmare, but yes, I care how I'll look up there on the witness stand as she stares at me from the defense table—or looks away and refuses to acknowledge that I am there. I read somewhere that people tend to remember what they were wearing at the most important moments in their lives, but this will be one outfit I'll want to get rid of as soon as I wear it, erase it from my memory and never have to think about it again.

Of course I remember the ivory satin gown—floor length, no train—I wore when I finally got married. And the hideous purple and yellow flowered maternity dress I wore home from the hospital after Todd was born, bitter because I couldn't wear the jeans and white shirt I had packed, believing I'd be a size seven and 110 pounds again immediately after I'd given birth. The zipper on them wouldn't close for another month, and when Mae was born

1

two years later, I didn't even try, going home instead in the same maternity jeans and ugly green tent-like top I had been wearing when I realized labor had begun.

I remember what I was wearing when I got the job with the paper. It was a rust-and-teal plaid skirt, a teal blouse—oxford cloth—and a rust corduroy jacket. With it I carried a big leather bag filled with notebooks and pens that I thought made me seem more serious than a small clutch with just my comb and lipstick would have. If I'd known then what trauma would come with that job, I'm not sure I would have bothered. It turns out there are several ensemble-related memories I could do without.

I wore tan pants and a chocolate-brown sweater the first time I went out with Peter. It poured down rain that night, and we got soaking wet as we ran from the auditorium where we had heard a lecture on French filmmaking to his car, parked in a far corner of the lot. We gave up our plan of going out for a drink and went instead to his nearby house so I could slip out of my clothes and put them into his dryer before I froze. I remember changing into a red plaid flannel bathrobe that hung from a hook on his bathroom door and sipping a glass of brandy awkwardly with him while we waited for what seemed like hours for the clothes to tumble around and around.

Funny. He has always had a red plaid flannel bathrobe hanging on the back of the bathroom door—not the same one, of course.

After we were married I spent hours browsing in lingerie stores for lacy underpants and nightgowns to complement my fair skin and red hair. That was in the '80s, when we were all having our colors done, and I had learned that shades of peach and gold and salmon were the ones that made me look the best. For a while I foolishly thought I had to compete with the beautiful women with whom Peter worked every day, and I wasn't taking any chances.

I gave away the taupe suit I wore to my mother's funeral. It had been my favorite, but after that I repeatedly pushed it to the back of the closet because it reminded me of the pain of losing her so unexpectedly, of standing by an open grave between my father and my brother, gripping both of their hands, all of us in a state of disbelief. Eventually I gave up and put it in the bag for the local women's shelter. Maybe somebody staying there wore it to an interview and landed a job. I like to think that's what happened.

So back to this trial. Should I wear something I love to give me the confidence I'll need for the hardest thing I've ever had to do in my life, or something I no longer care about so that it can join the taupe suit in the cemetery of clothes that recall too many bad memories to ever be worn again? Should I have bought something black, my sallow skin tones notwithstanding, or would that be too hopeless? Is green too cheerful and optimistic? Brown too somber and dull? A suit to show I mean business—or maybe pants? Maybe it should be knit so it will pack easily into my suitcase and when my testimony is over I can wear it home on the plane before I donate it, too.

I saw her on television right after it happened. She was being arraigned, and she wore a blue coverall with some numbers sewn on a patch over one breast pocket, but my stepson, Jack, who is an attorney now, says they'll let her dress in her own clothes for the trial. I wonder what she'll wear and if her lawyer is giving her outfit as much thought as I'm giving mine. If he isn't, he should be. These things matter to people. The jurors could change their minds over silliness like this.

Maybe he's instructing her to appear too attractive and well-groomed ever to have purposely pulled a trigger and taken another person's life. Maybe they'll decide on a simple gray dress with long sleeves and an innocent touch of lace at the throat, like the one my grandmother was buried in, one last-ditch attempt to convince the jury that she's a harmless middle-aged matron who just had a moment of temporary insanity. In fact, she will most likely be as buried in the living hell of a women's prison somewhere as my grandmother is in the Santa Rosa Memorial Park.

I'll only be in the courtroom once. I didn't want to go at all, although I knew I'd have to because of the twisted set of circumstances that brought us to this point in the first place. The prosecuting attorney said he understands the grief I have suffered and promises I'll only be called on once. If they need anything more from me, he said, they'll take a deposition so I don't have to face it all again. They're sorry to put me through it, he told me, but surely I understand that my testimony as an eyewitness is crucial.

And so, if she goes to prison for the rest of her life, which seems inevitable, what I wear to her trial will be the last thing she'll ever see me in. These events have so changed the relationship between us that I can't under any circumstances imagine myself ever traveling to a prison where the two of us would sit on opposite sides of a window and speak into telephones as if we were still best friends and separated by several states. Once my testimony is over, I never want to see her again.

If she is found guilty, and surely she will be since seven other people besides me actually saw her take the gun out of her handbag, close her eyes tight, and fire, will she remember what I had on the day I helped to put her away? Will she lie in her iron bunk as we age simultaneously and picture me always as I'll look in the courtroom? Will she remember what she wore each day as she sat at the defense table with her attorney and watched the chances of her freedom dwindle? And when it's over and they outfit her in the overalls again, what will happen to the suits and dresses, the blue jeans, bathrobes, and evening clothes from which she still, for these last few days, has a choice? Will they be donated, too, so that some unsuspecting woman can wear them to work or to a party, proud of the designer labels and unaware that she is clothed in the castoffs of a convicted killer?

How will she cope with the memories of summers spent in bathing suits and capri pants, of the long skirts she wore when she and Richard gave their famous cocktail parties, of tasteful and ever-more-expensive dresses and jackets worn to chair meetings and while sitting on boards as he climbed in his profession and she followed along? If she is sentenced to life, she will spend the remainder of her days in prison clothes and never again have the luxury of standing in front of her closet as I am today and making a simple decision about what to wear.

2

You never know which of the hundreds of little choices you make every day will be one that will end up shaping your life—whether for better or worse. The freeway exit where you get off to look for a hotel, the one apartment you choose to rent from the three or four equally as close to your office, the doctor you select online. Will a truck T-bone you at the bottom of the exit ramp, or will your new neighbor give you the job of your dreams? Will the doctor solve your problem or make it worse? You acknowledge and make peace with the big decisions, like your major in college and whom you marry—although how you met that person was probably the outcome of some random, spontaneous urge to go to a party or call the owner of a lost dog. But it's the little ones that will get you. If it turns out well, you'll sing out merrily about synchronicity, but if it goes the other direction, you may forever wish it could be undone. In some ways life seems like one big crapshoot.

In my case it was a computer that made the decision that would color so much of my life, spinning and whirring and spitting out the card that matched me with my freshman roommate at UCLA, Cynthia Morgan.

It was hot and smoggy the day we moved into the dorm in 1973. My parents and I drove down from Santa Rosa in one day, leaving at five in the morning and stopping just once at a drive-in restaurant for hamburgers at lunchtime. Mom wanted to leave the day before and stay overnight somewhere along the way, but Dad didn't want to leave my clothes and records and my precious birthday stereo in the car overnight, so there we were, dodging coat hangers and boxes of clothing and stuffed animals, eating our sandwiches in the hot car in order to protect my few modest belongings.

I hadn't yet met Cynthia, but we had written a couple of letters over the summer at the suggestion of an orientation volunteer who sent us each other's addresses. From what I could tell we were nothing alike, but my mother, always the optimist, said our differences would make my college experience just that much more rich and interesting. Cynthia was an only child, and she had graduated from a private school in La Jolla. Her mother had died when she was in middle school, and she lived with her father, who was a gynecologist. A housekeeper and her gardener husband who rounded out the household lived in the guest house behind their ocean-view home. Cynthia's hobbies were drawing, horseback riding, and sailing. For graduation her father sent her and a friend on a cruise down the Mexican Riviera. She especially liked Cabo San Lucas.

The chronology of my life bore no resemblance to Cynthia's. I grew up on a dairy farm with my parents and my brother, Bradley, who was three years younger than I was. We weren't exactly poor, but there was no guest house and no housekeeper to live in it if there had been. I had never thought to organize what I did into the category of "hobbies," but I liked to read and listen to music. I had written some stories that were published in the school paper and worked on the yearbook staff my senior year. For graduation my parents gave me the suitcases that were packed in the trunk of the car when we pulled into the loading zone in front of Hedrick Hall. It would be years before I would take them to Cabo.

The air conditioner in the car had conked out two days before the trip and there was no time to get it fixed, so when I finally climbed out in Los Angeles my T-shirt was damp and wrinkled, and the hair I had set hopefully on jumbo rollers the night before had reverted to its natural state of uncontrollable frizz. My face was red. The eye makeup I believed transformed my small, close-set eyes into something you could actually locate on my face had sweat away, leaving black smudges that made it look as though I had been beaten up. My parents, terminally cheerful in their enthusiasm about my being the first child in our family to go to college, could hardly wait to meet my roommate.

I prayed she wasn't there yet, but of course she was, since their trip had been only two hours instead of nine. She was already in the cramped room that would be our home, wearing a white shirt with the sleeves rolled up, cutoffs, and strappy leather sandals—expensive, I could tell—with a delicate gold chain fastened around one ankle. Her smooth, pedicured feet made me think she had never gone barefoot in her life and also made me grateful that I had worn sneakers. She had selected the bed and desk closest to the window, which gave me a pang of regret, and she was lining up books on her shelf when we came through the door. For a moment her back was to us, and all I saw was poker-straight, luxurious deep-brown hair I would have died for.

Then she turned around and smiled. Her bangs were wispy, her face tan, her eyes wide and dark. Her teeth were perfect and white except that one of her front ones overlapped the other just the tiniest bit. It made her feel a little self-conscious, she told me when we knew each other better, but it hadn't been a big enough deal to get braces, even though her family could clearly have afforded them. I thought it gave her character, and Richard told me, years later, that he had found it so sexy it almost drove him crazy when he first met her.

"All I could think about was kissing that mouth," he told me then. "It was like she was a mouth with a person attached."

He shook his head. By that time he had stopped wanting to kiss Cynthia ever again, and we were having a drink together in a bar near my house because he wanted to tell me his side.

While I was admiring Cynthia and gushing about her cute bedspread and apologizing for my appearance, our fathers were shaking hands and introducing themselves. Her father wore a white shirt and a tie, despite its being a hot Sunday afternoon.

"I've got to stop at the hospital and make rounds on the way back into town," he explained, as if he needed to apologize for what he had on to my father, who wore jeans, work boots, and a short-sleeved red plaid shirt. Even as he said it he was picking up the jacket that lay across the bed that now by default would be mine and moving toward the door like he couldn't wait to get away. It seemed as if now that he had had a look at us and we passed inspection, he was free to go.

"What about dinner, Daddy?" Cynthia asked him. Her smile disappeared and little frown lines appeared between her eyebrows.

"I'm sure you girls are eager to try out the dorm cafeteria," he told her. He winked over at my mother like the two of them were conspirators sharing a private joke at our expense.

"It doesn't open until tomorrow," Cynthia said.

He frowned and looked at his watch.

"I really need to get back, sweetie," he said, his tone becoming just the tiniest bit strident even as he addressed her with a term of affection.

My mother saw what was happening and spoke up. She had embraced Cynthia as a motherless waif the day her first letter had arrived.

"Why don't you go with us, honey?" she asked. "We're spending the night and driving back tomorrow, so we'll be going out later for a bite."

Cynthia didn't move her wide, questioning eyes from her father, but he saw his out and took it. He gave her a quick hug and was gone.

Over the months that followed, I figured out that the one thing Cynthia and I did have in common was that neither of us had a lot of friends. It wasn't that I had been unpopular in high school. I'd had a lot of casual friends, especially when I started working on the yearbook. But our farm was outside of Santa Rosa, so in the summertime, when all of my classmates were going to the movies and the swimming pool together and hanging out at each other's houses, I was working on my 4-H projects and doing chores with my dad or helping my mom with the garden and the canning. During the school year I worked hard. I really, really wanted to get into UCLA. I had a social life, but I didn't make the kind of friendships that sometimes last beyond graduation.

At first I credited Cynthia's solitude with her having gone to an exclusive private academy, which meant her classmates from several states and Mexico all scattered when the school year was over. Once I knew her better I realized she was often moody and could be vindictive, her personality capable of switching on a dime, but it seemed to me that she had good reason. She had no mother, and her father never came to see her and seldom called. When she needed money she left a message with his receptionist, and within a few days a typewritten check, signed by his accountant, appeared in the mail with no letter to accompany it.

At the beginning of the semester she had a boyfriend she'd met at a neighbor's beach picnic the summer before. He had stayed in San Diego to go to San Diego State, and she wasn't much interested in meeting new men. He drove up to see her once in September, and for the rest of the month and much of October, he called and sent letters and begged her not to forget him. Then just before Halloween he wrote to say he had met someone new and would she please return his class ring.

"Oh, right! I'm sure going to do just that," she said, laughing humorlessly, and she yanked it from the chain on which she wore it around her neck and charged out the door and toward the bathroom down the hall. When I realized what she was doing I ran after her, but I was too late. Even before I pushed the door open I could hear the sound of flushing.

Nevertheless, she played "Misty," which had been their song, on my stereo over and over, often reaching out from under the covers to replace the needle on the record long after I thought she had finally fallen asleep. On a couple of occasions I heard her crying into her pillow late at night.

"Cynthia?" I whispered the first time.

"What?" she sniffed.

"What's the matter?"

"Nothing. Why?"

"I heard you crying."

"No, you didn't. You were probably having a dream. Just go back to sleep."

The next time it happened she said, "Not that again! You're hearing things, Maggie."

But whatever the flaws that I began to see creeping around the edges of her perfect exterior, we had each other, and we did form a friendship that would have been lifelong, except for everything that happened.

Friendship notwithstanding, our paths continued to go in different directions. Some people described me as a hippie. I didn't use drugs except for the occasional hit off someone's joint at a party, but I wore gauzy cotton Indian-print shirts and wrecked jeans, and I spent weekends making signs for women's equality and civil rights. I also spent a fair amount of time at protest marches against the Vietnam War, which was still raging at the time. I was in love with my freedom and being at school, and while my mother asked me from time to time what on earth I had on when they came down to visit, I knew my liberal parents were proud of me. They had hammered into Bradley and me all our lives how important it was to become engaged in the world and leave it a better place than we found it, and now here I was faced with the opportunity to actually do what they had asked. I often pleaded with Cynthia to join me, but she'd wrinkle up her nose like she smelled something that had spoiled, and I'd tear off across campus alone.

Cynthia was conservative in every sense of the word—quiet when I was loud and boisterous, well-dressed in her Bobbie Brooks skirts and matching sweater sets, even if she was just running out to her evening botany lab, her hair always magically smooth, her lips touched with just enough lipstick that never seemed to wear off. I asked her once about her politics, and she answered, "Rich people are all Republicans. Didn't you know that? As my dad says, 'We vote with our pocketbooks.'"

But despite all that, we quickly became much closer than most of the other roommates we knew. We snuck up food from the cafeteria for each other, and one day when I had the flu she went to my classes as well as her own so that she could take notes for me. When she got back late that afternoon she was soaking wet.

"Where have you been?" I croaked from the bed where I lay strapped to a heating pad and reeking of Vicks salve, defaulting to the homespun remedies by which my mother had always sworn.

From the paper bag she was carrying she produced a takeout container of hot and sour soup, which she handed to me in the manner of someone awarding a prize.

"Where on earth did you get this?" I asked her. I took off the lid and began to eat immediately. The spicy broth made my throat feel better at once, but I knew the dorm cafeteria had never produced anything that tasted this good.

"China Castle," she said, like it was no big deal.

"China Castle is a mile away," I said. "And it's pouring down rain!"

She shrugged her shoulders and disappeared down the hall with her towel and the pink bag that held her soap and shampoo. She could be like that—so kind and thoughtful and then five minutes later a rattlesnake.

We talked about our childhoods and high school and our futures. She was planning to major in psychology and I in journalism, an ambition born when I saw my byline in the high school paper for the first time. She wanted to work in a clinic that treated disturbed women.

She often mentioned her mother but never the circumstances under which she had died, and I figured it would be impolite to ask. I finally found out the whole story at Thanksgiving in the most unhappy, uncomfortable way possible. Cynthia's father called to make sure she was coming home for the holiday and then asked to speak to me so he could invite me along.

"It's a long trip up to Santa Rosa just for the weekend," he boomed through the phone, "and we can't eat a whole turkey by ourselves."

As it turned out, the "we" to whom he referred was not just himself and Cynthia, which was precisely why he wanted me along. I knew this trick. I had used it myself when I was a child, taking a friend home with me to mitigate my parents' anger if I had done something wrong and thought I might be in trouble. He met us at the train station on Wednesday evening by himself, but when we got to their house, high on a cliff overlooking the Pacific, a tall woman in black silk pants and a shiny coral blouse—clearly not the housekeeper—was tossing a salad in the kitchen. She had straight, dark hair shaped into a geometric cut that I would have killed for but that would have been impossible with my frizzy mop. It was enough like Cynthia's that if I didn't already know her mother was dead, I would have sworn they were related. Twinkly earrings that I was pretty sure were real diamonds dangled from her ears.

Cynthia's father told us to leave our bags in the foyer for the moment. There was someone he couldn't wait for us to meet.

"This is Caroline," he said, his eyes riveted on Cynthia, as if sending her a telepathic message that dared her to be anything but cordial. "We were introduced by the Crosbys. Caroline teaches art history at the university with Lynn."

I learned later on that night that Lynn's husband, Paul, was Dr. Morgan's partner, but at that moment, with tension thickening the air between us, I didn't care who they were. Caroline moved forward, smiling hopefully, and put her hand out to Cynthia, who fussed with a zipper on her jacket instead of taking it. I handed her the little gift I had brought for Dr. Morgan—a tissue-wrapped package of paper Thanksgiving napkins that my mother would have loved but I realized right off would never be used in this kind of house. I had been taught to take a small gift when I was a guest in someone's home for the first time, but this one seemed out of place and pathetically cheap. Caroline didn't open it then, and my using the gesture to break the silence hadn't worked. I looked from Caroline to Cynthia to her father and then down at my shoes.

"If you don't mind, I think I'll go unpack," I said finally, wanting nothing more than to pick up my suitcase and go right out the door and back to the train station.

"I'll help you," Caroline said, smiling too brightly. I had given her an out, too. "We'll give John and Cynthia a little time alone together."

She insisted on carrying my bag upstairs to Cynthia's room, where she laid it on one of the twin beds. A window across the room looked out over the ocean. Far below, a ribbon of surf snaked along the beach in the moonlight. A bouquet of roses sat on the dresser, and a banner strung across the closet doors said "Welcome Home!" From downstairs we could hear voices rising, first Cynthia's and then her father's, but we couldn't make out most of what they were saying. I did hear Cynthia say something about her mother, and then her father said, "This is exactly what she would have wanted." There was no ignoring Cynthia's shouted "Bullshit! This is exactly what killed her."

Caroline pushed the door closed and winced apologetically.

"I don't think our idea was such a good one," she told me. "But I don't know what the right time would have been. Since John's first wife died I think I'm the only person he's even dated very seriously. We knew it would be hard on his daughter, but he's only forty-seven. He has needs."

All I could do was nod stupidly, warming to this woman who seemed only to want to do the right thing but feeling disloyal to Cynthia and uncomfortable talking about her father's needs since I figured out right off the bat what some of those might be.

"It's not like you got married or anything without telling her," I said, grasping for something—anything, however lame and useless—to say instead of just continuing to nod my head. So far I had nodded so much that I figured this woman wondered if I had a disorder that rendered my head too ungainly to sit quietly on my neck for any extended length of time. Unfortunately I had selected exactly the wrong words with which to break my silence. She flinched as if I had raised my hand to slap her.

"I'm afraid we kinda did," she said, and then she launched into a breathless self-defense that sounded rehearsed, as if she had been waiting to recite it to Cynthia but under the circumstances I would do.

"John didn't know quite how to do it," she began. "He felt Cynthia had been traumatized enough by her mother's hideous death. I've never been married before, and I would have liked more of a wedding with Cynthia and my family involved, but he wanted to keep it as simple and quiet as possible. A couple of weeks ago, we flew up to San Francisco for a weekend. John has a friend who's a judge there, so he married us in his chambers, and then he and his wife took us out to dinner. We spent the night at the St. Francis Hotel and flew back the next day in time for him to make evening rounds. End of honeymoon." She smiled sadly. "I believed him when he said it was the best thing for his daughter, but judging from the argument I hear going on downstairs, I'm not sure we made the right choice."

Voices below us still rose and fell. I hadn't paid much attention to anything Caroline said beyond the words "hideous death."

"I don't know anything about her mother's death," I said, hoping she would tell me more. "She told me her mother died, but I don't know how."

Leaning against the dresser, Caroline folded her arms and shivered as if she were suddenly chilled.

"It was a suicide, carbon monoxide poisoning. She killed herself in this very house, down in the garage, in her car. She was bipolar and apparently not always regular about taking the medication her doctor had prescribed. She had delusions that John no longer cared for her, that he was having an affair with another woman, although he swears that wasn't the case. Anyway, she did it on a Saturday afternoon when she thought Cynthia was going to spend the night with a girlfriend. I guess she wanted John to find her, some sort of punishment, I suppose. But Cynthia got sick, and her friend's mother brought her home. The mom just dropped her off at the end of the driveway and left, and as Cynthia got closer to the garage, she could hear the car's engine."

She hugged herself even more closely with her folded arms.

"The point is, she found her mother dead all by herself. John had been called to the hospital for an ectopic pregnancy—funny the details people remember in situations like that. He was in the operating room and couldn't be reached for a couple of hours. The housekeeper and her husband had the day off, so Cynthia had to call the police and handle it all on her own. I think she was twelve or thirteen at the time. By the time her dad got the message, Virginia—that was her name—had been pronounced dead. Cynthia was waiting here alone with a police officer to find out what funeral home to call. She was in counseling for a couple of years. Apparently she blamed herself, thought if she'd been here, it wouldn't have happened. Of course, there was nothing she could have done, but she was devoted to her mother, and she looks just like her. Virginia was dark and beautiful. I didn't know her, of course, but John has shown me pictures."

My heart went out to Cynthia, and I forgave her whatever little obstacles had marred our three-month-old relationship. I was glad she had the bed near the window, glad she was pretty and got more offers of dates than I did. I thought now I understood her mood swings and promised myself I'd be more understanding. Just the week before, she had gone for a whole day without speaking to me for no reason I could think of, and when I slammed out of our room on my way to class the next morning, I yelled back over my shoulder that she could either get a grip or start looking for a new roommate. She had run down the hallway after me, crying and holding out her arms like a broken-hearted child. I wouldn't ever say anything like that to her again.

Suddenly I missed my own mother. How I had taken for granted her easy laughter and her endless projects. I could see her now, surveying the garage full of tables and chests in various stages of being stripped or finished, a chair she was trying to reupholster with the aid of a book she had checked out of the library and propped up behind a paint can, a dozen seed catalogs that she'd pore over all winter and order in the spring, when she would borrow a neighbor's rototiller and get her garden ready.

"If I live to be a hundred, I'll never get everything done I want to do," she had often said. And how many times had she hugged Bradley and me when we brought her our pitiful offerings of dandelion bouquets and collages glued together from old magazine photographs and said, "I'm the luckiest woman in the whole wide world."

I looked at my watch. Seven twenty. As soon as I could I would slip away and give her a call and let her know how much I appreciated her. Meanwhile Caroline, as if reading my thoughts, said, "It's too late for me to be any kind of real influence in Cynthia's life, of course. I'll never be a mother to her, but I'm hoping maybe we can eventually be good friends."

I nodded again.

"I'm sure you can," I said weakly.

I wasn't sure at all, but it was the only thing I could think of to say at the time, and Caroline was looking at me hopefully, as if my reassurance would make it so.

I followed her back downstairs and out onto the deck, where Dr. Morgan had started to cook shrimp on the grill and Cynthia watched from her perch on a redwood stool pulled up to a portable bar under a string of white twinkling lights. Her eyes were red and her nose still runny, but she smiled shakily.

"Congratulations," she said. "I'm sorry about my reaction earlier. It was just a surprise, that's all. Of course I want Daddy to be happy."

Dinner was polite, if not the celebration for which Caroline and Dr. Morgan might have hoped. It was too chilly to eat outside, so while Cynthia carried in the shrimp and her dad shut off the grill, I helped Caroline bring the salad and bread into the dining room. We drank wine with dinner, which seemed incredibly urban and sophisticated to me. At my house dinner, which we would have called "supper," would have been served hours ago, and my mother would have poured milk for Bradley and me and iced tea for herself and Dad. Here, though, the wine at least had the effect of loosening everybody up a little. Later there were truffles from a fancy chocolatier, and then I excused myself to call my parents. I said the lines would probably be tied up the next day and I wanted to be sure to wish them a happy Thanksgiving. Caroline directed me down a long hallway to her husband's study.

"I miss you guys," I whispered furtively into the phone as if my feelings were a shameful secret. I didn't want the Morgans to think I didn't appreciate their hospitality, and now that I knew the burden Cynthia carried, the last thing I wanted to do was hurt her feelings. Still, I wished desperately that I had taken a plane home to Santa Rosa as my parents had wanted me to.

"Is anything wrong, honey?" Mom asked.

She could tell from my whispering voice right off that something was.

"Cynthia's mother killed herself—that's how she died."

Mom gasped at the other end of the line.

"And her father just got remarried two weeks ago without telling her. When we got here, he just sprang it on her. His new wife is really nice, but they should have told Cynthia beforehand."

"Oh, honey, I wish you had come home. You've never been away from home on Thanksgiving before. I can't imagine making dinner tomorrow without you here to roll out the pie crust and sample the stuffing. And now this."

I imagined the crease that formed between her eyebrows when she was worried or trying to work out the solution to a problem.

"I know," I said with conviction. "I wish I had, too."

"Do you want to try and get a plane out of there late tonight or early tomorrow morning? I could call the airlines and see if there's anything still available."

"No," I said regretfully. "It's not that bad, and I think Cynthia needs me here with her. She's pretty upset."

"She's lucky to have a friend like you," Mom said.

"Well, I'm lucky to have her, too."

"Maybe we can have her up here next year," she said.

"I'd like that a lot better than being here," I whispered back, but that was never to happen.

Later that night, after Dr. Morgan and Caroline had gone to bed (probably to meet some of his needs, I thought), Cynthia and I soaked in their hot tub. After their talk she seemed to have accepted her father's marriage, and Caroline certainly seemed nice enough. Below us the lights from other houses twinkled on the hillside that sloped down to the beach, and I could hear the waves pounding onto the sand and the occasional squawk of a gull. Cynthia poured us another glass of wine left over from dinner, and the long weekend started to look much more inviting than it had a few hours ago.

"I think your dad and Caroline are really neat people," I said.

"She's a bitch," Cynthia countered matter-of-factly. "I'll bet she just married him for his money and he married her for sex. I'll bet they're up there fucking their brains out right this very minute."

Just after Thanksgiving Richard Bartolucci, who had an English lit class with Cynthia and had been admiring her kissable mouth all semester, finally got up the courage to ask her to his fraternity's holiday formal and changed all of our lives forever. He was a senior, a science nerd in pre-med, and he wore the obligatory horn-rimmed glasses, but behind them his eyes were deep brown and often smiling. He was tall and had curly dark-brown hair that he parted and combed to one side until Cynthia convinced him to leave off the hair cream and let it fall naturally across his forehead.

"He has definite potential," she said the night she told me he had asked her out.

In the beginning I think I was a little jealous. He was exactly the kind of guy I hoped I would someday meet. But I knew that first night, as they were leaving for the dance, that something special was about to happen. When Cynthia ran down the stairs to the lobby in her short red satin dress with the bouncy bubble skirt, her dark, glossy hair flying out behind her, it was like the air was charged with an energy that if ignited might explode into spangles of purple and gold. Richard felt it, too, he told me much later. He stood dumbly below us in a black tux, holding a cellophane box in which lay a red-and-white carnation wrist corsage and staring up as if he couldn't believe what he saw. I followed behind her, dateless in sweatpants and a blue UCLA T-shirt, a lady in waiting, witness to the moment it all began.

She folded herself into his old blue Plymouth with the grace of a queen arranging herself in a carriage, and he fussed over her dress, making sure it didn't get caught in the door and closing it gently, as if he were a footman and Prince Charming rolled into one. I watched them drive away with longing. It was as if instead of going to a dance they had left me to travel through time.

She didn't come in at all that night. I hovered by the Coke machine near the front door as the one o'clock curfew came and went. Several girls who had been to the same dance came in, one crying, one with a large stain that looked like spilled red wine spreading across the front of her long white gown, another wrapped around her date until the last minute and coming inside with swollen lips and a red mark on her neck just as the RA came with her keys to lock the door for the night.

Cynthia slipped in not long after the doors were unlocked the next morning at seven. Even with her makeup gone and carrying her stockings and shoes, the magic from the night before remained. Richard had obviously gotten his wish to kiss Cynthia's extraordinary mouth and a whole lot more.

"I did it with Richard," she announced before she said hello. "I've never done it on the first date before."

I had been asleep when her key turned in the lock and woke me up, but I was wide awake and alert now. I still hadn't done it at all, which I had been embarrassed to tell her when she had recounted her exploits in the back seat with Mark, the boyfriend whose ring she had dispatched through the sewer pipes just a couple of months before.

"I'm nuts about him," she told me. "I know it's crazy. I mean, we've only had one date and he doesn't seem at all like my type, but I think we're in love, and so does he. We didn't dance very much last night. We just sat and talked."

"About what?"

"About everything. What we want to do in the future and how we feel about children and everything else, too."

"Did he ask you out again?" I asked her. I still labored under the theory that if you did it on the first date, no matter what he said, you wouldn't be the one a guy called again and took home to meet his mother.

"He's waiting downstairs in the car for me to shower and change. We're going for a hike and a picnic, and I may not be back tonight, either."

"Where did you ... ?" I made circles in the air with my upturned hand, waiting for her to fill in the blanks of my unspoken question.

"He has a friend who lives off-campus in an apartment. It's a two-bedroom, but the guy's roommate transferred to another school and moved out at the beginning of the semester, and he hasn't found another one yet. He's looking, but he said until he finds someone, Richard and I can use the place any time we want. Even if he finds someone, that fraternity house is a loose place. They have a housemother, but once she goes to bed guys sneak their girlfriends in all the time, and Richard said even if she knows, she has kind of a 'boys will be boys' attitude."

She took a record-breaking quick shower and pulled on jeans and a sweater.

"I'll see you tomorrow," she said and was gone.

Some college roommates drift apart, exchanging Christmas cards for a while or looking each other up on Facebook, now that that's an option, or losing touch completely and not even remembering one another's names. But Cynthia and I grew ever closer. I had worried about our differences that summer before we met, but now I think our differences helped bind us more tightly together. She had everything I wanted, and, strangely enough, I think she would have traded it all for the life I had. Selfishness alternated with generosity, laughter with tears. Poor Richard often showed up horny and lovesick, only to find that in an angry snit she had decided not to go out with him at all and even she didn't know why. The clues were all there, especially the bipolar suicidal mother, but I didn't know anything about mental illness back then, and by the time I learned what I needed to know, it was too late to help my friend.

While I appreciated my own average family in Santa Rosa, I envied her ocean-view house in La Jolla, her rich, sexy father in his maroon Jaguar, the department store credit cards with which she had carte blanche. It wasn't sick, green-eyed jealousy but rather a comfortable pleasure, delighted at being included in her life, Trixie Belden to her Honey Wheeler. She didn't socialize with anybody except Richard and me, and when she moved through the cafeteria line or negotiated the combination that opened our mailbox, I often saw people watching, wondering. She was silent and distant and seldom smiled except with the two of us. I felt privileged somehow to be her only friend, as if I were the sole member of an entourage for a misunderstood rock singer or a lonely movie star. Once I overheard some girls down the hall ask her if she and I wanted to review for an exam with them.

"I'm sorry," she said, and I could tell from my side of the door that she kept on walking as she spoke. "We've already made plans to see a movie tonight."

She didn't realize that I had heard and didn't mention it when she got back to the room. In fact, no such movie was in the cards. We stayed in our room and studied for the same test, and when I went to the soda machine later, she didn't seem to care that I might run into one of the other girls, which I did.

"I thought you and your roommate were going to a movie," she said.

Even then there wasn't much I wouldn't do for Cynthia.

"We were going to," I lied, "but she's not feeling very well, so we stayed in."

Most of all Cynthia missed having a sibling and a stable family. That's what she wanted for herself, she said to me repeatedly that first semester: a big house and two children. She wanted to get her degree and work for a while, but eventually she would set her career aside long enough to have babies, a boy and a girl like we all thought we'd have, and then go back to work, maybe part time.

And the house! It wouldn't be the angular glass and marble and chrome box she had grown up in, a house run by a housekeeper for a moody, withdrawn mother and an absent father. Hers would be big and rambling and have two stories with grass out front and trees lining the driveway. She was going to wallpaper every room, she announced one day as she was flipping through a decorating magazine my mother had left behind during one of her visits, and there would be geraniums in clay pots and a porch swing. The floors would be hardwood covered by interesting rugs, not the antiseptic white wall-to-wall carpeting with which she had grown up.

"When my children run in with muddy feet," she told me one gray afternoon, sitting on our heating vent and watching the rain bang against the window, "it will be just fine with me."

Her eyes clouded and she bit her lip with her overlapping front teeth, and I knew better than to ask any questions.

Once she started dating Richard, she incorporated him into her plans as if he had arrived on some kind of cue to fill the role of the handsome, sensitive, well-to-do man who would support her privileged life, and as their relationship intensified I could tell she had made up her mind about the outcome, even if it wasn't all that clear to him.

As for me, I had also thought ahead to the details of how my life would play out. I wanted a husband and kids someday, too, but first I wanted to be Brenda Starr, traveling around the world with my camera and notepad, packing my white blouses and khaki pants into a worn canvas suitcase and catching planes headed for exotic locales in the dead of night. And when I met the man of my dreams, he would share exactly my vision and we would live in an apartment filled with books and typewriters, someplace that we could leave at a moment's notice when duty called to the office or overseas.

For now I was content to date the geeky fraternity brothers with whom Richard fixed me up, seldom seeing any of them more than once or twice, both they and I forever the less attractive friend with the great personality. One, in fact, confessed to me that he had a crush on Cynthia and had only gone out with me to be close to her.

At winter break Cynthia took Richard home to La Jolla to meet her father and Caroline, and when they came back they were engaged. I had gone home to Santa Rosa and got back to our room the Sunday night before classes began a couple of hours before she did.

"You're not going to believe what I have to tell you!" she shrieked as soon as she opened the door and sailed through. Without saying anything more she held out her left hand, on which sparkled a tiny diamond. My first reaction was a stab of regret. I wanted her to be happy, of course, and her being with Richard seemed inevitable, but now I thought I would lose her and our good times together would end.

"Have you set a date?" I asked her. I tried to sound as excited as I could.

"This coming summer. My dad wasn't happy about it at first because he said he wanted me to finish school. But when I convinced him that I didn't plan to drop out, he was okay with it. And he's thrilled that Richard's in pre-med."

"How are you going to carry this off?" I asked.

"We'll live in the married students' apartments, and we'll just both go to school. My dad said he'd give me the same tuition and board money I get now, and Richard's parents will, too. In a way it will be cheaper—two living for the price of one."

Talking about money brought her back to the subject of the ring. She stretched out her hand and looked at it, frowning, as if she hadn't really seen it before.

"It's really small," she said, "but Richard says when he has his own practice he'll buy me something nicer."

"I think it's beautiful," I said. That much, at least, was true.

With the new semester our routines naturally changed. Now we had no classes together, with most of mine on Monday, Wednesday, and Friday and hers on Tuesday and Thursday. I took some beginning journalism classes and began spending time in the newsroom at the campus newspaper. Hooked on the smell of ink and the feel of newsprint, I was happy to answer phones, check facts, and pick up lunch. In my senior year I would be the features editor for the paper, but I didn't know that then, and I was happy just to be allowed to hang around.

Richard studied constantly since he was getting ready to graduate and didn't want to jeopardize his admission to medical school, and now Cynthia studied with him, usually at the fraternity house. More nights than not she stayed over, and often several days went by before we saw one another again. I began using her bed—the one by the window, now wasted—to store my laundry or lay out reference books for term papers, never expecting her to show up, always surprised and glad when she did.

You'd think that with all that time apart, with our interests growing in opposite directions, each on her way to a major and a career path and a life, Cynthia embroiled in her love affair and now her engagement with Richard, that we would have pulled apart, but we became closer than ever. They say in every relationship one person cares more than the other, and looking back now I realize that was me. Nights when she did come home were special events. We'd linger over starch-packed dinners in the cafeteria or walk to the taco shop six blocks away. Mostly she talked about the wedding plans, in which I was to play the role of maid of honor.

"It will be small but elegant," she said, acknowledging from the outset that she didn't have enough close friends to fill a church or a reception hall. "Since Richard is Catholic, we're going to have it in the church in Riverside that he's gone to since he was a little boy. I think we'll do it in the morning and then have a brunch at some nice restaurant."

She hauled a thick bridal magazine out of her book bag and flipped to a page on which she had turned down the corner.

"Here's the dress," she said, poking at it with her finger. "Antique lace over ivory satin with a cathedral train. I've dreamed of this dress since I was a little girl. I couldn't have designed it myself to be any more perfect."

She leaned over and hugged me impulsively.

"You're the closest thing I've ever had to a sister," she said. "I'm going to have the most beautiful wedding in history, and you're always going to be my best friend."

❧

But neither was to happen. On a cold, windy afternoon in early March Richard was waiting for me when I came out of my music appreciation class.

"Richard!" I said, my tone telling him how surprised I was to see him. His science classes were held in the laboratory buildings at the other end of campus.

"Do you have time to get a cup of coffee?" he asked me.

By now Richard was my friend, too, but he was busy with his classes and spending time with Cynthia. He wouldn't come all the way to where I was in the cold without a reason.

"Is anything wrong?" I asked him as we started walking to the student union.

"I just need to talk," he said, "and you're the best person I could think of."

We went through the cafeteria line in the commons and got our coffee. When we were settled at a small table in an out-of-the-way corner he began.

"This is really tough," he said. He ran a hand through his hair, which now, under Cynthia's supervision, was much longer and looser than it had been when they met. "I guess the only way to start is just to jump right in."

I couldn't think what he might be getting at, but I was pretty sure I wasn't going to like it.

"I don't want to marry Cynthia next summer," he blurted.

"Oh, Jesus," came out before I could edit my response.

"I know. I need for somebody else who knows her and cares

about her to help me figure out how to tell her. She's not like other people, you know what I mean? She's fragile, and I don't want to hurt her."

"Of course you know she's got the dress picked out and her stepmother has been to Riverside to look at the church with your mom."

He nodded miserably, shutting his eyes and grimacing as if he were in pain.

"It's just that I don't think that's reason enough to get married if you don't think it's the right thing to do."

I waited silently. I couldn't argue with him there.

"I still want to marry her at some point. I'm crazy about her, but right now I'm getting ready to start med school, and there's no way I can explain to her how difficult that's going to be. I'll be studying night and day, and later on I'll be on a hospital service and staying overnight sometimes on call or with a critical patient. The letter of acceptance to med school even talks about the commitment it takes. The idea of having a wife just complicates everything and makes it seem overwhelming. She says now that it wouldn't be a problem, but you know Cynthia as well as I do. If she wants your attention, she wants it now, and if you happen to have an anatomy exam the next day, she wants it now anyway. And I'm worried about my parents. They're struggling to pay my tuition as it is. They own the bakery, but it's hard work. As corny as it might sound, I want to make them proud. I don't ever want them to be sorry they put so much confidence in me. Cynthia has probably told you I had an older brother who was killed in Vietnam, and now all of their hopes are pinned on me. Cynthia and I can stay engaged, and when I finish med school we can get married then."

"I'm so sorry," I said. "I can see why you don't want more responsibility. Everything you say makes sense to me. My parents are working hard for me to be here, too, and I feel the same way. I don't think it's corny at all, but Cynthia is not going to understand. She's been through a lot, but at the same time she's always been wealthy. I don't think work and money mean the same things to her that they do to you and me."

"I wouldn't hurt her for the world," he said, "but wanting to protect her from pain isn't a reason to rush into a marriage, either. I just want to postpone the wedding for about four years. Even then I'll be facing internship and residency, and they're ball-busters, too."

"Then start out by telling her that. Use the word 'postpone' because once you tell her the wedding's off, she's not going to hear anything else you say."

He told her that night, and the next day he caught up with me on campus again. Cynthia had not come home the night before.

"It went a lot better than I thought it would," he said. "I did it like you said: First I told her I love her and want to marry her. Then I said I wanted to put off our wedding until after med school. She cried a little and said she didn't know what to tell our parents because my mom and Caroline have already started the plans. But then she was okay, and she seemed to understand. In fact, it was her idea to stay the night with me. We were as close as ever, if you know what I mean, and everything was great."

At the beginning of May, Cynthia shook me awake one night just after the one o'clock curfew.

"I'm pregnant!" she told me. "Richard and I are getting married in two weeks."

3

Years later Richard and I were huddled on the bar stools at Brady's Bar and Grill in my West Los Angeles neighborhood when he was in town for a medical conference. His suited shoulders were hunkered down over a Manhattan that he stirred continually with a swizzle stick as he stared into it and poured out everything he couldn't say to anyone else but me. He told me he realized right away that Cynthia had planned the whole thing. We were trying to sort out what had gone wrong, how she had managed to change so much and finally to run completely amok. The real horror still lay coiled in the future but was probably even then gathering form in her nightmares and plans.

"I'm convinced she has a mental illness, probably inherited from her mother, but she's never been diagnosed," he told me. "I blame John for not recognizing that and having her treated. I like him, and he's always been good to me, but he's a doctor, for God's sake. You'd think he might have spotted this a long time ago and gotten treatment for her so that none of us would have to be going through this. But he is also all about himself and usually has his head up his ass. And I think maybe he was in denial about having a child who wasn't quite perfect. And her mother's suicide didn't help matters, either. Cynthia has such a fear of abandonment."

By this time he had been in practice for several years. He was an internist, but still he had seen his share of unhappy, neurotic, and downright psychopathic patients.

"When I first met her she seemed so unusual and different, so aloof from everyone else," he said. "That added to her mystery and her attraction. But the reality was that she desperately wanted security, and she knew I could give it to her—emotional and financial. She didn't want to take a chance on losing that." He laughed humorlessly. "I was such a nerd, and she was . . ." Unable to find the word he sought, he paused to take a sip of his cocktail. "She knew I never dreamed I could land somebody like her, and she thought she'd never have to worry about losing me. When it looked like I wanted out, she panicked. You know her mother suspected John was being unfaithful, and I think Cynthia believed it, too. It's the only way she could cope with what her mother had done. She couldn't bear to think her mother had died over nothing—that she just wanted out of a life she no longer thought she could handle."

He stared into space for a few moments and then shook his head as his consciousness returned to the reality of the bar and he continued.

"The first time we had sex was on our first date. I'm sure she told you that."

I smiled in acknowledgment.

"I used an old condom that had been in my wallet since high school. Every guy from about thirteen on carries one that he hopes he'll get to use sooner or later. Usually they just make the imprint of a ring on the leather, and you hope when you open your wallet for something else whoever is with you will notice and think you're a real player, you've been around. Mostly it is just proof that you've never had a chance to use it, which was exactly right in my case. I never really thought I'd get the opportunity to use the thing. I'm surprised it was even still any good. I didn't date much in high school. I took a girl to the prom my senior year but only because the daughter of one of my mom's friends needed a date. She was as geeky as I was, and we shuffled miserably around the dance floor a couple of times and never went out again. In college all I could think about was making grades and getting into med school. I was a nervous wreck just asking Cynthia to the fraternity dance. But she said yes, and then there she was in that red dress. Do you remember that night, Maggie? Jesus, I was nuts about her. And I still am nuts about who she was. Do you know what I mean?"

I nodded and toyed with the glass of chardonnay I was nursing. By that time I had had my own share of loving and losing, of seeing a man change and betray me as if aliens had taken over his body and the person with whom I was in love had been locked away in a cellar somewhere that I would never be able to find. I had learned that it was possible to know a living, breathing shell while the person I cared for had abdicated and was as good as gone. And I, too, had figured out that it was possible to cut your losses and move on.

"Anyway, that first night I never dreamt something like that would happen. When it did, I hauled out my trusty old condom and put it to use. After that I bought more, but when we got serious and it looked like we were going to stay together, she got a diaphragm. It was in a little round pink case that looked like a compact. She wanted to finish school, and I wanted her to. But then all of a sudden she tells me she's missed her period and she goes to the doctor and bingo, we're having a baby. That's why she got so cozy with me the night I told her I wanted to put off the wedding. She knew exactly what she was doing."

"Diaphragms aren't foolproof, Richard," I said, still a little defensive of Cynthia's honor even then. "You, of all people, should know that. So maybe that explains it."

But he didn't buy it and neither did I.

"We were going at it like rabbits," he said, chuckling at the memory. "I was a virgin at my peak. And she . . . well, I think she genuinely loved me back there in the beginning. We couldn't get enough of each other. And when we weren't doing it, we were talking about it. You know, where she was in her cycle or when we could get my friend's apartment for a weekend. No, she knew what she was doing."

"And you couldn't have asked her to end the pregnancy because that wasn't legal yet."

He shook his head vehemently.

"I wouldn't have anyway. Her plan worked just like she knew it would. She would never have considered getting rid of a baby she thought would ensure her future. And I don't have any regrets on that score. Even knowing what she pulled, I loved Cynthia, and I'm crazy about my girls. I couldn't ever have asked her to abort a child we had created together. You remember that my family was Catholic, and back then I was serious about it, too. I'm not religious anymore, but I still feel a little sad when one of my patients feels she has to make that choice."

"It sounds like you've left the church," I said.

This surprised me. I remembered their wedding at which Richard's family's priest refused to officiate because of the sinful circumstances, the problems that had arisen as a result of Cynthia's haphazard Protestantism, the arguments over whether the baby would be christened, and the black wooden rosary beads Richard's mother gripped tightly throughout the wedding ceremony. During my visits to their apartment Richard and I had held long discussions about religion and philosophy, but Cynthia had steadfastly declined to take part, often telling us we were too deep, way over her head.

"Yeah, I did," he said. He ran his hands through his hair in the gesture that I recognized from other talks years ago and massaged the back of his own neck as if to relieve some tension I had caused there with my question. "I don't like the church's position on social issues, and I just don't buy the stories anymore. I believe in something, but it doesn't have anything to do with organized religion."

"So what caused you to make the break?"

"It was fairly recently, but it was a long time coming. My parents trotted me to Mass every Sunday from the time I was born, and I just figured that was the way it was. I started having questions while I was still a kid, but you know my parents. I sure wasn't going to ask them anything. My mom would have had a stroke. What happened was that Saint Christopher was defrocked. My middle name is Christopher because in Catholic tradition your child's name has to include a saint's name. I always wore a medal with his picture on it around my neck and I had a little statue of him in my car. He was supposed to protect travelers, you know. But then the church decided there wasn't enough evidence to show that he deserved sainthood and demoted him, just like that. Like he had been sainted in error. My guy, the one I'd been named after who was supposed to protect me everywhere I went, was suddenly a nobody. There was some question about whether he had even existed. How could an institution like the Catholic Church make such a mistake? As I got older, I kept wondering what else they got wrong. How could they think someone was so special for so long and then find out they'd been so wrong?"

He realized instantly what he had said, and he reached over and squeezed my hand. His new wedding ring sparkled even in the dim mirrored light over the bar.

"I've got to go," he said, his voice husky. "Kim should be out of her meeting by now, and I've got an early one tomorrow morning."

He took some bills out of his wallet and folded them under the glass he had just drained. Then he slid off the stool and headed into the night, through the dark, toward his waiting bride.

But the day of Richard and Cynthia's wedding nobody could have guessed that their marriage would completely disintegrate later on. There had been some rumblings from Richard's parents about Cynthia's not being Catholic, but she laid them to rest by simply agreeing to raise her children in the faith and to take instructions with the goal of converting.

"How could you do that so easily?" I asked her the night before the wedding, when we were once again ensconced in her room above the sea in La Jolla. "I mean, okay, if you believe all the stuff they believe, but do you? This is a real commitment we're talking about here, especially with Richard being devout and a baby coming. You must have had to think about it a lot to come to a serious decision like that."

She looked at me squarely, and I saw the same ice in her dark eyes that I'd seen when she flushed the class ring.

"I didn't think about it at all, Pollyanna," she said evenly. "It makes Richard and his mother happy, and that's all that matters. I don't want his parents to have any reason to think I'm not the perfect bride for their precious son."

The next afternoon we gathered on the same deck where we had barbecued shrimp during the awkward Thanksgiving visit not all that long ago. In lieu of a priest, the Morgans' judge friend from San Francisco flew down, and earlier, standing beside me in his long black robe while we waited for Cynthia to finish dressing, he told me it wasn't often he got to marry father and daughter within just a few months of each other.

A harpist from the university played the wedding march, and first I in a purple satin number that I would never wear again and then Cynthia processed down the steps from the bedrooms above, across the living room and dining room, and through the open doors that led out to the deck. There hadn't been time to order the satin and lace creation that Cynthia had dreamed of during the evenings when we had pored over the bridal magazines, but she was as radiant in an off-the-rack dress we'd found at a mall as she had been in the red bubble dress that had ignited Richard's passion in the first place. Below us the Pacific rolled up on the shore, and the sun broke weakly through a light mist that lingered from morning. The deck was ablaze with red roses that Caroline had arranged, and a small, suitable cake waited on a table that was now draped in white.

The only other attendant was one of Richard's fraternity brothers—the one who had confessed he dated me just to be near Cynthia. Behind us stood tuxedoed John and glamorous Caroline on Cynthia's side and Richard's plump parents on his—the consequence, I supposed, of running a bakery for years. His mother wore a cheerful dress covered with bright flowers, although she wept openly as she worked systematically through her beads.

If Richard still had any doubts about the marriage, you wouldn't have guessed it that day. They joined both of their hands before the judge told them to, gripping each other like victims of a shipwreck clinging to a raft and staring into each other's eyes as if they found there Truth itself. I thought it was the most beautiful wedding I'd ever been to, and I started to hope that someday a man would look at me the way Richard had looked at her. You could put up with a lot if somebody cared that much about you, I thought, and later, while we ate cake and toasted with champagne, I heard Richard's mother say to his father, "It was a pretty wedding. Maybe it will work out after all. Heaven knows I hope they prove me wrong."

Cynthia's father gave them a honeymoon in Hawaii, but when they got back reality set in. Richard's middle-class family continued to pay his tuition and give him a housing allowance, as they had planned all along, but they couldn't add any more. John Morgan, happy his daughter had married a budding physician, continued to send a monthly check, too, but it wasn't enough to make ends meet. Cynthia's fantasy of two living for the price of one turned out to be just that. The semester was over, anyway, and the day after finals she signed on with a temporary agency that sent her to substitute for typists, clerks, and receptionists in offices all over the west side of LA. Richard took a summer job with a construction company and continued to work with them occasionally all through med school.

I spent the summer in Santa Rosa working part time in the circulation office at the local paper but mostly soaking up time with my mom and helping my dad out on the farm. I had spent much of my freshman year on an emotional roller coaster with Cynthia's ups and downs, her grand passion with Richard, and finally their hurry-up wedding at the end of the year. I had benefitted from Cynthia's frequent absences by studying more and making the dean's list, and I would start to work seriously on my major in the fall.

Cynthia decided to drop out of school—just temporarily, she said—and she and Richard fell into a pattern of marriage as predictable as if they had copied it off a television sitcom. She had begun to show, and for the most part she wore jeans with a stretch panel sewn in and voluminous maternity tops. She patted and stroked her belly constantly as if the child inside were already fussy and had to be consoled. After work she shopped for groceries and made casseroles laced with canned chicken soup and brownies from red and yellow boxes of prepared mix. Richard, tan and muscular from a summer spent framing a new apartment complex, turned up at six each evening, and they ate dinner, took a walk, watched a little TV, and went to bed. Sex, Cynthia reported to me, wasn't quite as exciting now that it was sanctioned and legal, and Richard was always at some lab or library until late at night. She said she was sure that would change once the baby was born.

For the next three years, their tiny apartment in the married students' complex was my home away from home. Before the baby was born, Cynthia and I browsed for hours in department stores for her layette. I had all the fun of anticipating the baby's birth without experiencing the weight gain and thick ankles that eventually played havoc even with Cynthia's trim figure. We sorted through shelves of tiny white T-shirts and thick quilted crib pads and delicate flowered nightgowns. Cynthia went to Lamaze and nursing classes and arranged for a cloth diaper service to begin delivery as soon as the baby was born. At first she was determined to be a purist—no plastic bottles or disposable diapers for her—although those romantic notions would quickly dissipate when the realities of motherhood settled in. Since Cynthia had made no other friends at school, worked at temporary jobs, and had no siblings, there was no one to invite to a shower, so I tried to make up for the void by bringing over small baby gifts each time I came to visit —a rattle, a bib, a pair of socks. I didn't have much money, but I felt so sorry for her that I took it upon myself to be a one-woman maternity celebration.

They had me over to eat at least once a week, and our evenings together usually ended with Cynthia and me playing a game of cards or Scrabble while Richard studied. When he had to go back at night to work in a lab, Cynthia always called me up to keep her company. Now that she had no homework of her own, she was bored when everyone around her did, and even when I had studies of my own to attend to it was hard to resist her urging.

"It will just be for a couple of hours," she'd say, or "You can study over here," although I seldom did. Sometimes we watched television. Usually we just talked until Richard came home and walked me across campus late at night. Only then did I start my own work.

When Chloe was born in January, just after the winter break, I instantly became "Aunt Maggie," and the three of us were closer than ever. I couldn't get enough of the tiny bundle who looked enough like Richard to be his clone, and Cynthia seemed genuinely happy, both with having had his baby and with the pure delight of the child herself. We sang songs to her, nibbled on her toes, and snapped pictures of each other holding her in our arms. We started a photo album and wrote every new development into a white quilted satin baby book that Caroline had brought when they came to the hospital. Cynthia nursed her openly in the comfort of our little group, but occasionally I got my turn at giving her a bottle of the milk Cynthia had pumped and watching her suck hard until she became drowsy and her tiny wet lips slid from the nipple and grew still. When the two of them wanted to go out, I grabbed up my schoolwork and galloped across the campus to babysit as if I had won the lottery.

In March, Cynthia stunned us both by announcing that she wanted to go back to school. It was a rainy, overcast Sunday. We had made chili and eaten it sitting on cushions on their living room floor. Richard had been at the medical library all afternoon, but now he lay lazily with his head in Cynthia's lap while she toyed with his hair. I was sprawled on the sofa. Two basketball teams played a silent game on the television set Cynthia had turned down so Chloe could get to sleep in her closet of a room just a few steps away.

"I called admissions today," she blurted out, apropos of nothing.

"Mmm. What for?" Richard mumbled. He had been up early that morning to make rounds with a team of interns and residents, and he was about to fall asleep on the pillow of Cynthia's widened thighs.

"I think I'll start back to school in the fall," she told him. "If I take a full load every semester and go to summer school each year, I'll be able to finish at the same time you're done with med school. We can graduate together."

She had obviously given this project a lot of thought but without consulting Richard, who now sat upright, his eyes wide, anger replacing the need for sleep.

"No," he said simply.

"What do you mean, 'No'?" Cynthia asked him. She caught his mood, and her own temper flared. Her cheeks were red. His eyes were narrow. I had never seen them fight, and I didn't want to. This was none of my business, and besides, I didn't want to see a crack in the porcelain flawlessness of their perfect love and their new, idyllic marriage. The tone of both of their voices hurt as much as if their anger had been directed toward me.

"I mean you've got a baby to take care of, in case you've forgotten," he shot at her. "What do you plan to do with her?"

Cynthia had worked out that angle, too.

"There's a day-care center right on campus," she told him. "I called and talked to the director. She said they accept children as young as six months old. I'd start in the fall and arrange my classes like I did before, with all of them concentrated on two or three days. If you really don't want me to, maybe I could just go part time."

"There's so much wrong with this I don't even know where to start," Richard said. He laughed, but his voice shook as if he might at any moment start to cry. "You can't put a baby who's practically a newborn in a day-care center. Jesus, Cyn, think about it. They've got kids over there of all ages. She'll have every childhood disease known to man before she's even out of diapers. And how do you plan to keep breast-feeding if you're off in some lecture hall when it's time for her to eat?"

"I'll probably be done nursing by then, but if I'm not, I'll pump some milk and drop it off with her."

"And when you're home with her, what then? If you take a full load, you'll have schoolbooks in one arm and a baby in the other. You can't predict when she'll need you or when she'll be sick and the day-care center won't take her."

"You seem to manage quite nicely," she snapped back. "Of course you have a housekeeper and a nursemaid working for you. Those are luxuries I wouldn't have."

"That's not fair. You know I've got to work hard these next few years so we can have the life we want for us and Chloe and whatever other kids we have. We talked about this before we got married and again when you left school."

"I said that was temporary. Now what you're saying is, you're the man and you can do whatever you want, and my job is to stay here and keep the home fires burning."

"Fine, you go to medical school," he shouted. "I'll stay home with Chloe."

"So is this the way it will always be? You with the upper hand, pronouncing judgment on any idea I have of doing something for myself because you'll be the rich, busy wage-earner and I'll be the housewife waiting at home to grovel at your feet."

"You might have thought about this when . . ."

"When what?"

"Nothing. All I'm saying is that I thought we were a team," Richard said, his voice deliberately level now. "We talked about how I'd go to school and when I finished you could go. Christ, I'll make enough money that you can hire people to help you with the housework and babysit. And when our kids go to school, your time will be completely your own. But now . . ."

His voice trailed off in frustration.

"Fine," she said, setting her overlapping front teeth down hard on her lower lip to form a word she most certainly did not mean. "Just forget I ever said anything."

I furtively crammed the books I had brought over into my book bag as if I were ashamed of them, which in a way I guess I was. Cynthia, still mad at Richard, glowered at me like I had done something wrong. Richard disappeared into the kitchen, and I heard the snap and hiss of a beer can opening. He didn't volunteer to walk me home, she didn't suggest it, and I didn't ask. I think we all realized that a subtle shift had taken place—something between the three of us—and between them an obstacle had begun to be erected that would never go away again.

❧

Since it's Cynthia's story I'm trying to make sense of here, I've probably made it sound as if I had no life of my own during this time. It's true she and Richard were my best friends and I spent a lot of time at their place, especially after Chloe was born. When I had an emergency appendectomy they insisted I stay with them for a few days when I got out of the hospital. But they were a married couple, after all, and on most weeknights when Richard was able to be home, they wanted to be alone and that was fine with me. I had become a news junkie, enchanted with journalism, and I hung around the newsroom at the campus paper even after the next morning's edition had gone to bed and there was nothing left to do but drink coffee and talk world events with others of my kind. I had occasional dates, mostly with other J-school students, mostly in groups where six or eight of us went to a movie or out for a pizza. It was the free-wheeling '70s. We prided ourselves on our identity as a group, the absence of a need to pair off and possess one another as our parents had done.

During my junior year, with beginning reporting and copyediting classes behind me, I started working on the paper for credit, grabbing up extra issues that contained my stories to send to my parents and present like offerings when I went for weekend suppers with the Bartoluccis.

"This is so great, Maggie!" Richard said, tapping at my byline with his index finger.

I had covered the hearing of two upperclassmen about to be expelled for cheating, and the story had made the front page.

"Let me see, honey," Cynthia said. She had been in the kitchen making a salad to go with our hamburger and noodle casserole, and she came out wiping her hands with a dish towel. Richard handed her the paper.

"Neat," she said to me, and then she scooped up Chloe, who had been clinging to the mesh wall of her playpen in the hope of just that. "Your Aunt Maggie is going to be famous someday," she told her. "People will want your autograph just because you know her."

I had a family here, separate from the biological one up north, who cared about me and were proud of what I accomplished, who were almost as thrilled by my little successes as I was—or so I foolishly thought at the time.

I went home for the summer before my senior year. It wasn't what I had wanted to do initially, but my little brother was turning eighteen and would start college in the fall at UC Davis, where he planned to become a veterinarian. My mother had the idea for us all to take one last family vacation together before I graduated and got a job, and so we did, a train trip through Canada to see the glaciers and stay at the hotel in Banff that had been on her wish list for as long as I could remember. When we got back I wangled a job as a temporary part-time reporter at the *Santa Rosa News*. It didn't pay much, but I covered city council meetings, a gas station holdup, and a fire where the owner of the house trailer tried to make a move on me as we stood together watching his home burn to the ground. It was the scut work nobody else wanted to do and it didn't pay much, but it allowed me to collect the clips I figured would give me an edge when I started applying for real jobs the next year.

Since I was going to be the features editor for the fall semester, I went back to LA three weeks before school started. I moved in early to the apartment I had rented in Westwood with three other women and worked eight-hour days going over the advertising budget with the faculty adviser, getting beat assignments figured out, and planning the edition that would welcome students to the campus on the first day of classes.

I bumped into Ian Halliday on Wednesday of registration week. I had seen him around the year before, but he was a graduate student and we had never even spoken, let alone considered dating. He had a degree from a small Illinois college in political science and had come to UCLA for a master's in journalism with an eye to working someday in Washington. From my vantage point of covering campus protests and speeches given by visiting dignitaries, both his demeanor and his ambition were intimidating and made him seem as unapproachable as he was intriguing.

But now I was an editor at the paper and he was the adviser's teaching assistant, and despite his brooding looks, his black turtlenecks, the ponytail caught at the back of his neck with a rubber band, and the cigarettes that dangled Jackson Pollock–like from the corner of his mouth when he worked, we seemed more like equals.

"We'll have to get together sometime," he said that day as we waited to pick up the orange computer cards that would admit us to the classes we needed. He was looking for a place in a graduate seminar on ethics in journalism—ironic, as I look back on it now—and I was hoping for an evening class in investigative reporting. The lines were next to each other, and we talked while they inched ahead.

"Sure," I said. "That would be fun."

The night before the first issue went to press we worked late, folded and frowning over a light table, measuring and pasting up last-minute bits of copy, and having a final look at the proofs long after the rest of the editorial staff had gone home.

"How about a beer?" he asked me.

I nodded in agreement. I was exhausted, but I had been waiting for the moment he would ask. We had flirted constantly since our meeting in the registration line. He made cracks about a woman being an editor at a newspaper, and I fired back with remarks about men who had to prove the size of their body parts by backing into parking spots. That morning when I had gotten to campus, his red convertible was already parked in the lot outside the newsroom, its "Hell no, I won't go" rear bumper sticker facing the fence next to the sidewalk instead of the rest of the lot.

Prior to that evening, our exchanges had been more like those between a couple of silly twelve-year-olds than those between a dark beauty in a red bubble dress and a pre-med innocent falling in love for the first time. In our case Ian was the beauty who had been around, and I was the geek who had spent the first three years of college chasing stories and making grades. He teased me for being skinny and observed in his midwestern drawl that I was no bigger than a bar of soap after a week of washing. He flipped rubber bands at me and sailed paper airplanes in my direction like a schoolboy—to the delight and envy of other women students in the room with us at the time. He typeset a dummy headline that said "Maggie Patterson Hired by *The New York Times.*"

Despite its being an era of free love and abundant, open sex, my virginity was still intact, not for lack of several dates' trying or any particular moral or philosophical stand on my part, but just because I hadn't found the right partner. My mother had preached saving it for marriage. I didn't plan to do that exactly, but I was holding out for love. My standard was the intensity I had watched firsthand between my two best friends. I wasn't going to squander myself on a casual relationship.

We drove to a bar at the edge of campus and drank two beers apiece.

"I remember seeing you last fall," Ian said after we had swilled down the first and were waiting for the second to be delivered. "I thought you were cute then, but I was busy and already seeing someone."

"And what has happened to 'someone' since then?" I asked, almost afraid to hear the answer. I didn't want to know there was a girlfriend waiting somewhere for his call or worse, lying in his bed at this very moment, waking occasionally to turn over and check the time on an illuminated clock.

He lit a cigarette and smiled lopsidedly.

"There's only one way to put it," he said. "She dumped me. She went home to San Diego for spring break and met some hotshot Navy pilot whose parents were friends with hers. She moved back there, and they're getting married next year."

"That's too bad," I said.

I hoped I sounded properly sympathetic and not as if I suddenly felt like turning cartwheels around the bar.

"I thought so, too, until I saw you again at registration."

I remember what I had been wearing that day, too—cutoffs and a blue work shirt with the sleeves rolled up, my makeup gone and my hair frizzed as usual in the summer heat, despite the ubiquitous fans that had oscillated continuously.

The beers came and he paid without taking his eyes off of me.

"There's something about you," he said. "You're wiry and intense and serious, and yet you don't let the pressure down there get to you. I would have killed that reporter who misspelled the mayor's name, for Christ's sake."

I shrugged my shoulders and made a face.

"He's just a sophomore," I said. "And that was only the second story he ever wrote. I talked to him about it, but I don't want to scare him away."

"See, that's what I mean. I guess what I'm trying to say is that you're a nice person and I like you," he said, catching my fingers, still cold from holding my glass, into his. I didn't pull them away.

"I like you, too," I said.

And so, like Cynthia and Richard, we did it on the first date, although it probably wasn't as earth-moving as their first time had been. In fact, if Ian ever looked back on that night, I suspect it was with annoyance more than fondness. For one thing, I was totally without a birth control device of any kind. I had never had a reason to take pills or carry a diaphragm in my purse like some of my friends did, as if they were likely to be yanked into a phone booth for a quickie with no time to run home for their supplies. I announced this to Ian only after we had necked on his living room sofa for the better part of an hour. My lips were cut and sore, my blouse was unbuttoned, and he was working at the zipper on my jeans.

"Aw, shit," he said and pulled away. "I don't know if I've got anything, either."

Apparently the ex-girlfriend who was now going to be a Navy wife had come better-prepared than I did. Nevertheless, he went into the bedroom, where I could hear drawers opening and banging shut one after the other, and emerged with a foil wrapper, triumphant and ready to go. He held out a hand to pull me up and led me back to his unmade bed. I slid out of my blouse and kicked off my jeans as smoothly as if I did this for a living. Ian unfastened my bra and moved one hand into my underpants while he undid his belt buckle with the other. He unrolled the condom onto himself and rolled over onto me, but now, naked and ready, he discovered the truth.

"You've never done this before, have you?" he asked me after a couple of thrusts had failed to make their mark.

"No, but I want to," I whispered. I didn't know exactly what the right response would be in a situation like this.

"Oh, man," he said and pulled away. He sat up on the edge of the bed and reached for a pack of cigarettes that lay between a stack of books and a glass of old soda on the bedside table.

"I wanted to save it for somebody I really cared about," I told him, sounding to myself like a Girl Scout or a character straight out of a Victorian novel. Cynthia's accusing me of being a Pollyanna flashed through my mind.

Suddenly I wished I had done it with everyone who ever asked, that I was loose and lubricated like a pro. He smoked in silence, holding the cigarette out in the darkness a couple of times and considering it as if he could find the answer to our dilemma in its molten glow. I didn't know what would happen next, whether I should get up and dress or try to arouse him again. By lifting myself up on my elbows and checking between his legs, I could tell his erection was gone. The condom hung limply off its tip like a tiny, ridiculous hat. I ran my fingers up and down his back. He stubbed the cigarette out in an ashtray on the floor.

"Are you sure?" he asked me. I nodded my head vigorously. "Then we've got to find some kind of lubricant," he said. He went into the bathroom and turned on the light. Something fell into the sink and broke. He swore and came back empty-handed.

"Shit," he said. "I can't find anything."

I remembered the small jar of Vaseline I carried in my purse because I had read somewhere that it would make my pale eye-lashes glisten.

"Wait a minute," I said.

I groped in the darkened living room for my purse and returned with the potion that would save the day.

The first time hurt. My discomfort slowed Ian down but didn't thwart him completely, and when it was over he lay heavily beside me, kissing my shoulder and murmuring apologies until he fell asleep. When I woke up the next morning he was gone, but a note on the kitchen table said he was doing an errand and would be right back. When he returned, he had two coffees, a bag of doughnuts, and a box of prelubricated Trojans. By midafternoon I had gotten the hang of it, and we were—as we said back then— together.

4

In the last photograph ever taken of Richard, Cynthia, and me together, we all look stunned. We are smiling—at least our lips are curled in the right direction and in Richard's case there is an excessive show of teeth—but our eyes give away that something is terribly wrong. It was taken on Thanksgiving Day, 1990. In the foreground, on the table, is a wicker cornucopia from which spill real bananas, apples, oranges, and grapes. By that time Cynthia had the art of homemaking down to a science. The perfect turkey was decked out in white paper frills. She had piped sweet potato puree into hollowed-out orange-peel cups and topped each one with toasted brown sugar and a candied cherry. The cranberry sauce was fresh and homemade, and so were the pumpkin and apple pies she had produced from scratch.

Cynthia warmed our dinner plates in the oven and changed wines between courses. The napkins were linen, each embroidered with a symbol of the holiday—tiny turkeys, Pilgrims, Native

Americans, a pile of squash, a colorful ear of corn. I cringed, still embarrassed about the tacky paper holiday napkins I had taken the first time I went to Cynthia's house. In the background their stereo system softly played the first carols of the Christmas season.

We started the meal with a shrimp cocktail and champagne. Coming from a family that put the potatoes right onto the table in the mixing bowl in which they had been mashed and gauged the servings of jellied cranberry sauce from the indentations left by the can, I thought it was going to be one of the most elegant holidays I had ever spent. The one at Cynthia's dad's house in La Jolla didn't count since the whole meal had been delivered by a caterer and nothing tasted quite like the Thanksgivings I was used to. Even the pumpkin pie had been garnished with some kind of bourbon-laced whipped cream instead of sprayed from a can. It might have been fancy and expensive and the table with its gleaming china and sparkling silverware like something off a magazine cover, but it just didn't seem real. Also, I had been homesick and everyone else at the table was virtually silent after the events of the night before.

On the same page in our album are other photographs taken that day, most of them giveaways that it hadn't turned out exactly as we had hoped. My husband, Peter, appears in very few of the pictures because he was the one with a camera so he took most of them. In the two or three in which he does turn up I can tell he is annoyed, although he, too, is attempting to smile. He didn't like Cynthia from the beginning, and now this.

There is only one of my stepson, Jack, who had just turned nineteen and is sitting in front of a televised football game and sipping a technically illegal can of beer. He is laughing because the picture was taken before dinner by Chloe, who triumphantly believed she had caught him doing something he wasn't supposed to and planned to blackmail him with it.

"Maybe you can sell it to a beer company for an ad in a magazine," he told her. He had asked permission, so now the joke was on her.

"Hmmm, not a bad idea. I could get you put in jail," she said, and then she snapped the picture.

I realized when I looked through the pictures again not long ago that they were flirting, even way back then.

In one the children are posed in a group. Chloe was just about to turn sixteen, and Lorraine, her sister, would have been eleven. My Todd was eight and his sister Mae was six. Of all of us, she is the only one making no attempt to hide her feelings. She is obviously crying. Her mouth is upside down, and one fist in which she clutches the sleeve of her sweater wipes at tears. Todd stands behind her with a protective hand on her shoulder, trying to look brave. Richard and Cynthia's girls look tense and worried. I figured out later that this wasn't the first time a meal at their house had taken a wrong turn, and they look in the pictures as if they know others will, too.

The problem stemmed, I thought at first, from Cynthia's working too hard to get everything ready for our arrival. I hadn't been to visit for several years, and Peter had never been to their home. I could see when we walked in the day before that while the house was spotless and the guest rooms fitted with fresh flowers, thick fluffy towels, and my favorite lily-of-the-valley soap, she was frazzled. Maybe if she hadn't been so tired, she would have tried to control the demon that even then was threatening to ruin her life. As it was, her defenses were down, and when she thought Richard had insulted her, she let him have it.

The conversation started out innocently enough, with us talking about some volunteer work Cynthia had started doing. With her children's activities and Richard's career making so many demands on her socially, she had never gotten around to finishing college, but a shelter for battered women had opened up in Kansas City, where they had lived for several years by that time, and she had started working just the month before as an unpaid coordinator.

"I work there three days a week—Monday, Tuesday, and Wednesday," she told us.

We had just filled our plates and begun to eat. Since she had spent the past two days in the kitchen, she understandably wasn't as interested in the feast she had prepared as we were. She rested her elbows on the table and folded her hands above her untouched plate. Obviously what did interest her was talking about her new volunteer job.

"I go in at eight and stay until three. That way I can pick the girls up at school and be home when they are. At lunchtime we send out for sandwiches or bring in potluck. We eat with whatever women are staying there at the time. You'd be surprised how much more they open up when they realize we want to be their friends and not just deal with them on a professional basis."

Richard told me later that day—and on several other occasions when my loyalty had shifted to him and he had called me to talk—that he never intended the cruelty that his next remark inflicted, but he had been insensitive and his timing couldn't have been worse. Without even acknowledging what Cynthia had said he launched into a story about how he had had to fire a nurse in his office who had countermanded the orders he had given to several patients. On one occasion she told a woman with financial troubles that if she broke her tablets in half and just took a partial dosage each day, they would last longer and thus cost her less. On another an elderly man had opted to follow her instructions for a mustard plaster instead of taking the antibiotics Richard had prescribed, and he could have lost an arm to infection. He was fed up, he said, with people who lacked the proper training giving advice to his patients and putting them in danger. The nurse had let her job go to her head, he said.

"If she wants to be a doctor, let her go to fucking medical school," he said by way of wrapping up. Then he glanced at the children at the other end of the table and winced. "Sorry!"

"So we were talking about my job," Cynthia said, frowning slightly. "What does that have to do with what I do at the shelter?"

"Well, what I'm saying, honey," he said, "is I wouldn't exactly call what you do professional. Laypeople can do as much damage as they do good if they're not careful, especially when it comes to dealing with the kinds of issues those women have."

He held a forkful of sliced turkey in one hand and the corner of a roll in the other and was still chewing as he spoke. Cynthia's enthusiastic smile froze.

"Well, I guess it depends on how you define 'professional,'" she said.

Her voice was icy. I shot a sideways look at Peter, who was sitting next to me, and then one across the table at Jack. My younger children hadn't caught on yet, but Chloe and Lorraine were sitting up straight and tense, in fight-or-flight mode, waiting to see what would happen next.

"Usually professional means an advanced degree or some kind of specialized training," Richard said. "You haven't even finished your bachelor's."

I wanted to scream at him to stop talking, but by then it would have been too late anyway.

"Advanced degrees and specialized training like, for example, you have?"

"Well, yes, if you want to put it like that. I did finish college and then go to medical school, internship, and residency to be able to do what I do," he shot back. "How many people at your shelter can make that claim?"

"The director has her doctorate in psychology."

"Yes, but the rest of you are just office staff or unpaid volunteers. You can't call yourself a professional if you don't make any money at what you do."

"But I am trained. I had to go through a three-day workshop before I could start working there."

"I'm just not sure that handing someone a stack of sheets and a ham sandwich and telling them everything is going to be okay qualifies as 'professional.'" He looked at Peter and me for confirmation, but by that time both of us were completely engrossed in what was on our plates and wishing we had stayed home.

"Really?" she countered, with the accent heavily on the first syllable.

Their eyes were riveted on one another as if none of the rest of us was in the room. These two were legendary lovers, but when they fought you had to wonder if anyone would survive. I had learned that lesson all too well back at their campus apartment.

The rest of us were silent, silverware and glasses stopped in transit from table to lips. There was no question of trying to take sides or to interject that the conversation was pointless and perhaps not worth ruining Thanksgiving dinner over. There was no laughing nervously and trying to move on to another topic.

"My point is just that if we're trying to define 'professional' here, I would say what you do probably isn't. It's generous and kind for sure, just not professional in the dictionary sense."

"So if I could have gone back to school at any of the points I wanted to, maybe by now I'd have a master's or a doctorate. Maybe I'd be the director of the center rather than one of those disgusting unpaid volunteers. Maybe then you'd think I was 'professional.'"

"Nobody said anything about 'disgusting,' honey, but well, yes, I suppose so. But that's not what happened, and any way you look at it, a three-day seminar does not a professional make."

"You condescending son of a bitch," she cried.

And then, without regard for the rest of us, without stopping to think that the china had been her grandmother's Limoges and the pattern long since discontinued, she picked up her plate and hurled it at Richard. This time she screamed, "You fucking son of a bitch!" and ran crying from the room and up the stairs to their bedroom on the second floor. The whole house seemed to shake when she slammed the door.

Richard tried to make light of the situation as he used a teaspoon to scrape potatoes, turkey, stuffing, and cranberry sauce off the front of his shirt. The antique plate had come mercifully to rest in his lap in one piece.

"Gee, do you think it was something I said?" he asked, chuckling without humor. And then, when no one spoke, he pushed away from the table and headed in the direction Cynthia had gone. "We'll be right back," he said.

But that rosy June of 1977, when we had just finished school and our futures stretched out long before us, those tense moments were still years away. Earlier in our photo album is a picture of Richard and Cynthia, Ian and me, taken by a waiter at a hotel restaurant in Beverly Hills. In it we are raising glasses toward the camera. They are filled with champagne, and we are laughing, our prospects so good, so filled with bright, shiny bubbles of hope. We had just graduated—me from college, Ian with his master's, and Richard with his MD. Ian had landed a job at the *San Francisco Examiner*, and when he had found out they needed two more people he suggested me. I flew up the next day for an interview and got one of the jobs.

"As long as we're here, we might as well look for a place to live," he had said that night over bowls of thick clam chowder and chunks of sourdough bread in a tourist spot at Fisherman's Wharf.

At first I didn't catch what he meant.

"I can't afford much to start," I said. "I figure just a studio somewhere as close to the paper as possible since I don't have a car."

"I was thinking maybe we could find a place together," he said.

I missed the meaning of that, too.

"You mean get married?" I squealed in surprise.

We had been dating exclusively and sleeping together the whole year, but never once had we talked about making it permanent. Our futures were too shaky. There was always the chance that we'd find jobs at opposite ends of the planet, and something else I had already learned from Richard and Cynthia was that I wasn't prepared to have what I wanted to do with my life come a distant second after my husband's plans or maybe not at all. Instantly I realized that wasn't what he had in mind.

"God, no!" he said. "I just mean live together. You know, shack up. I've got the car and some money saved, and we're going to be working at the same place, so it just makes sense. But, hey, don't try to rush me into anything. I'm not saying we won't get married someday, but I'm not ready for that kind of heavy commitment shit now, just when I'm making a beginning."

I wasn't ready, either, but I had liked the idea of his proposing to me, and maybe for a moment I entertained the idea of walking down an aisle and wearing a wide gold wedding ring and hyphenating my name. His fast retreat hurt my feelings a little bit.

"Nobody's rushing you into anything," I said, biting my lip. "I just wanted to make sure I understood what you meant. I don't know if I'm even ready for that much. Let me think about it overnight and we can talk about it in the morning."

In the end I agreed, and we signed a year's lease on the top floor of a green-and-yellow Victorian whose kitchen window looked out onto a narrow view of the Bay Bridge that sliced between two tall office buildings facing the street behind us. The night of the champagne photograph we had just shown Richard and Cynthia pictures of our new home, and they had announced they were moving to Kansas City.

"Kansas City?" I said to Cynthia. I was more than a little surprised. I had always assumed her two-story wallpapered dream house, while very different from her parents', would nonetheless be somewhere on the West Coast.

"It's only for a year," she said. "I wouldn't be this excited if I thought I'd be stuck out there permanently, but it's great for Richard's career. You two should come and visit us while we're there."

"Well, honey, it could be longer if I stay there for my residency," Richard said to Cynthia. "We'll just have to see how everything goes."

Then he turned back to us.

"I think I told you that I had applied to three internship programs, and I got accepted by two—one of them was here in California," Richard said, "but Kansas City Samaritan is the best. With credentials from there I'll be able to write my own ticket. We'll be able to settle wherever we want, especially if I stay on for the residency. It was a tough choice, but I think I made the right one. "

"And I'll finally be able to finish my degree," Cynthia said.

"Not right away, though," Richard said. "There's really no point in taking a lot of classes out there that might not transfer if we come back here at the end of a year."

"Well, whatever," she told him brightly. "You're right. Let's just see how it goes."

∽

None of the plans we made that happy night turned out exactly as we thought they would. They would move and I would go to Kansas City to visit them, but Ian would never see either of them again. Richard and Cynthia worked furiously to pack up their apartment in just a few days. It had come furnished, so they were able to pile their belongings—books, dishes, records, and clothes—into the back of their hatchback and a rented trailer that Richard drove away toward their new life in the Midwest. Meanwhile Cynthia and Chloe took the train to San Diego for a visit with her father and Caroline in La Jolla. They would stay for a few days, she told me, and fly off to join Richard the following Monday.

"Can you see me driving off across the Mojave Desert with a baby?" she asked, tapping pink fingernails that even in those early days were perfectly manicured on the Formica table in the coffee shop at the train station. "I don't think so."

I had driven them downtown in Ian's convertible, and after our coffee I helped carry their luggage to the platform while Cynthia pushed Chloe along in a collapsible stroller. Just before they got on board she hugged me tightly.

"I don't know what we would have done without you," she said. "Any of us. We're all going to miss you."

Chloe giggled and pointed to the train.

"I'm going to miss you, too, Cyn," I told her. "You and Richard and now Chloe have been like family ever since we met. Please let's not let that go."

She had tears in her eyes, but she laughed them away in embarrassment.

"Hey, kid, no chance of that," she said. "You aren't going to get rid of us that easily."

She scooped up Chloe, and I folded the stroller and handed it up to a waiting conductor. As they turned and disappeared into the car I heard her call out, "You write first."

I did write in those pre-email days, and so did she, volumes at first—letters, postcards, birthday and anniversary and Christmas greetings. Sometimes hers included photographs, sometimes articles out of the newspaper naming Richard the head of some medical board or applauding Cynthia's charity work. I sent back clippings of my best stories. Her family's importance to me never faded, but the details of my own life filled much of the space that had once been reserved for them. And the gradual disengaging that must naturally take place between friends who live far apart began that very afternoon. Their train pulled out at 3:07. I found their window and waved for as long as I could see them, Cynthia waving Chloe's hand as well as her own. Minutes later I was back on the freeway, the list of things to do in my head already crowding out the sadness I felt at telling my best friend goodbye.

Their move was now well underway, but ours was still unfinished and chaotic. There was the matter of deciding whose belongings to keep and whose to drop off at the thrift shop on campus. We had both lived in furnished places, too, so our belongings consisted primarily of the same accumulation of lamps and pillows Cynthia and Richard had—many of them duplicates. Ian and I packed, we argued over whose coffee pot we'd keep and whose pillows were firmest and whether we needed the rug I'd had beside my bed, and then we made up.

Three days behind Cynthia, Ian's car with a trailer of our own was packed, and we drove as joyfully north as Richard had east. For Ian and me it was a little like a honeymoon before we started living together. With the pressure of getting away behind us and the stress of our new jobs still lying ahead, we stretched the seven-hour trip into two days and planned to treat them like a real vacation before we went to work. We drove up the Pacific Coast Highway and spent the night at a seedy beach hotel, sitting on our rickety balcony until nearly two in the morning drinking wine and then making love with the window open, despite the noisy air conditioner, so we could hear the waves wash up on the sand below.

When we woke up it was nearly noon, and now that we were rested and pointed away from LA, we both wanted nothing so much as to get to San Francisco and settle into our new home. We feasted on fresh strawberries and cantaloupe we bought from a roadside stand for breakfast and a bag of hamburgers for a late-afternoon lunch, otherwise stopping only for gas.

For the rest of the week before we had to turn up at work, we bought furniture—the rough-hewn wood and corduroy sling chairs that were popular then, a matching sofa, a thick brown-and-white braided rug for the living room, two used desks for the second bedroom that would now be our office, and a waterbed that we christened as soon as it was set up and filled, forgetting at the outset that it hadn't had time to heat. When we were finished the clammy chill quickly cooled the heat of our passion and sent us back to the chores at hand.

∽

The next Monday I followed in a cloud of musky perfume behind Andrea Stone, a thirty-ish, tall, no-nonsense, '50s-looking blonde in high heels, huge hoop earrings, and bright red lipstick, as she threaded us through a maze of desks and filing cabinets in the newsroom. A few reporters and editors looked up curiously or stood up and shook my hand; most were too busy pounding on typewriters or answering ringing phones to notice. At last we arrived at the cubicle that would be mine.

"Home sweet home," she said, smiling fleetingly and waving her hand in the direction of a banged-up wooden desk separated from its neighbor by a sheet of corkboard studded with thumbtacks that would now be mine. "It's not much, but it's about all anybody has."

The editors and their assistants, of which she was one, had space in a cluster of glassed-in offices. Behind their windows I saw people laughing into telephones or having conversations with each other beyond our hearing. I looked at them longingly and wished for a quieter place to work. *Someday*, I thought, but for now I was thrilled with what I had—a real job at a big newspaper right out of college. I had been luckier than most of my classmates, and I'd make it to the glass offices in my own good time.

Andrea broke into my reverie.

"The morgue's at the end of the hall when you need to do research," she said. "Supplies are in the cabinet on the opposite side of the newsroom. Any questions?"

"I don't think so," I said. "Thanks for the tour."

"Okay, then, I've got one for you," she said. "How well do you know Ian Halliday?"

Ian and I had rehearsed this part carefully. The paper had a strict policy against married couples working together. We weren't sure how that applied to our situation, so we decided to play it safe and keep our relationship secret until we tested the waters. We weren't willing to blow good jobs for the privilege of holding hands at the copy machine.

"Pretty well," I said. "We had several classes together in J-school, and we worked together on the campus paper. I guess he thought he knew my work well enough to recommend me for this job."

She arched her eyebrows.

"Hmmm. Do you know if he's seeing anybody?"

My stomach lurched and the insecurities against which I constantly struggled came instantly to the surface. My eyes hadn't gotten any bigger or farther apart than they ever were. Neither had my wild head of red frizz decided to settle down into anything even remotely resembling a hairstyle. The bond that had brought Ian and me together had been the newspaper business. If she had looks as well as that, I might as well disassemble my half of the sofa and hit the road right now.

"I think he has a girlfriend, but I'm not sure," I said.

"Well, that's too bad," she said and then, as if it were an afterthought, "Oh, the big guy wants to meet with both of you at eleven o'clock this morning."

That night, perched on new barstools in our kitchen and eating takeout Chinese right from the square white cartons, I handled the Andrea situation in the worst possible way.

"I think Andrea Stone has a crush on you already," I blurted out.

He frowned. "What makes you say that?"

"She asked me if you had a girlfriend."

"And you said ...?"

"I said I thought so, but I wasn't sure. Then she said if you did, it was too bad."

A smile played at the corners of his mouth.

"Well, good," he said.

"What is that supposed to mean?" I asked. The sinking feeling in my stomach had never completely gone away.

"It means I have an advantage, however small. It means if I want to do a particular story or need some help from her boss, I'll probably get it."

"It also means the first time things aren't perfect between us you've got someplace else to go," I said.

I was insecure and pathetic. He was my first real boyfriend and the one to whom I had given my dubiously precious virginity. And the fact was, I loved him, or thought I did. I didn't have any practice in being cool and disinterested. There was no way I could pretend that if he left me, my life would move right on along. I didn't know then how to take the upper hand, how to make a man think I didn't care in order to make him care for me more.

"No chance, cupcake," he said, reaching across the counter to fondle my cheek with the back of his fingertips. "We're in this thing together. We're Clark Kent and Lois Lane. And we're going to do such a good job that when we finally do tell the world we're a couple, they won't be able to do without us."

For the next few months I had no need to worry. I was ambitious, but Ian was completely driven, and because we shared a home and a car, I learned to keep the same hours he did, earning myself the same workaholic reputation he had. We got to work by six thirty every morning, ate lunch at our desks, stayed late, and took work home. Even on weekends, everything we did was connected with our jobs. We carried notebooks everywhere, jotting down ideas and taking notes. At story conferences—his in the news department, mine in features—we came up with enough ideas for everyone. The pieces we wrote were so long and packed with information and colorful detail that editors hated to cut them, often preferring instead to divide them into a series or put the most outstanding facts into a sidebar or box. We supplemented news stories with profiles and background items. We helped each other, so every story really had two people working on it, but of course no one knew that.

Ian still talked about Washington being his ultimate goal, but we had both fallen in love with San Francisco. At the Christmas party we told people we were dating, a month later that we had moved in together, and no one seemed to care. We began to entertain occasionally, having other reporters in for fondue and wine, but mostly we ate on the run and worked so hard that if Ian had wanted to see Andrea on the side, it would have had to be between two and six in the morning. And that was if he hadn't stayed up all night to read, long after I had snuggled into the waterbed, wrapped in one of my mother's handmade quilts, and fallen into an exhausted sleep.

Richard and Cynthia were due to move back to California the following June, but on a foggy Sunday morning in January the phone rang. Ian and I were sprawled in sweatpants and T-shirts on our braided rug with the newspaper spread out between us, drinking newly replenished mugs of hot coffee. Earlier we had scrambled eggs with green pepper and onion and eaten them with sourdough toast and homemade strawberry jam. Now that I lived closer to Santa Rosa my mother brought us something almost every time she came into the city. The remains hardened on wheat-colored pottery plates that now were stacked on the coffee table.

"Cyn!" I cried happily when I heard her voice. Medical interns didn't get paid much more than we did as reporters, and back then long-distance calls were expensive and nobody could afford to call unless it was important. We wrote, but I hadn't heard her voice since New Year's Eve. "What's up?"

In the pause that followed I heard her crying.

"Cyn?" I said again. "Are you okay?"

"Oh, God, Maggie," she said. I could hear her blowing her nose and then sniffing. "We're not coming back in June."

"So when are you coming back?" I asked. "And what is there to cry about?"

"I mean I don't think we're coming back at all. Overachieving Richard made such an impression on the staff at the hospital here that they asked him to stay on for his residency. When he's done with that, one of them has already made him an offer to join his practice."

"Has he decided for sure?" I asked.

"Oh, yes," she went on. "In fact, he asked me what I thought, but there was no question what he wanted, so I told him to go ahead and sign the contract."

"It sounds good for him, but did you tell him it wasn't what you wanted?"

"Sure, but I didn't have a leg to stand on. He pointed out what a great place the Midwest is for raising kids. And if he joins that practice, he's going to make a fortune. With the cost of living so much lower here, we'll be able to buy a house a lot sooner than we had planned. In fact, we're already looking."

"So you think this is really permanent?"

"It's a lifetime decision, Maggie. You don't change medical practices like you do clerical jobs. No, this means we're here forever. And you're out there, and my dad's out there, and the ocean's out there, and I'm here in the middle of some goddamned corn patch."

I could hear her crying again. I was disappointed, too, but there didn't seem to be anything to be gained by siding in her despair.

"Let's look at the good points," I said to her brightly, as I supposed Richard must have done when he told her what he wanted to do. "Richard's certainly right about raising kids out there. There's less crime, less pollution, less traffic, fewer people."

"I didn't call to hear your annoying optimism," she snapped. "I notice you're not rushing out to the middle of nowhere to set up shop."

"Only because our jobs are here," I said, not altogether truthfully. "I've never been to Kansas City, but I've heard it's beautiful. They have an opera there and a really good art museum."

"Like those are reasons to stay."

"Maybe not, but they are some of the advantages to staying. And I do understand Richard's not wanting to turn down such a good position. And you're wrong about there not being anything good about this. For one thing, now we can come and visit you, like you said. For another, doesn't this mean you can start back to school?"

"I could have done that in California," she said dully. "But, yes, I guess that's what I'll do. I've got to have something to keep me from going completely crazy or dying of boredom."

But she didn't. In the couple of years that followed I got more letters from her than I ever had, and the long-distance calls picked up, too, made possible by Richard's ever-increasing paycheck and a determination to keep his wife happy at any price. Then there were pictures of a rambling two-story house on an exclusive street called Ward Parkway, which Cynthia told me was one of the best areas in the city.

"It's old money," she bubbled during one of our phone conversations. "But we got the house at a steal. It needs some work, of course, but it has five bedrooms and a formal dining room. The kitchen floor is red ceramic tile, and two of the bathrooms have the original claw-foot tubs. We had planned to wait for a while, but this came along and we couldn't afford to pass it up. Daddy gave us the down payment, and we can afford the mortgage because of Richard's income."

The anger and reluctance of her earlier call seemed to have evaporated, and in its place I detected a tone of superiority.

"Have you looked into starting back to school this fall?" I asked her.

"No time," she said cheerfully, as if the whole prickly situation were no longer an issue. "I called the university and had them send me a catalog, but by the time it came we were in escrow with the house, and now there's so much work to be done. I'm going to spend this year getting the house in shape, and then when Chloe starts kindergarten, I'll start back, too."

"You sound a lot happier about being there than you were at the beginning," I said.

"I am. Yes, I guess I am. I mean, Richard's delirious he's so excited. His work is going great, and now that we've got the house. . . . You were right. I've got a lot to be happy about. I really do."

Not long after that I began to be suspicious of Ian and Andrea Stone in earnest. It was nothing I could really put my finger on. Ian worked late, like he always had, but so did I, so I was usually around. Now that everyone knew about us, we could wait for each other openly instead of leaving separately and waiting in the night chill for the other one to come out. There were no lipstick stains on his collar, no unexplained nights away, no hurriedly finished telephone calls when I came into the room. It was just a feeling I had, based more on Andrea's behavior than on his. She and I had never become best pals, but we had been friendly and occasionally had lunch together, and once we went for a beer after work when Ian was out of town on assignment.

Now I noticed she no longer sought out my company and actually seemed to try and avoid me when I sought out hers—even when it had to do with work. Once, when we were alone together in the elevator, she acted like a trapped animal, desperate to get out. She checked her watch, stared frantically at the illuminated numbers above the door, and bolted when we reached our floor.

"I just hate elevators," she giggled nervously over her shoulder. We had ridden together in this very one countless times before and she had been fine.

After that I realized that when we actually needed to talk about something or when we ran into each other in the hall, her eyes slid from mine as if they had been oiled and couldn't stay on track in their sockets. Her conversations now seemed aimed at my jacket pocket or my earrings.

Meanwhile, life at home also changed in small, almost imperceptible ways. It was looks Ian gave me or the station he played on the radio. Suddenly he was wild about country-western music and said my preference for jazz, which he had always shared, was "narrow." Just as suddenly he developed a passion for Greek food and paisley ties. And abruptly he quit smoking. I knew something was changing; I just couldn't pin down exactly what it was. The giveaway was the day in March when I went into Andrea's office to ask for a phone number and found Ian digging through her purse.

"Jesus, Ian, what are you doing?" I asked him.

"Borrowing five bucks for the basketball pool from Andrea until I can get to the bank this afternoon."

"I've got five dollars you can have," I said, although this was not at all the point.

"I know, but you were out doing an interview when the guys in sports asked me if I wanted in. I asked Andrea, and she said just to get it out of her purse."

It was such a small thing, but I knew how I guarded my purse—not for security but simply because my cache of lipstick, hair pick, and tampons was not public domain. Cynthia and I had never even looked into each other's purses, and I was taught from childhood that my mother's handbag was private, which had made all the more mysterious and special the suckers and chewing gum and tissues she pulled from its depths.

Early the next morning, after a night in which I had not slept, I confronted Ian point-blank. His look was incredulous.

"Oh, God, are we back on that? I thought we laid that one to rest a long time ago."

"Well, then Andrea was still talking to me, we still listened to jazz together, and you weren't rummaging in her purse."

"This makes absolutely no sense," he said. "I think you're working too hard. You've never taken a day of vacation. Why don't you take some time off, maybe even try to get away? Your folks would love to have you come up and stay for a few days."

"Oh, right, so you can move Andrea right in here and not have to limit your romance to flirting when I'm not in the newsroom."

I knew I sounded like a harpy, but I couldn't stop. I knew I was right about this.

"Women only let people they're really close to get into their purses," I said, beginning now to cry despite my best efforts not to.

"And it's other little things that seem insignificant one by one but taken together add up to a pattern. I just wish you'd tell me and get it out in the open. I can't stand lies, and I don't want to be in a relationship with somebody who doesn't want me."

He sighed as if I had made him very tired.

"Okay, you're partly right," he said. "I needed some help with the research on that piece I was doing about the state legislature, so I took her with me the day I went up to Sacramento. I took her out to lunch, and she probably thought it was supposed to mean something."

"That's all? All of this intimacy and purse-searching stems from one lunch in Sacramento?"

"She organized the data for me, and I picked it up at her place."

"And when was this?" I asked.

"I don't know. Three weeks or so ago."

"The weekend you were supposedly in the office until four in the morning? The weekend we had to cancel going to the media awards dinner because you were on a deadline?"

"That might have been it. I don't remember."

"But instead of being at work while I waited for you here, you were at Andrea's apartment, right?"

"All right, yes."

"And all that time you were just working away on data you collected about the legislature."

"No." His voice was low. He had given up the fight. "I also fucked her."

Between two and six in the morning, just like I had joked.

"You're kidding me!" I yelled, although I already knew that he wasn't. I could accept and forgive a crush, maybe even a kiss. I had worked late myself with other guys, had covered a movie premiere one night with a photographer who invited me to his place for a nightcap. I knew about temptation, but I had never given in.

"No, but right now I wish I were."

"So what happens next?" I asked him. It was not a rhetorical question. I could see our life disintegrating in real time, as if an earthquake had hit our apartment and our books and our carefully chosen pillows and china were rocking into the bay.

"I don't know. I guess that's up to you," he said.

"Are you in love with her?" Corny as it sounds, that's all that mattered to me. If he had said no, I could have pulled his sad, pathetic face to my breast and relegated Andrea to the past.

"I don't know," he said.

"Are you in love with me?"

"I don't know that, either."

"Then I think you'd better pack your things and move out."

I heard myself say this to him. My brain was still paralyzed with the image of Ian locked in a naked, sweaty embrace with Andrea, her bleached curls against the pillow, her arms and legs wrapped around him, her red nails digging into his back as clear to me as if I had been there watching the night it happened.

"Look, let's not be melodramatic about this," he said. "Just give me a couple of days to think it through. I'm not crazy about throwing away everything we have."

I wasn't sure whether he meant the stereo system and the waterbed, or the feelings and body fluids we had exchanged, but I was sure I wouldn't fight Andrea or anybody else for Ian. Our bond of trust had been broken, and if he didn't know, then my decision was easy.

"If you can't decide between us, then she can have you," I said. "Now, I'm going to work, and when I get home tonight, I want you out of here. I'm staying in the apartment. You can have anything else you want. Take it all."

He knew there was no negotiating. When I left a few minutes later he was already emptying his drawers in our bureau. We never even said goodbye.

I made it my business not to find out how the affair between Ian and Andrea progressed. He had had enough decency to leave behind the furniture and dishes, the posters and rugs with which we had feathered our nest, so at least I had someplace to retreat to each day after seeing both of them at work and still trying to maintain my reputation as a pro, someone whose personal problems didn't get in the way of her more important career. It was rumored around the newsroom that the assistant features editor was about to retire, and I didn't want anything to get in the way of being considered for her job if she did. If I could land that, I'd be on my way up the career ladder, and, almost as important, I'd work in one of those glass offices where I couldn't hear the talk about the happy couple.

Ian was a gentleman at work, too. The only way I knew for sure the two of them were even seeing each other was through a gossipy copyeditor who couldn't keep his mouth shut and thought I would want to hear the juicy details. They kept their distance from me, and if they ever moved in together, they still came to work in separate cars. Meanwhile I took the bus, arriving back home every evening emotionally drained, lighting candles and playing music and drinking too much wine and eating too little food, a wounded animal taking refuge in my lair.

Eventually I even began dating again, but I never brought anybody home. Already Ian had left his mark on every bedspread and sofa cushion as surely as if he had lifted his tail and sprayed. I didn't want to look at the rug on my floor and remember a man sitting there, lifting a glass in my direction, smiling as he selected records or ran his finger along the spines of my books. I didn't want anybody to drink out of my coffee mugs or look into my refrigerator. Most of all, I didn't want another man in my bed. If it happened somewhere else, fine, but I didn't want more memories that I would have to work this hard to forget. I didn't want to remember the smell of a man's desire or the sound of his satisfaction as I hauled our spotted and aromatic sheets to the laundromat at the end of the block. I didn't want to think about the silhouette of a naked man in the moonlit bathroom doorway, his pants and jacket tossed carelessly across my chair.

It finally did happen, but I was far away from home when Stan Cohen, the photographer who had tried to seduce me before, finally had his way. Knowing that Ian and I had broken up, he asked me without ceremony or pretense to go away with him for a weekend. His parents had a condo at Lake Tahoe, he said, but they were in Europe for the summer and with the ski season over, the place should be peaceful and quiet. The idea of getting away to a spot where Ian and I had never been was reason enough, but I was also ready to have sex with another man. Ian was still the only person I had ever slept with, and if I couldn't scald away his traces with an acid douche, I would obliterate them in the only way I could.

We drove up on Friday night and had dinner at a French restaurant on a pier that extended out into the lake. I drank enough wine to make sure I didn't have second thoughts later. It wasn't that Stan wasn't attractive. He was—in his own short, slightly overweight, bearded way. He was married to his work, which is why his wife had left him—always in a rush with a camera bag slung over his shoulder and wearing a khaki vest with canisters of film tucked into his pockets, but he was a pal, and I still carried around the ridiculous idea that lovemaking should be with someone I loved.

Back at the condo we went straight to it, the first time against a rough carpet on the living room floor and later in his parents' bed, which might have bothered me had the tables been turned but didn't seem to faze him. The next day we hiked and picnicked until midafternoon; then we came back for another bout in the bedroom. My lack of involvement emboldened me. I smoked a joint with him, then I poured wine for us in the nude. I drizzled some of mine across my belly and invited him to lick it off, a favor he promptly returned with a different body part. We napped for a while, then barbecued steaks out on the deck before going at it again as if we had set out to break a record or to finish a job so arduous it allowed only enough time off to eat and sleep. But now I was sober, and I knew this would be the last time. When we had finished I went into the bathroom and cried. When I came back to bed, Stan was propped up on one elbow, waiting to talk.

"Look, Maggie," he started out, fumbling for words that I could easily have supplied. "Jesus, you know how much I like you, but you know I've just been divorced for about a year, and I'm not looking for a girlfriend or anything permanent here."

"I'm fine," I said.

"I heard you crying. Maybe it was a bad idea coming up here, but I knew you and Ian had broken up, and I thought maybe, you know, we could just have a good time together. I don't want to hurt you, but I don't want you to think that this, you know, means anything."

"I don't think it means anything, Stan," I said, smiling now. "I certainly don't."

In the middle of the summer, the managing editor called everyone into the conference room to announce that the assistant features editor would retire at the end of the month.

"I'm delighted to be able to tell you that our own Ian Halliday will be moving over from the news side to carry on the fine tradition of high-quality feature stories we've worked so hard to build here at the *Examiner*," he said. He said a lot more, too, but I had no idea what. I was staring at Ian, who was smiling modestly and later accepting congratulations. Andrea stood by his side beaming.

When the meeting was over, I followed the managing editor back to his office.

"I have to tell you how disappointed I am," I told him. "If I had known for sure Sadie was retiring, I would have applied for her job. I didn't even know it was open."

He leaned forward in his chair and frowned.

"You know, I mentioned you to Andrea. You were my first choice. I thought this sounded more like something you'd like a crack at than Ian, to tell you the truth. But she said she had asked you about it and you said you weren't interested. In fact, she said you were holding out for a job in one of the bureaus—maybe Washington, DC."

Ian's tenure in his new job was not to last long, however. During a drive down the coast that autumn to interview someone about the new phenomenon of the Silicon Valley, he lost control of his car and crashed down an embankment. The convertible top was down, and he was thrown out, then crushed by his own car and killed instantly.

For a few days I worked in a fog. I had never completely gotten over him, and when I heard he was dead I thought I loved him still and might never recover. *What if I'd stayed with him,* I wondered. Would he have worked through his feelings for Andrea and decided on me? Would we have been cooking breakfast together in our apartment that morning when his wheels left the pavement and he found himself airborne?

Andrea came back to work the day after his funeral, her eyes red and swollen. Everybody in the office stopped what they were doing to hug her or squeeze her hand and express their sorrow. She was as close to a widow as he had, but had he ever cared about her at all, or did it all have to do with getting an edge on Sadie's job? I'd never know now.

I loved him, I hated him. I wanted to grieve, but I couldn't. That position had also been filled. Our colleagues didn't know what to say to me, so they said nothing. At night I came through my front door crying; then I iced down my eyelids so that by morning no one would know. Finally I picked up my phone and dialed Cynthia's number. This time I was the one crying when someone else answered the phone.

"Cyn?" I said when I heard her voice. "I'm coming to Kansas City."

5

The weather was clear for the flight over Nevada and Utah, but by Colorado we were above thunderstorms, and so, as we crossed over Kansas and approached Missouri, I was not prepared for the spectacle that panned out below us when we broke through the clouds. The airport was several miles away from the city itself and surrounded by trees, a puzzle of asphalt, and concrete amid a thousand intense shades of green tinged with just the first hints of yellows, golds, and reds. Except for the trip to Canada, I had never been out of California. My mother was an avid hiker who claimed that if you lived in a state that had Yosemite and the ocean, you really didn't need to go anywhere else, and we never did. There were other reasons, too, mostly having to do with money and the farm. My dad always said it was more trouble than it was worth to go away for more than a few days at a time. When I left, much of the state was parched after a summer with no rain, but now this—a panorama of luxurious colorful foliage for as far as I could see.

Cynthia met me at the gate—we could still do that then—and hugged me tight. She was excited and looked wonderful, although a little heavier than I remembered. After Chloe was born she'd never fully recovered the tiny figure she'd had in college, but now she looked healthy and good. Her hair was different, too, up in a twist on the back of her head, which gave her the look of a serious wife and mother.

I couldn't have gone home to my mother with my current situation. Although she had liked Ian and was sorry when we broke up, she had never quite approved of my living situation with him, and I had never told her all the details of our split. Even in my anger and pain I didn't want my family to think I had been shacked up with a jerk. What I needed now was some plain talk with a girlfriend so I could get my job and my life back into some kind of order. Being here with Cynthia, with her taking charge, insisting on lugging my carry-on bag, and herding me toward baggage claim, seemed like the next best thing.

"I love your trees," I babbled while we waited by the carousel that for several minutes failed to produce my graduation suitcase. "I couldn't believe it when the plane came out of the clouds. You know what it's like in California at this time of year."

"Remember you said that when we get outside," she said.

She was right. I was as unprepared for the Indian summer heat and humidity that blasted us when we left the air-conditioned terminal as I had been for the trees. But just after we got back to her house the thunderstorm that had been threatening broke, slicing through the atmosphere and leaving everything washed and shining and cool. Lightning flashed and thunder rumbled in a display that thrilled me as much as if it had been the Fourth of July.

"I guess you can take the girl off the farm . . . ," Cynthia teased.

"I know, I know," I said. "But you've got to realize what I've just been through. These simple pleasures are a balm for my soul."

She was instantly serious and understanding.

"I know, honey, and you've come to the right place," she told me. "I thought we'd have some lunch first. We've got three hours before Chloe gets home from preschool, so start spilling your guts while I make some Bloody Marys."

It was easy to do. Cynthia's big old house was truly a mansion with the vintage character of its heyday still intact but Cynthia's mark firmly imprinted. The same décor would have been just as appropriate in the California home of which she had dreamed, although I was surprised to see that the living room was carpeted in white. A red-and-white peppermint-stick striped sofa anchored a conversational grouping of tables and chairs in front of the white-bricked fireplace, and nearby bottles of cognac and sparkling snifters waited invitingly. The dining room was purple and white, and shelves behind glass doors held china and silver. The table was already set for dinner, and a crystal basket held a profusion of purple and white blooms that reached nearly to each plate. Beyond a swinging door that led to the kitchen I could hear the clatter of plates and the sound of someone humming. Cynthia stopped at a wet bar tucked into a corner to mix our drinks.

"I told Hattie we'd have lunch out on the front porch," she said matter-of-factly as she poked frilly stalks of celery into our drinks. "I know people in California eat on the patios in back of their homes, but here we sit right out in front where we can see what's going on."

"Hattie?" I whispered as I followed her through a massive wood-paneled foyer and onto the porch. "Who's Hattie?"

"Oh, my maid. You probably heard her singing in the kitchen."

"You have a maid? Jesus, Cyn!" I knew she had grown up with a housekeeper to care for her father and her, but in college she had vowed she would always do her own housework. She didn't want strangers touching her food and going through her things. Apparently she and her dad had had some unfortunate experiences along the way that she had now been able to forget.

She looked a little sheepish and shushed me silently. Hattie, a sturdily built Black woman wearing a blue uniform, moved efficiently through the door carrying a tray that held our lunch. On the table between us she set out fruit salads, warm slices of a freshly baked quiche, and a bottle of chilled white wine for when we were finished with our cocktails. I felt as if we were in a 1950s movie, and it was all I could do to keep my mouth shut until Hattie went back to the kitchen.

"Will that be all, miss?" she asked Cynthia when the tray was empty and she was ready to go.

"Thank you, Hattie, yes. You might check back in a few minutes, and then I'll let you know when I'm ready for you to clear."

I raised my glass toward the door through which the woman had disappeared.

"Miss? Good God, Cyn, where are we, Tara? So much for power to the people."

"You were the protester, my dear, not me. And it's not as bad as it looks. I am giving someone a job, after all, and she only comes three mornings a week—Monday, Wednesday, and Friday. Since she was going to be here today anyway, I asked her to serve our lunch so we could talk uninterrupted."

I wolfed down what was on my plate, and when Hattie magically reappeared with a second slice of quiche, I ate that, too. I hadn't eaten much since Ian's death, but right now my life in San Francisco seemed very far away. I was keenly aware of its details—the roughness of its surface, the sharpness of its edges—but my problems were like creatures locked away in a glass cage, like the snakes at the zoo, where they couldn't hurt me here.

Outside the wide, screened-in veranda the rain had started again, and cars going past slowed and splashed through puddles, causing sprays that came up over the curb. Across the street a black Mercedes turned into the driveway of another huge red-brick home surrounded by a manicured lawn and brick walls and disappeared when the garage door silently opened and then closed behind it.

We moved from the glass-topped table and iron chairs to a white wicker swing—at least *that* fit in with the dreams she had always told me about—and settled against cushions in opposite corners, our feet up and knees nearly touching, like bookends, as we had sometimes done when we were roommates.

"I guess the trouble is I don't know how I'm supposed to feel," I told her. "I mean, I was doing okay as long as I could be mad at Ian, and I had good reason to be mad. First he had an affair with a woman at the paper, so there I was trusting him and working with both of them and they slept together while he was still living with me."

Cynthia nodded her agreement. "Tacky," she said.

"But that's not even the worst part of it," I went on. "I don't know if he really was in love with her, or if he was just using her to get this job that he wanted and that he knew I would want if I knew it was open. I wish I knew. I wish I could go someplace and ask him. Somehow it would make a difference if I knew either that he loved her madly and the job thing was just a coincidence or that he loved me all along and was too insecure about his abilities to get the job on his own merit or if he was just a jerk."

"It's hard being mad at someone who's dead," she said quietly. "Even if they left you on purpose. Believe me, I know."

"Of course you do," I said, feeling instantly guilty for not considering the memories my comment might evoke for her. "But that's not the whole thing, either. I never did get over him, despite my anger. And when I found out he was dead, I couldn't tell anybody how I felt. Everybody at work was gushing sympathy all over Andrea. They all seemed to have forgotten that Ian and I had ever been a couple. I guess that's how good a job I did of acting normal and convincing everyone I was over it."

"You know the expression 'A new love replaces the old'?"

"Yes, well, I tried that. I went to Lake Tahoe with a photographer from work and we screwed our brains out."

"Great!" she said. "Then what happened?"

"We sort of shook hands and announced to each other that it was meaningless sex, a zipless fuck of the highest order."

Fear of Flying had come out while we were in the dorm, and we had read it and talked about it endlessly, but a zipless fuck had not been the answer to my problem.

"I do get lonely and horny as hell," I told her, "but I'm old-fashioned enough to think sleeping with a guy should mean something."

"I know how difficult this is for you, I really do," Cynthia said. "But you'll meet somebody else. If Ian hadn't died, the healing process wouldn't be so complicated. You could just hate him and that would be that."

Just hearing someone else say what I already knew made me feel better, and I was grateful for a best friend like Cynthia in whom to confide. But then she leaned toward me and squeezed my knee companionably.

"This sure makes me appreciate what I have with Richard," she said. "I really am one lucky woman."

Zing.

❧

At a few minutes after three, a yellow minibus stopped in front of the house and Chloe ran across the yard and up the steps to where we were. The rain had stopped, but the grass was soggy and the sidewalk wet, so when she clomped across the porch, she left wet footprints behind.

"Is she here?" she squealed in delight, seeing that I obviously was. In the time since I'd seen her she had grown from a toddler into a little girl. Her dark hair was in twin ponytails, and she wore the red-and-blue plaid overalls of her parochial kindergarten and dragged a blue sweater on the floor behind her. Her brown eyes danced. I couldn't have loved her more if she had been my own.

"Chloe!" her mother snapped. "You know better than to come onto the porch without wiping your feet on the mat, and stop dragging your pretty sweater. You've been in school less than a month, and it's going to be ruined by Christmas."

Chloe's smile fell abruptly off her face as if an unskilled puppeteer had pulled the wrong string, but I gave her a wink and motioned for her to come to where I was hiding the teddy bear I had brought for her. I snuggled her into my arms, and she looked woefully out at Cynthia.

"Sorry, Mother," she said.

Not long after Chloe's arrival Richard's car pulled into the driveway. Cynthia looked at her watch in annoyance. He ran around the house and onto the porch, pulling me up to him in a bear hug.

"You're sure early," Cynthia said, frowning and apparently forgetting for the moment what a lucky woman she was. Richard still had his arm around my shoulders.

"My last patient canceled, and I wanted to get home and see Maggie," he said. "And I must say she's looking good."

I could have said the same about him. He had contacts now and looked thinner than when I had last seen him. He had been downright skinny when I first met him, but married life and medical school had added a few pounds. Now he wore a gray suit with a red-and-black striped tie. He tossed his jacket across one of the chairs when he came onto the porch.

"You guys look great, too," I said to both of them. "And Chloe's so grown-up, and your house is beautiful. It's like everything turned out just the way it was supposed to."

That night the three of us cooked dinner together, and it seemed like old times when we were back in their cramped apartment on the campus. Cynthia had been marinating chicken breasts all afternoon, and now Richard carried them out to the deck off the kitchen and put them on the grill.

"Don't say anything interesting while I'm gone," he called back over his shoulder, and Cynthia and I laughed. She was chopping salad at a butcher-block island in the middle of the room and had given me the mindless task of arranging olives and artichoke hearts on a small glass tray. Through an archway into what had once been a formal parlor but was now the family room, Chloe fed imaginary cookies to her new teddy bear and watched television.

"I can't tell you guys how good this is for me," I said when Richard came back. He was as close to me as his wife was, and I had no secrets from him, either. I wanted both of them to know how grateful I was for their support. When I got together with other women friends we often had to wait until their husbands or boyfriends were out of the room to talk about anything important or personal, but Richard was different. I had once told him he was just one of the girls.

"Oh, great. Now there's something for every man to aspire to," he had groaned.

But he knew what I meant. Here I could blither on about Ian and my feelings and my job and know he wouldn't fade away to switch on a ballgame or putter in the garage. Now he squeezed my shoulder as he passed me on his way to the sink to rinse off the meat platter.

"This is a tough one, Mags," he said. "But you're strong enough to get through it. Are you going to stay on at the paper or try to find something else?"

"It's in my blood," I said. "I love the work and I love San Francisco. I was so lucky to get this job in the first place, and I'm a big enough girl to work with Andrea, unpleasant as it is. I'm hoping that as time passes and people aren't catering to her so much, we'll get back to normal and I can just avoid her. It's a big place."

"And you're close to your family," Richard said. "It must be great to have them just an hour or so away."

I made a face to show my embarrassment.

"I haven't been home since all of this happened," I said, "but I'm going to have to face the music sometime. My mother didn't like that we were living together. We argued about that when he was alive, and now that he's dead, I just haven't been up to talking to her about him."

Cynthia had stopped chopping. Her knife was poised over a cucumber and she was staring at me intently.

"You should be very glad you have a mother to go home to, Maggie," she said. "Some of us don't have the luxury of picking and choosing what we talk to our mothers about and when."

"Jesus, Cyn!" Richard said, obviously as shocked as I was at her sudden change of temperament. He frowned and shook his head at me as if he wasn't quite sure himself what the trouble was, but just then the doorbell rang and Cynthia ran to answer it. "I don't know what that was all about," he said to me.

"Don't worry about it," I told him. "It's not the first time I've said something stupid about mothers or loved ones who have died. I keep forgetting about Cynthia's mother."

"That all happened a long time ago, and she had no right to fly off at you. Most people who have losses like that pull themselves together and move on—like you're trying to do."

"Really," I said. "It was my fault. I'm the one who should be sorry."

When Cynthia came back she was all smiles and holding hands with a man whose black suit and white collar announced that he was a priest. He was blonde but balding and a little pudgy with a round, pink cherubic face.

"Father Tom Hannigan, meet Maggie Patterson," she sang out. He held out a soft, well-manicured hand to shake mine. "Or maybe I should say old best friend meet new best friend. I've told Tom all about you, Maggie, and about how close we've been since our freshman year in college. Now he's the one who keeps me sane stuck out here in the Midwest."

She poured a glass of the wine we had been drinking and handed it to him.

"Actually, I'm the one who benefits from knowing Cynthia," he said with an accent that was faintly Irish. "She has taken over our altar society, and she organized a parish library and helps edit the monthly newsletter."

"She spends more time at the church than she does at home," Richard said, and I couldn't tell whether this pleased him or not. Certainly Cynthia's conversion must have made him and his parents happy. "If I call home and nobody answers, I know I can reach her by calling Tom's office down at the rectory."

Cynthia shrugged.

"I've got to have something to do," she said. "I can't just sit around the house and watch soap operas. I like to think I'm contributing a little something to the world, even without a degree."

Over dinner I found out that Father Hannigan also escorted Cynthia to the symphony and that the two of them had taken an overnight trip to the Ozarks together. Richard chewed and smiled, seemingly unconcerned. Much later, after we had eaten slices of Key lime pie and had coffee and cognac in the living room, Father Hannigan rose to leave.

"Don't forget lunch on Wednesday at the club," Cynthia reminded him.

"I'll be there," he said. Then he shook my hand and Richard's, kissed Cynthia on the cheek, and was gone.

"Club?" I asked, incredulous. "As in country club?"

"It's important to Richard's practice," Cynthia said. She was moving around the room, gathering glasses and wadding up the embroidered linen napkins.

"And how does that work?" I snorted. "Don't people just get sick and come into your office? Or are you hoping to collect up all the golfers who get struck by lightning?"

"It has to do mostly with referrals," Richard said. "I play golf with other physicians in town, we get to know each other, and then if they have an overload or are out of town and need someone to cover, they give me a call. It's just a way to get to know each other. And it gives Cynthia a way to meet the other wives. That's important, too."

"So it doesn't have anything to do with how good you are or they are—it's just who's the most cordial on the links?" I teased.

Richard laughed.

"That's a little bit of an oversimplification," he said. "Certainly a guy's reputation is what matters most, but basically yes. A lot of medical politics takes place on the golf course or in the bar afterward."

"Geez, I just can't imagine you two hobnobbing at a country club," I said. "First a maid, now the country club. Next thing I know you'll tell me you have a fur coat."

"Of course I have a fur coat," Cynthia said with a touch of condescension. "But it's not all as black-and-white as you make it seem, Maggie. Surely you've figured out that real life isn't quite the way we thought it was going to be in college. It isn't just one long freedom march."

I hadn't forgotten her icy look and the pointed comment she had given me earlier in the evening and dreaded the argument that might be coming, so I took the easy way out.

"You're telling me," I said.

For a while I forgot that my own depression was what I had come here to work out. Once again it was Cynthia's delicate psyche that had to be considered, Cynthia's unfortunate past that we needed to help her forget.

༚

The next morning when I arrived in the kitchen Cynthia was making coffee. Richard, in shorts and a T-shirt, was lacing up a pair of running shoes.

"I've been running for about six months," he told me. "Even did a 10K and came in fifth in my age group—not bad considering that there were more than two hundred of us."

"That's so cool!" I said, genuinely impressed. "That must be how you've slimmed down. I noticed that when I first saw you yesterday."

"Don't give him a bigger head than he already has," Cynthia said. She reached over and flipped up his gray athletic T-shirt. "But he'd also like for you to notice his washboard stomach."

"Well, why not?" he shot back, grabbing her and kissing the top of her head. "I've lost about twenty pounds, and it's been hard work. But I like the running. It gives me a rush and clears my head. I do a lot of thinking while I'm pounding the pavement. I work out at a gym, too, but that isn't quite as much fun."

"Do you ever run with him?" I asked Cynthia. Since she had on a bathrobe and slippers, I guessed the answer was no.

"It's Richard's time to be alone," she said. "I need to lose some weight, too, but I do a stretch class at the club twice a week. I'll get there."

"Hey, why don't you go with me, Maggie?" Richard said.

"No," I said quickly. "If you like to be alone, I understand that."

"Ordinarily yes, but it would be fun to have you along, and that way I could show you around the neighborhood. I stay pretty close to home."

The idea of breaking out of my routine, of being outside and starting an exercise program of my own, was tantalizing. After all, the reason I had come here was to climb out of the rut where I was wallowing in self-pity. I looked to Cynthia for approval.

"Sure, go ahead," she said, maybe just a little too brightly.

Just then Chloe bounded down the stairs and into the kitchen. She was wearing pajamas and rubbing her eyes.

"Chloe and I will fix breakfast," Cynthia said, putting her hands on her daughter's shoulders, "and by the time you two get back I think it will be warm enough to eat outside."

I ran upstairs to change and caught up with Richard as he was running in place on the porch, waiting for me. Then we headed out to the street. We did three miles instead of his usual five, and even then I knew I was slowing him down, sometimes even to a walk. He pointed out his neighbors' homes, occasionally telling me what a house cost or something about its history. As we were heading home he abruptly changed the subject, as if he thought this might be the only chance he'd have to talk to me alone.

"Do you think Cynthia's okay?" he asked me.

"What? Sure, I guess so. What do you mean?" I asked. I hadn't been prepared for this.

"I mean, do you think she's happy? She really wanted to go back to California, but this situation here was ready-made for me. Out there it would have been a struggle—graduating to the bottom again. I'd never be making what I'm making here this early in my career, and we'd probably never in our lives be able to afford a house like we live in here."

"She seems fine to me," I said and meant it. She'd had her little flare-ups the whole time I'd known her. I didn't think they were an indication she wasn't happy. "She's obviously busy and she's made some friends."

He knew who I meant and smiled.

"One gay priest?"

"Sure. Why not? I mean, she volunteers at the church and goes to the country club. She's done a great job on the house, and she told me she volunteers at Chloe's school. It doesn't sound like she's pining away for California to me."

"So . . . she hasn't said anything?"

"The only thing she's said is that she's lucky to be with you. That doesn't sound like an unhappy woman to me. She hasn't had much of a chance to say anything because I've been dominating the conversation with my own problems. I plan to change that, though. You guys have made me feel better already, and I don't want to spend my whole vacation obsessing about Ian and boring you into oblivion."

"But if she says anything about being unhappy, you'd tell me, wouldn't you?" he persisted, as if I hadn't spoken.

"Well, sure, if you think that might happen."

"I just want to make sure," he said. "We probably look like a couple of stuffy old married folks to you, but this is everything I've ever dreamed of. And I'm still nuts about Cynthia. If being here really made her miserable, I'd figure out a way to go somewhere else."

"I think she's still crazy about you, too," I said.

"Great," he said, picking up the pace a little, although we were within view of his own driveway. "That's just great."

Later that afternoon Cynthia and I were in the car headed to the city's historic Country Club Plaza.

"It's really beautiful, and it's supposedly the oldest outdoor mall in the country," she told me as she backed her silver Volvo out of the driveway and onto the street. The used car Richard had driven to Kansas City was nowhere in sight. "I need to look for a birthday gift for Richard's mother, and I thought we'd go shopping there so I could show it to you."

"Sounds good," I said, and I turned to wink at Chloe, who was fastened in her booster seat behind me. "Maybe we'll be able to find a store that has some I-C-E C-R-E-A-M."

"Ice cream!" Chloe cried, clapping her hands.

"You're too smart for me," I said. "No keeping secrets from you anymore."

It only took a few minutes to get to the Plaza. Cynthia pulled the car into a parking spot and we got out to walk, window-shopping mostly, each of us holding one of Chloe's hands as she skipped between us. At a department store we found a scarf and a handbag that Cynthia arranged to have gift-wrapped and shipped. Then we located an ice cream shop and sat on a bench outside eating our cones. In front of us water from a fountain splashed against colorful Mexican tiles.

"So, did you enjoy your little run with Richard this morning?" she asked me suddenly. I could hear the edge in her voice. Like Richard, she seemed unable to broach a subject about which she was uncomfortable with any grace.

"Yes, it was a lot of fun," I said, hoping I was mistaken about her tone. "As a matter of fact, I may try to keep at it when I go back home. People I know at work run up and down the hills in San Francisco. They say it's the best possible way to stay in shape."

"Did he talk to you about me?"

I understood immediately that my physical fitness was not what she wanted to talk about, but I felt loyal to Richard, who had seemed so sincere and vulnerable and who had, after all, talked to me first.

"What do you mean?" I asked. "He pointed out some houses where people you know live, and he told me about the cocktail party you gave right after you moved into yours."

"I mean, did he talk about us—our marriage?"

I was in a difficult position. I didn't want to betray Richard or lie to Cynthia.

"He just told me how happy he was," I said. "Everything seems to be going well for him here. It looks to me like you two have it made, and I believe he thinks so, too."

"Did he come on to you?"

She licked a trickle of ice cream that had started to drip down the cone, looking off into the distance, as casually as if she were commenting on what someone was wearing across the street.

"Cynthia!" I glanced at Chloe, who was trailing her fingertips through the water in the fountain, not paying attention to us and so she hadn't heard. "No, and I can't believe you asked me that."

"It's not that I don't trust *you*."

"Well, you should certainly trust Richard. God, he's as much in love with you as he was in college. And he's laying the world at your feet. How can you even ask a question like that?"

"I just need to know. We've been married almost five years. You weren't with Ian that long, and you were never married. It isn't all sex and roses, you know. I know how hard he works, but that keeps him away from home a lot. I guess I just need to know he's not looking for it somewhere else."

"No," I said emphatically, truly annoyed. "Now, why don't we head back."

In the evening the muscles I had taken out of storage that morning began to stiffen and ache. We were sitting on the front porch with coffee after a takeout Chinese feast, and I was rubbing my calves.

"Starting to pay the price, huh?" Richard asked. He sat beside Cynthia on the swing, his arm draped casually around her shoulders.

"They really hurt," I said and grimaced. "What does the doctor order?"

"For now, some aspirin just to alleviate the pain. Then, before you turn in, a good long soak in the tub, and tomorrow morning we do it again. Hair of the dog, as the saying goes."

Later, when we had said goodnight and they had gone down the hall to their room, I ran a deep, hot bath and poured in some of the bath salts Cynthia had left in a basket on the vanity. Richard was right. My sore legs felt better as soon as I sank in, and so did the rest of me. I slid down to my chin in the water and closed my eyes. I had nearly fallen asleep when I heard a gentle thud, and I thought someone was coming down the hallway. Then it became more pronounced and rhythmic, and I knew what I was hearing. The thud increased to a bang, the unmistakable sound of a headboard hitting the wall over and over, faster and faster. Then Cynthia's voice, louder than it needed to be.

"Oh, Richard, oh, honey, oh God."

I could hear the murmur of Richard's voice, too, but I couldn't make out the words, and I guessed he was telling her to keep it down.

I gave way to tears that probably had needed to be cried for a long time anyway. I had been trying to hold myself together since I'd been here, but now, here, alone in a bathroom far away from home, on my way to an empty bed, what I had to face seemed suddenly insurmountably bleak and overwhelming. I was still in love with someone who couldn't come back to me even if he changed his mind, and down the hall my best friend was rubbing it in by having sex at a decibel level there was no question I'd overhear.

It disappointed me and made me angry to think Cynthia would deliberately go out of her way to mock my loneliness. Ian and I had once had sex when friends of his were in town and staying over. I knew it was possible to stay quiet even when you wanted to scream with pleasure. I even recall his propping one hand against the wall to stabilize our headboard. Why couldn't Richard and Cynthia do that now? And why did she feel the need to flaunt everything she had, the fact that she had a husband most of all?

Lying there in the quickly cooling bath water I felt the aloneness of an astronaut walking in space or a passenger train crossing the plains in the dead of night. I wanted to bellow out from the bathroom, "All right, Cynthia. I know you're having sex. Yes, you have it all—a great husband, an adorable daughter, a beautiful house, and you're still prettier than I am. Now, would you settle down so we can all get some sleep?"

But Chloe beat me to the punch.

"Mommy?" she called out, sounding frightened.

"It's okay, honey," Cynthia called back, and I could hear laughter in her voice, as if she and Richard, having finished now and lying smugly entwined beside their wet spot, had an intimate secret that neither their daughter nor I could share, as if in awakening Chloe she could be sure their sounds had carried to me. "Mommy just had a bad dream."

I had come to be healed, but Cynthia's increasingly icy thoughtlessness was not helping. I resolved to call the airline and reschedule my return ticket. I could take an evening flight out and be back in my office on Monday to save vacation days I had earned for another time or change the ticket to Jamaica or Bermuda and lick my wounds privately in some sun-splashed clime. For all its warm, comfortable moments, the Kansas City visit wasn't turning out as I had hoped. Besides sorting out my feelings about Ian's death, I was also on the first break I had taken since starting my job, and I didn't want to spend it walking on eggshells, forever on guard against saying anything that might hurt Cynthia's feelings or recall her own sad memories. And I didn't want to be constantly reminded of my solitary state by Cynthia's insensitive comments and their raucous, inconsiderate lovemaking.

But when I came downstairs in my bathrobe Cynthia was in high spirits. She had obviously already showered. She wore a pink terry-cloth robe, and her long hair was still wet. She had on no makeup, and it seemed to me that she still retained the glow of a woman who had been well-loved the night before.

"Good morning, sunshine," she sang out, raising her coffee cup in my direction. "Where are your running togs?"

"I thought I'd just stay here and talk to you while Richard runs," I said. "I really slowed him down yesterday, and my legs are still sore."

"This doesn't have anything to do with what I said when we were out shopping, does it?"

I shrugged.

"Maybe," I said. "But it doesn't matter. I came here to spend time with you, didn't I?"

A little smile played around her lips.

"Well, I don't want to be selfish, but of course I'd rather have you here with me. We can take some coffee out onto the porch and wait for him to come back, and then we'll all go out for brunch."

She poured a cup for me and picked up a calendar and a pencil with which she had already started planning our activities for the week. Back at the iron and glass table outside, she started reeling them off.

"Tomorrow I'm invited to a kickoff luncheon for the Christmas benefit for Children's Hospital, and I'm taking you as my guest," she said, tapping at the square on the calendar with the eraser end of her pencil as if saying it would make it so, as if she could already see us seated in a hotel banquet room with other well-dressed women, making polite conversation and munching portions of Cornish game hen stuffed with rice and accompanied by watery tomato aspic.

"Tuesday we'll go to the Nelson Art Gallery. You won't believe how good it is. Their Chinese collection is one of the top three in the country. I know you'll enjoy that. While we're there we can have lunch in their tearoom. Wednesday, of course, we'll meet Tom for lunch. I want you to see that the evil old country club isn't quite as bad as you think. Thursday morning I have a doctor's appointment, so you'll be on your own for a couple of hours. When I get back I'll cook my famous lasagna, first perfected in married housing at UCLA. Then Friday night we're having cocktails with some friends and later taking you out for dinner."

She looked up and smiled, obviously delighted with the careful planning that would allow me to meet her friends and see her city.

"I'm so glad you came," she said suddenly. "This visit is as good for me as it is for you. I've missed you so much. I love you just like a member of my family, Maggie."

"I love you, too," I said, and I did. I had forgotten my plan to leave and was wondering what to wear when Cynthia introduced me to the ladies who lunch.

For the next few days the visit was good. I slept well, and if Cynthia and Richard were down the hall fucking themselves blind, it was wasted on me. The autumn days were still warm, and when we weren't keeping to Cynthia's schedule I could usually be found on the front porch, sipping iced tea and talking to her or reading while she consulted with Hattie about what we'd have for dinner or what chores needed to be done that day. One day I sat on a stool and talked to Hattie while she cleaned the kitchen. It turned out she was a widow who had moved to Kansas City to live with her daughter's family. She took the job with Cynthia, she confided, just to get out of the house for a few hours, and that knowledge helped me better deal with being waited on, although I still didn't like it.

Cynthia had announced at the beginning of the visit that she intended to spoil me, and she did. One day it was breakfast in bed, another evening my favorite lemon crepes with fresh strawberries for dessert. She listened and nodded sympathetically while I droned on endlessly about my life with Ian and its doubly untimely end. I knew I was beginning to heal when I fell asleep one afternoon right in the middle of a sentence. I was lying in the swing with my eyes closed, and we had gotten to the point in my story where Ian had helped himself to Andrea's purse. Cynthia tried not to laugh but couldn't stifle the giggle that snapped me back to consciousness.

"God!" I said. "I've bored my own self senseless."

I endured the charity luncheon, loved the art museum, and was curious about the country club. Late Wednesday morning Cynthia came downstairs wearing a red linen suit, black patent-leather heels, and a matching set of silver earrings and brooch.

"You look great!" I said. I was wearing khaki pants, flats, and a yellow T-shirt.

"Chanel," she said.

"What?" I wasn't quite sure I had understood what she said.

"Chanel. It's a designer label."

"I know about Chanel. We poor reporters can't afford the clothes, but we do read about them and look at the pictures."

She smiled and shook her head as if I had told her I was out of a job or homeless.

"Would you like to borrow something of mine?" she asked pointedly.

"No, thanks," I said, feeling the snub. "I think I'll wear what I've got on."

As it turned out, the most extraordinary part of our chicken-salad lunch was Cynthia's shameless flirting with Tom Hannigan, making me think maybe Richard's assessment of the priest's sexual orientation was wrong. When friends of hers stopped by our table to say hello, she introduced him as she might a celebrity, often completely forgetting to mention me. I realized that my being along was secondary to her enjoyment.

"Tom's the gem I drag off to the opera when Richard won't go," she chortled to one friend, and to another, "Tom's the one I went to the Ozarks with last spring. We love car trips. We only meant to be gone for a couple of days, but it turned into more than a week, didn't it, Tom?"

On Thursday morning Cynthia left for her appointment before I got out of bed. She had warned me the night before that she'd be going early.

"Why don't you sleep in tomorrow?" she said. "I haven't really let you do much of that this week. I keep forgetting that you have to get up to an alarm most mornings of your life."

I didn't know if she was ridiculing my lifestyle or admiring it, but in any event some time alone sounded good. I woke up when I heard the garage door go up just after eight, then rolled over and slept for another hour before the sun hit my window with full force and woke me up again. Downstairs Cynthia had left a plate of fresh cheese Danish covered with a cloth napkin beside a note that said juice was in the refrigerator and the coffee still hot. I put it all on a tray along with the morning paper and headed for my usual spot outside. The house was empty. Richard must have taken Chloe to school on his way to work.

An hour or so later, Cynthia's car pulled into the driveway and toward the garage, which she had already opened with a remote control. I waved to her as she passed the porch, but she was looking straight ahead and apparently didn't see me. A few minutes later I heard her rattling around inside the house. The door from the garage into the kitchen slammed, and then I heard cupboard doors banging and the clatter of ice falling into a glass. Several more minutes passed before she joined me in the swing. She was carrying a glass of tea, which was already half gone, and she had the glazed look on her face that I had gradually come to dread. I hoped I was wrong.

"So, how did it go?" I asked her.

"Fine," she said.

"I didn't even ask you why you were going. I figured it was just your annual poke and prod."

"Well, yes, he did quite a bit of that, too."

"I've had a great morning," I said. I heard myself being too cheerful, talking too fast. "It's lucky I don't live here because I'd never come in off this porch. I'd never get anything done. I'd even be out here in the wintertime. You'd probably find me one day frozen to death and with icicles hanging off my nose."

Shut up, Maggie, I told myself. I seemed incapable of stopping the mindless string of chatter. I laughed shrilly, but she wasn't amused.

"But you don't live here, do you?" she said.

Since her question was obviously rhetorical, I didn't answer and she went on.

"Icicles aren't a problem where you live, are they? I'd say in a Victorian apartment in San Francisco you could probably sit outside and enjoy the view of the Bay Bridge most months out of the year, couldn't you?"

She was talking to me in the tone a prosecuting attorney might take with a defendant on the witness stand. I remained silent, frowning in apprehension.

"The tragedy is, of course, that you can't sit on your porch or deck or patio or whatever it is you have because you're too busy with your exciting career. Isn't that the case?"

I wondered where this was going.

"I'm busy," I said carefully. "I think that's one of the reasons I've felt so relaxed here."

I hadn't, of course. The eggshells had reappeared, and I was measuring my responses to her questions, not sure where we were headed. I wished there were a black-robed judge present who would smack down a gavel and demand that she make her line of questioning clear. Since there wasn't, I had to do it myself.

"What's all this about, Cyn? Is something wrong? Does it have to do with your doctor's appointment?"

She ignored my questions and pecked with a manicured red fingernail at a photograph in the newspaper I had been reading, which now lay between us. I had read the article already, and evidently she had, too. It was on the first page of the features section, an interview with a psychologist who had just written a book about dealing with troubled teenagers.

"That might have been me," she said, jabbing at the photo again, harder this time. "If I could have finished school, I would have been in my career now, too. Maybe I'd have written a book and be traveling around the country giving lectures like she is. Or maybe I'd just be at a clinic somewhere, quietly helping women straighten out their lives. But I'd be doing *something*. I wouldn't be rotting out here in the middle of nowhere, filling my days with ridiculous social events, dying of boredom while I watch my life inch past me. My husband goes off to save lives, you're out there writing all those articles you send us, and I'm going off to charity luncheons with a bunch of old biddies who want their names in the paper a whole lot more than they care about raising money for sick children."

I made a note to stop sending clippings of the articles I had written. Now tears were running down her face, and she sobbed and shook as she spoke. I reached over to hug her, but she pulled away.

"Look, honey," I said. "There's nothing wrong with your life. Sure I kidded you about your fur coat and the country club, but I think you've got it made. You're raising a great kid, and you're helping Richard with his career. I see now how important all of this socializing is. It's true I wouldn't care for that part, but I see it's something you have to do, and Richard appreciates it. You're a team. And finally, you're not exactly over the hill. You told me when you got settled here and the house was done and Chloe was in school, you were going back to school."

I waved my hand toward her finished product, a home that might have been featured in an *Architectural Digest* layout.

"Voila, you've done it. You're there. You've put together a beautiful home. So go back to school, and in three years you'll be doing whatever you want."

She waved her hand in a dismissive gesture.

"Finish school, and in three years you'll be doing whatever you want," she mimicked in a high falsetto voice. "Oh, it's all so easy for you, isn't it? No strings, no kids, no house, no husband. You don't even have a boyfriend to consider anymore."

"That's mean, Cyn," I said.

She glared at me without speaking.

"This is what you've always wanted," I went on. "You told me a career would be secondary, that what you really wanted was a marriage and kids."

"Well, I was wrong."

She was looking right at me now, and her eyes were blazing.

"Yes, I wanted that, too, but I didn't want my life to be utterly meaningless. And I didn't want to spend it in the middle of nowhere."

"This is a very exciting city," I said, too amazed at her outburst to address any but the most trivial of her concerns. "And if you're that unhappy, you should tell Richard."

"Don't oversimplify everything I say," she snapped. "There aren't easy answers to anything. Richard can't just close up his practice and go somewhere else. He's worked too hard to get established here, and I've worked too hard to help him."

"Okay," I said slowly, trying not to let her bitterness seduce me into an argument I would regret later. "But what's wrong with going back to school? They need psychologists in Kansas City just like they do everywhere else."

"What's wrong with that idea is that I'm pregnant again," she said finally.

She lifted her face from her hands and looked at me as if she hated me.

"Congratulations!" I said. I knew this wasn't what she wanted to hear, but what was I supposed to say to an announcement like this?

"This is exactly what Richard wants," she said. "Watch what happens when I tell him tonight. And his blessed mother will at last be pacified. It makes her crazy to think we might even use birth control. I think she keeps better track of my cycle than I do. And I'll be kept down once again and not able to do the things I dream about."

"When's the baby due?" I asked.

"Next summer. Late June."

"So why don't you start taking some classes now if it's so important to you? You could probably still enroll for this semester, and by the time the new baby comes you'll already have several hours under your belt."

She shook her head.

"I'm tied up with this hospital benefit until Christmas. I could take some courses next semester, but what would be the point? With a new baby, I won't be able to go back for a long time."

"I'm just saying that with every three-unit class you take, you're that much closer to what you want to do," I said.

The steely glint was back in her dark eyes.

"Well, Miss I-Know-All-the-Answers, it just isn't as easy for everybody else as it is for you. You must think you're such hot shit." She laughed humorlessly. "You're still thin as a reed, you live in a great place and have a great job. And somewhere out there is a great guy that you'll meet someday, but in the meantime everybody you fuck will be some movie star you meet in an interview or a Pulitzer Prize winner who sits at the desk across from yours. I'd be smug, too, if I were you."

"I don't have to listen to this," I said. "I should have left the first time you laid into me. It's not going to happen again."

I left my coffee cup and part of the Danish behind and ran inside and up the stairs to my room, too angry and hurt to cry.

Later, downstairs, I could hear Cynthia clattering dishes and banging pans, and I guessed she was fulfilling her promise to make the lasagna despite what had happened between us. From the telephone in the upstairs hallway I called the airline and asked for the first flight out. All the non-stops to San Francisco were booked until the following morning, but I signed up for the first one I could get. Then I spent the afternoon packing.

We ate dinner almost wordlessly.

"The lasagna's delicious," I said to Cynthia, mostly for Richard's benefit so he wouldn't catch on that something had gone terribly wrong between us and start asking questions in front of Chloe.

"Thanks," she said and smiled fleetingly without looking at me. Then she took a deep breath.

"I have an announcement to make," she said, but before she could go on, the phone rang. Richard got up to answer it.

"It's for you, Maggie," he said. "A guy."

I frowned at him questioningly as I took the receiver. I couldn't imagine who might call me here, certainly not a guy. It turned out to be the managing editor at the paper. I looked at my watch. It was still late afternoon on the West Coast.

"We'd like to offer you Sadie's job as assistant features editor," he told me. "I don't want you to feel like our second choice. As I told you before, if we'd known you were interested, you would have been the choice in the first place. We need to get that slot filled, and you're the logical person. And just for the record, Andrea is gone, too. She lied to me about you, and that's one thing I won't tolerate. I don't run that kind of shop."

I didn't comment on that, although I could feel relief mingle with my surprise and joy at getting the job I had hoped for.

"Of course I want the job," I said. "Thank you."

"There's something else, too," he said. "We've got an exclusive interview with Rosalynn Carter, but she's booked with other commitments for the next several weeks. The only time she can do it in the near future is tomorrow. Since you're halfway to Washington anyway, I took the liberty of booking you on a midnight flight out of Kansas City tonight. I'm afraid this cuts your vacation a little bit short."

"That's all right," I said. "I'm already packed."

6

In the months that followed, I had little time to worry about Cynthia, and when she did come to mind, I tried to block out the painful memories of our recent visit. When I had come back to the dinner table from my phone call that night and told them I had to go, she had already told Richard and Chloe about the baby, and I could tell from their faces—Richard's wreathed in smiles, Chloe's reluctant but hopeful—that whether I stayed or went had become by virtue of their family celebration completely inconsequential.

Cynthia begged off taking me to the airport, saying she needed to stay with Chloe, and besides she was exhausted and had a headache. She went up to bed before Richard and I left, and our only goodbye was a weak wave as she reached the top of the stairs, almost an afterthought now that she didn't need that hand for the banister anymore. Richard missed all of the implications, not able to see beyond his excitement, chattering all the way to the airport about what he perceived as his wife's good news.

"I am one happy man, Maggie," he practically sang. "I thought we had it all, but now this."

I recalled my promise to tell him if I thought Cynthia wasn't happy, but I couldn't bring myself to do it. *It's their marriage, their life*, I told myself. Despite their being my best friends, tinkering with the delicate web of deception Cynthia had constructed between them was not something I wanted to be a part of. Had she contrived this pregnancy, too, because she thought it was what Richard wanted? And if she had, why was she so upset about it? At this point I didn't even care. She wasn't the only one who was exhausted and had a headache.

After the trip to Washington there was the matter of moving into a new office and figuring out what my new job would require. Suddenly I had a lot more responsibility, and while I still occasionally wrote stories, now it was also my job to assign everybody else and work with the features editor to make sure the section was full of good stories and photographs seven days a week. There were days when I went to work at six in the morning and didn't get home until ten at night, but I loved it. It blocked out the memory of Ian and the new fissure with Cynthia, and there certainly was no one waiting up nights, begging me to rearrange my schedule so I could spend more time at home.

Then one day in late November Cynthia called.

"I really need to know that everything is okay between us," she said. "With the holidays coming, I've been thinking about you a lot. I'm sorry about, you know, some of the things I said when you were here."

I had mixed feelings about hearing from her. In fact, I'm not sure I would ever have called her. Still, I did miss her. The only man I had ever cared about had dumped me and then died. I didn't need to lose my best friend, too.

"Sure, Cyn, of course it is," I said. "With everything we've been through, I don't think anything could really come between us."

"Some of the things I said were true," she went on. "Not about you, but about me. I'm not sorry I married Richard, I don't mean that, but I wish it hadn't been under the circumstances it was. I think it would be a lot different if I could have finished my degree. I wish I had some control over my own life instead of just being the handmaiden to everyone else's. I'm Richard's wife and Chloe's mother, and now I'm going to be somebody else's mother, and I still don't know who I am. The people in this city who pay attention to me only do it because my husband's a doctor. I don't kid myself about that. If we split up tomorrow and he married someone else, she'd be the one they'd include in their committees and parties. Sometimes I feel like I don't even have a face of my own, like if I look into a mirror nothing will be looking back. It's horrible."

"I can see what you're saying, I really can," I said.

I didn't bother to point out to her that she had taken complete control and engineered her particular set of circumstances in the first place—if not the current situation, too. We had never discussed the sudden pregnancy that had led to her marriage, and it was a subject there was no point in bringing up and throwing in her face now.

"But those of us who love you know how special you are, and Richard and Chloe head the list. For your own peace of mind, I still say you need to get started on some kind of plan for yourself. Maybe school isn't the answer anymore. Maybe you could learn a skill or do more volunteer work. Or do some kind of artwork. You were always drawing when we were in college. Then at least you'll be too busy to sit around and obsess about all this stuff. You can have a life of your own, even with children and certainly without a degree. From the perspective of a single person, I could say you have it all."

"I know you're right," she said. "But I still say it's not as easy as it sounds. Since you don't have any kids of your own, you really can't understand how empty my life is."

"How are you feeling?" I asked. I wanted to change the subject before we got mired down in the same argument that had started all this to begin with.

"Great. I had a little morning sickness in the beginning, but that's pretty much over now. He'll be here before we know it."

"He?"

"I'm thinking positively. Richard wants a boy so bad he can almost taste it."

❧

I mentioned before the role of fate or coincidence or whatever you want to call it in anyone's life, and those same weird, unpredictable forces were apparently at work when I met Peter. Today we'd call it a "meet cute," since I wasn't actually supposed to meet him at all. I had assigned the interview to a reporter who called in sick the morning she was supposed to meet with him.

"Maggie," she croaked into the phone at seven that morning, "this is Lila. I've got the cold from hell and I'm losing my voice. Can you get somebody else to do the Peter Goldberg interview?"

I flipped through the assignment log on my desk and frowned. Everybody else was booked, but I could tell there was no way Lila could come in, let alone conduct an interview. The only person free at one in the afternoon was me.

"It looks like I'm your girl," I told Lila. "Everyone else is already out."

"Oh, Maggie, I'm so sorry," she groaned. "I know you don't have time to mess with this."

"It's no problem," I said, not altogether truthfully. "I don't mind at all, but you'll have to give me a little background. I'm not going to have time to do any research."

"Okay," she squeaked. "Peter Goldberg, movie director. *Five of Clubs* is his first feature film, but he's done several made-for-TV movies. Career started with directing PBS contribution campaigns. Thirty-five years old, graduated from Columbia University. Um, I think he's been married but isn't now. You'll have to ask about that."

I could hear her riffling papers for more information.

"That's enough," I told her. "I'll explain to him that I'm filling in for you and that you were fully prepared. It's just that I don't watch much television. Before this movie came out, I'd never even heard of the guy."

Peter's house was on Telegraph Hill, nestled just below the top, near Coit Tower. I left the office early to give myself plenty of time to find it, but I still arrived a few minutes late because it was so artfully hidden away and difficult to find. I parked on the narrow street and followed a brick path through a tangle of deep-green ivy to the front door. A woman with a dust cloth in her hand answered the bell and led me through the living room and onto a deck, where Peter sat at a table, writing in a notebook while he awaited my arrival. From here his view was a trapezoid of blue bay with a bridge on each side and Alcatraz roughly in the middle.

"Miss Campbell?" He stood up, smiling, and held out his hand. He was just a little taller than I was, and his straight brown hair was pushed straight back off his forehead. He took off the round tortoiseshell reading glasses he had been wearing when I arrived and laid them on the table while we shook hands.

"I'm afraid not," I told him. "Lila came down with a cold and seems to be losing her voice, so I'm filling in. I'm the assistant features editor, Maggie Patterson. She told me a little bit about you, but we're pretty much starting from scratch here."

"That's not a problem for me," he said. "Before we start, would you like something to drink—coffee or tea?"

He disappeared for a few minutes while I soaked in the view and returned with a tray that held a teapot and two cups.

"Okay," I said. "I know you started at PBS, did some television movies, and have now come out with *Five of Clubs*. I also know you went to Columbia University. That's it. Before we talk about the film, could I just get some personal statistics? I saw some pictures of a little boy in your living room. Is he yours?"

"Yes," he said, smiling. "That's Jack. He's seven now."

"So you're married," I went on. "What type of work does your wife do?"

"Was," he said. I looked up questioningly. "Was married. My ex-wife is an actress. We were divorced not long ago."

"I'm sorry," I said.

He put up his hands in a gesture of acceptance.

"These things happen," he said. "We gave it up before we started to hate each other, and I got custody of Jack because she has to travel so much, so I didn't lose all the way around."

Peter's assistant had told Lila he could only spare an hour. Two and a half hours after we started talking I looked at my watch.

"I can't believe this," I said, snapping my notebook shut and leaping to my feet. "I've way overstayed our appointed time."

"It has been my pleasure," he said. "You're very easy to talk to. In fact," he said, looking at me a little sheepishly, "I don't quite know how to ask this, but I do notice that you're not wearing a wedding ring. Is there a boyfriend in the picture?"

"No."

"Then maybe we could continue talking on a less formal basis some evening over dinner."

"I'd like that," I said.

"I'm not ready for a serious relationship yet," he warned. "I haven't even been divorced for a year yet. But I do find your company enjoyable."

"I'm in a similar situation," I said. "I was involved with someone who was killed in an accident not long after we broke up. I'm still trying to sort out my feelings, so I'm not in the market for anything serious, either."

"Oh my God, Maggie!"

He reached over instinctively to touch my hand, then withdrew it quickly when he realized what he had done.

"Can I ask what happened, or is it too painful to talk about?"

"He was my boyfriend in college and we both got jobs at the *Examiner* after graduation. He wound up falling for an editor at the paper, and I asked him to move out. Not long after that he was killed in an automobile accident. It has been a tough time."

Stop talking, Maggie, I told myself. *You're here to interview him, not tell him your life story, even if he did ask.*

"Look, if it isn't too soon, there's a lecture on French filmmaking this Friday that I'm interested in hearing," he told me. He had apparently missed my lapse of professionalism. "It probably sounds deadly boring to you, but it might tie into something I'm working on now. If you think you could bear to sit through it with me, I'll buy you dinner beforehand."

"Bribe accepted," I said. "You've got a deal."

❧

In the weeks following our first rain-soaked date, Peter and I saw each other whenever we could, and each time we learned more about each other and liked each other more. But more often than not our schedules kept us apart. His movie was opening, and he was all over the country and then in Europe to promote it. Besides the house on Telegraph Hill, he also had an apartment in LA, and that's where he lived most of the time when he was actually filming. When he came to San Francisco, it was usually to closet himself away and get work done on a script, and when he had free time, I was often out of town. Once when he called I was in London doing a piece on women in parliament, once in Hawaii to write about the cruise industry. Sometimes when we were both free he needed to spend time with his son. Although he didn't actually say so until much later, I could tell he didn't want to introduce Jack to every woman he dated. The child missed his mother, and Peter didn't want to cause him anxiety or raise hopes that he wouldn't be able to fulfill.

We had met in January, but it was late April before we slept together. We both wanted to—we had long since given up on insisting we were only friends and moved on to brushing fingertips and later to long, serious kisses, but the circumstances were never right. Then Jack went away with his mother for spring break, and we made our plans.

"She's picking him up after school on Friday," Peter told me. "So plan to come for dinner—and stay for breakfast."

He took me in his arms as I came through the door, then scooped me up and carried me to the bedroom as though we were characters in one of his movies. We had waited for this moment for so long that we dispatched with formalities and finished quickly without even working up a sweat. Afterward we made dinner together and ate it in bathrobes on the living room floor. By nine we were back in bed, and except to eat, we didn't get out again until Monday morning. Although I stopped by my apartment each day to pick up more clothes and check the mail, I spent the entire next week with him. It was Thursday night, over a pizza we had ordered, that he told me he loved me.

⁇

The phone woke me up at five in the morning. Before she spoke I knew it was Cynthia and that she was crying.

"The baby's here," she sobbed.

I pictured deformities, conjoined twins, perhaps a child born dead, a cord twisted around its tiny neck, its face pleading and blue.

"What's the matter, Cyn?" I barked into the phone.

"Oh, Maggie, it's a girl."

"Is everything okay?"

"Oh, sure. She's healthy and everything. She weighed over seven pounds, and she's got a headful of dark hair and all her fingers and toes."

"So why are you crying?"

"Because Richard wanted a boy so much. We only planned to

121

have two kids, and he was so hoping one of them would be a boy."

I felt angry that she had frightened me awake and that once again I had to consider her delicate feelings, the single, fruitless comforter to a happily married woman who has just given birth to a perfectly healthy second child. The position was a ludicrous one, but I didn't want this to be another issue that rocked the boat of our now-precarious friendship. Cynthia was like family—even when she did things I didn't like or couldn't understand, I didn't think I could just eliminate her from my life. Breaking with her would have been as unthinkable as tearing my brother's face out of our family photographs.

"Honey, he's been a great dad to Chloe," I told her. "I'm sure he'll love this little girl, too. What's her name?"

"Oh, sure, that's what he says, but I feel like I've failed him. Her name's Lorraine. It's his mother's middle name. I could at least do that much for him."

"This is textbook mild postpartum depression," I assured her. "Someday when we're out shopping for her prom dress we'll laugh about it. Besides, I always wished I had a sister, and I know you did, too. Your daughters will always have a best friend, even when the rest of the world fails them. I think it's wonderful."

"Oh, yeah, I suppose," she said, but I could tell either she didn't believe me or her attention had drifted on elsewhere. She blew her nose. "Now, tell me what's new with you. Is there anybody special in your life?"

We hadn't talked on the phone since her apology call before the holidays. I had sent a letter with my Christmas gifts, but I hadn't mentioned Peter. Cynthia's scathing predictions about whom I would date still remained in my memory, and my relationship with Peter was still too new at that point to be hashed over and dissected, even with her. I wanted to keep it to myself, to clutch it close to my heart like a locket. I was almost superstitious about it, as if discussing Peter might make him disappear. Now I didn't have any more of those doubts.

"Well, now that you mention it, yes," I said.

"So tell me about him."

"We've been dating since January, but we only started using the L-word a few weeks ago."

"Have you slept with him?"

"Yes, but only recently. We've been taking our time and getting to know each other before we moved forward."

Why was I explaining myself to her, trying to dash away suspicion that our romance might be based on physical attraction and nothing more to someone whose whole marriage had begun in a blaze of sexual passion?

"Do you think this might lead to something permanent?"

"I don't know. We talk about being together and neither of us is seeing anybody else, but we're both so incredibly busy with work that it's almost a joke. I saw a cartoon the other day of someone who was so busy that she had to have her assistant go out on dates for her. That's us. Last week the sum total of our contact was one phone call from Honduras."

In the late '70s and '80s we all justified our existence by being overworked and constantly busy, our calendars overbooked and rushing from one appointment or event to another.

"It sounds like you've got the best of both worlds," she said. "Somebody loves you and you love him, but you're left alone to do as you like and get your own work done."

"The grass is always greener," I said, laughing. "I'd kind of like to find out what it would be like to come home to him every night and wake up with him every morning."

"What does this guy do anyway?"

I had been hoping ridiculously that somehow this was a question she would forget to ask.

"He's a director," I said. "His name's Peter Goldberg. *Five of Clubs* was his film."

"Oh," she said. "How nice for you."

∽

It was another year and a half before Peter and I finally got around to getting married. We talked about it, and we kept planning to do it, but we never could find the time. Then one night as we lay naked in a post-coital tangle on his bed, he said he wanted to make definite plans.

"This is making me crazy, Maggie," he said.

He lowered his head to kiss each of my breasts—tiny, tender goodbyes—and then he pulled away and propped up on an elbow facing me so we could talk seriously.

"I've got clothes here and clothes in LA and clothes at your place. I love you, you love me, Jack loves you. I want us to have a home together. Let's just find a time and get married."

"I don't know if getting married will change much of the craziness," I warned him, "but you know I want to be with you. We may not see much more of each other than we do now, but at least we can eliminate one household."

"Then the answer's yes?"

"Yes, of course the answer's yes."

∽

"You're going to love Cynthia and Richard," I told Peter the night before our wedding, and I actually thought he would. The pain of my earlier visit with Cynthia had softened, and I was looking forward to seeing her again. He was fastening the clasp on my necklace in front of the mirror in our bedroom. I had given up my apartment and moved into his house several weeks before. Richard and Cynthia had flown in that afternoon so she could be my matron of honor, and checked into the bayside hotel where the ceremony would be held. They had left their girls in Kansas City with Hattie. Peter's mother had come in from New York, and my parents and brother from Santa Rosa. We were getting ready to meet all of them to run through the ceremony with the rabbi, and then we were going out for an informal rehearsal dinner.

"I'm not much of a practicing Jew," Peter had told me, "but with my mother coming and having Jack there, I'd like for the ceremony to be something more than just a legal formality."

"I love you for that," I'd said.

I wasn't much of a practicing anything. My mother had always bragged that our family believed in something, we just weren't quite sure what, and while I had found that agnostic philosophy embarrassing when playmates with meddlesome mothers had invited me to church picnics and vacation Bible school, now I found it explained what I felt exactly. I had formalized my thinking a little beyond my mother's loose interpretation of religious faith, but it still didn't fit within the confines of organized religion. I thought maybe standing under a chuppah with Peter wearing a yarmulke and crushing the glass would be exactly the symbolism that would carry us through and beyond the Andrea Stones who were sure to enter our lives. Ian was by now just a vague memory, just a boyfriend I had once had, a young romance with an unhappy ending, but the way the pain had felt would be in my memory forever. I didn't ever want to feel it again.

At first I didn't recognize Cynthia. She had arrived in the meeting room where our rehearsal would be held before us and was sitting on a chair in the front row, chatting with my brother. Richard was on her other side, and if he hadn't been there, I would have thought she was a stranger. She was frankly heavy now. She had apparently gained a great deal of weight with Lorraine and it was still there. She was no longer beautiful like she had been in college—very few people were—but she was still attractive. She wore an elegant suit, and her long dark hair was swept up into a kind of bun. Her hands now reached out to hold mine.

"And this must be Peter!" she said, smiling at him as she spoke. She was still unmistakably Cynthia.

He shook hands with both of them and then left me to go pick up his mother.

"You look fabulous!" she said to me.

"It's the radiant bride thing," I said. "You look great, too."

"Well," she said, "I've got some weight to lose. I signed up for an exercise class, but after the second one I stopped going. There just isn't time for everything I have to do. But, here, I brought pictures of our girls to show you."

Throughout the rehearsal, then dinner later that night and the ceremony and reception the next day, Cynthia managed to pull enough small tricks to lose Peter's favor before she ever even won it. During the practice, she stopped the rabbi twice to ask questions about where she would be standing and what her role would be. At the restaurant she sent back a perfectly done medium-rare steak, pronouncing it burned, and she monopolized the conversation with details of various charity events and activities at the country club, where she was now a member of the board. The ceremony began late the next day because she didn't show up on time, and during the vows she had a coughing fit that we had to stop for. At the reception in the hotel's garden we had to wait to cut the cake, with the caterer smiling nervously, while Cynthia showed baby pictures to my mother and Peter's—both of whom kept trying to find a way to shut her off without hurting her feelings.

"Maggie's never even seen my youngest," she said. "Much too busy with her career." And then, when she realized the group had silenced and was looking at her, she said, "Oh, I hope everyone's not waiting for me."

"That woman's a menace," Peter whispered into my ear.

We were circulating around the garden and visiting with our guests. Cynthia was holding court at a table with Bradley and an actor friend of Peter's. She hadn't moved for more than an hour, but she periodically held up her champagne glass and smiled in Richard's direction to show that she was ready for more.

"Haven't you noticed that she can't stand for the attention to be on you?" he asked. "It's our wedding day, and she wants every-body—even people she doesn't know or care about—to look at pictures of her children. Don't you think that's a little weird?"

As usual, where Cynthia was concerned, I became defensive.

"She wasn't always like this," I countered. "She can be wonderful, she really can, but she has a lot of problems."

I had never told him about the dust-up during my visit to Kansas City before I met him. I wanted him to like her. I wanted them to be his best friends as they had always been mine.

"She feels really insecure because she never finished college, and I'm sure she feels out of her element here."

"Well, she certainly goes on about herself like she has plenty to be proud of," he said.

"She does have, but truly she doesn't believe it herself. She's one of the luckiest people I know, but she seems always to concentrate on what she doesn't have." I was thinking of the times she had snapped at me for the gentle complaints I had lobbed at my mother. "She's told me before how intimidating I am to her because of my job and where I live, but she always had a home and family to hold over me. Now that I've got that, too, it will probably make the situation worse."

"You're too kind," he said. "And so is Richard. I don't know how he puts up with her self-centeredness. I think she's a prize bitch."

"You just need to get to know her. I've told you about her past. It's enough to screw anybody up."

We left before the party was over to catch the plane that would carry us to our honeymoon destination.

"You never told me where you were going," accused Cynthia. By now she had definitely had too much to drink and was truly obnoxious.

"Paris," I told her.

It was not an accident that I hadn't mentioned it before. She had a way of making me feel guilty every time something good came my way, as if I were purposely snatching it away from her outstretched hands.

"How nice," she said and raised her eyebrows in mock astonishment at the handful of people still at her table. "I thought you had already been to Europe."

"Just to England, and that was on business. I've never been to the Continent, and I've never been able to just relax and enjoy the trip."

"Of course," she said, "your incredible job would have kept you from having any fun before."

I ignored the sarcasm that dripped from her voice.

"Well, for whatever reason, I'm looking forward to it," I said. Then I looked at my watch. "And we've got to get going."

"Of course you do," she cried. "Mazel tov!"

I wouldn't see her again until the ill-fated Thanksgiving nine years later. I wasn't consciously avoiding her, but my feelings about our relationship had cooled again after the spectacle she made of herself at my wedding, and Peter made no secret of his feelings about getting together with them again. Besides that, all of our lives had become more complex, and time and circumstances just never allowed for it.

Peter and I wanted children of our own and started on that project not long after we returned from Paris. Our Todd was born a year later and his sister Mae two years after that. After *Five of Clubs,* Peter's feature film career took off so that he was constantly working, and after one of his movies was nominated for an Academy Award, he was even more in demand. When he wasn't actually directing, he was reading scripts or speaking at workshops. One semester he taught a class in filmmaking at UCLA and flew home to me only on weekends.

A live-in nanny now entered our lives. She was a widow whose grandson was at Stanford, so we fit into each other's lives perfectly. A couple of times we all joined Peter on location—once in Hawaii, once on a ranch in Wyoming—and we all went with him to Israel to do a documentary that had been his secret ambition for as long as I'd known him. It sounds like fun and it was, but it was also a hassle to arrange for all of us to go, and the fact was that he was so busy he didn't really have a lot of time to spend with us.

Much as I tried to arrange my life around Peter's, my own career was hectic and the children's lives were beginning to pick up steam, too. Jack, the image of Peter but tall and thin like his mother, started college and played as a walk-on on the freshman basketball team, and we made sure one or both of us—and often

Maxine Shulman, the nanny—were at his games to cheer him on. I wanted to spend as much time as I could with our kids. It seemed to me they grew whole inches every time I had to be away for a few days, and once they began to talk, their vocabularies doubled and tripled in my absence. Meanwhile I was promoted to features editor, and with a bigger office and more pay also came many more headaches and much more responsibility.

"You know you don't have to do all of this," Peter said to me late one Friday night. His plane had been delayed and all three kids were in bed. The two of us were enjoying a rare in-person conversation with a glass of wine in front of the living room fireplace. It was after midnight.

"Yes, I do, but it doesn't have anything to do with how much money I make or how well you provide for our family. You know that."

"I know, and I suppose your ambition and dedication are part of your charm." He pulled me closer to him. "But you've got so much going on with me and the kids in addition to your work."

I silenced him with a kiss, and for a moment I had a vision of Cynthia, whom Peter had taken to calling "Mrs. Doctor."

"I can't just be Peter Goldberg's wife. You know that. I've got to blaze my own trail."

"I know, I know, but if you do ever decide you don't want to do it all, I would support that decision. I'd welcome any change that would allow us to spend more time together."

"Me, too," I said, and I kissed him again.

❦

Cynthia and I almost got together once during that time, but it didn't work out. She had brought Chloe and Lorraine to La Jolla to visit her father and stepmother, and she called me in San Francisco.

"I'm at Dad and Caroline's," she sang through the phone, "and I just had the greatest idea. Why don't you come down and bring your kids? There's plenty of room here, and Caroline says it would be fine with them for you to stay for a couple of days. They'd love to see you. We could go to the beach and just relax and get caught up with each other."

While she talked I flipped through my calendar. It was an opportunity to see her again—and without Peter's having to be dragged along—but I didn't see how I could spare the time. Then I had an idea of my own.

"I don't think I can do that, Cyn, but I'd love to see you and Chloe and to meet Lorraine. I have to fly to LA to do an interview this Friday, and I was planning to come right back up here, but I could stretch it a little and stay over until Sunday. We have the apartment there, and Peter is in New York for meetings. Why don't you drive up Saturday morning and spend the day with me? You can stay over, and we'll fix brunch on Sunday morning before I go back. I'll book a late-afternoon flight."

"It sounds like you're much too busy to make time for me," she said. Her voice had become hollow.

"No, not at all, Cyn," I said. "I really want to make this work out, but I'm doing this interview on Friday and the story is due Monday. If you can come to me, I'll have time to get it done and still be able to spend time with you."

"Are you bringing your children?"

"No. I wish I could, but then I'd have to bring the nanny and all of their clothes and toys. This is just a quick trip for me."

"It sounds like everybody suffers because of your career."

That again, but I refused to take the bait.

"Nope," I said, keeping my voice light and with no trace of defensiveness, as if her intended slam had missed its mark. "I make sure that doesn't happen. That's why we have Maxine. When Peter and I have to be away, at least the kids have the security of their own rooms and their regular routines. I wish you could see them, but I hope you'll settle for a visit with me and some photographs."

"I don't think so, Maggie. It sounds like you're way too busy for me. I don't want you to have to change your plans."

"Cynthia!" I said in exasperation. But she had already hung up.

After that we still kept in touch but not with as much regularity. At birthdays and holidays she sent small gifts for all of us, and I went guiltily overboard with expensive pieces from Gump's and Saks and then worried that they weren't right. I shopped more carefully for Cynthia's family than I did my own. Would a less expensive gift seem like I didn't care enough about her to spend the money when she knew I had it? Would something nicer seem like I was showing off how much money I had to spend? Once I bought a charm bracelet with a tiny cable car on it and then returned it to the jeweler, not wanting to rub in that I lived in such a fascinating city.

I sent pictures of Todd and Mae and Jack but avoided photos taken at home in case it seemed like I only wanted her to see my house with a view of the bay or my apartment just minutes from the beach in LA. I spent as much energy trying to keep the facts of my daily life out of my letters to her as I did putting them into my correspondence with everyone else. Was that the way friendship was supposed to work? When Peter was nominated for the Academy Award, I didn't tell her, and when I went with him to the presentations, I hoped for a moment that the TV cameras wouldn't stop on me. If I didn't tell Cynthia, she'd say I was keeping things from her or ask why I hadn't shared my good news with her. If I did, I risked being accused of rubbing her nose in my good fortune. Eventually it became too draining, and I backed off, writing less often, sending fewer pictures, smaller and less personal gifts or just a box of chocolates for the whole family at the holidays.

Then she called and invited us for Thanksgiving, and the voice on the phone sounded like the Cynthia I had known and loved.

"It's been much too long," she said. "I know you and Peter are busy, but surely you're going to take a few days off for the holiday. Bring the kids and let's have a real family Thanksgiving."

Peter was reluctant, but I talked him into it, still trying to preserve the friendship that had once been so important to me, and at the beginning it seemed as if it would be as relaxing as I had hoped. He said he saw a side of Cynthia he hadn't observed at our wedding and that maybe he'd been wrong after all. But Thanksgiving night, after the dinner-plate episode, he said to me, "Never again. And this time I'm not kidding. I know she used to be a good friend of yours, but I don't know why you keep up this charade now. She's not your friend anymore, and I think the woman is certifiably nuts. And so is Richard if he stays married to her."

This time I couldn't disagree.

7

Richard stuck it out for five more years, and when he finally gave up trying, he had exhausted every possibility for saving the marriage that had once been so precious to him and brought him so much joy. He told me these things later at Brady's, but we had talked many times before that by phone, and I had figured out for myself that the person who used to be Cynthia just basically wasn't there anymore. She had kept me apprised of all the crisis-intervention steps they had taken, as if having a marriage counselor's card and a suicide hotline number stuck to the front of her refrigerator were status symbols of which to be proud.

"I'm in therapy," she sang through the phone lines in January after our disastrous Thanksgiving visit.

"Well, good, if you think that's what you need. Did Richard find a psychiatrist for you on the staff at the hospital?"

"Oh, no. I didn't want to see anyone we had ever met socially so I wouldn't have to worry about whether he's going home and telling his wife everything I've told him. No, this is someone I found on my own."

"How did you hear about him?"

"In a weird way, really. I was at the drugstore waiting for a prescription to be filled, and these other two women were waiting, too. I didn't mean to eavesdrop, but I couldn't help overhearing. One woman was telling the other one that she was seeing somebody and she felt like he was helping her a lot. I told her I couldn't help overhearing and that I was looking for someone to help me sort some things out. She told me his name, and I called him. It's funny how things like this turn up just when you need them. Well, you know some people say nothing is really a coincidence. I'm starting to believe that. What are the odds that I would find the answer to my problems in line at the drugstore?"

I was dubious even then, but if Cynthia really was getting help and if her spirits were higher than I'd heard them in several years, who was I to judge?

"What kinds of things do you talk about?" I asked her.

I wasn't sure if this was appropriate, but I figured she wouldn't have brought it up if she didn't want to talk about it, and all she had to do was tell me if she didn't want to say. This wasn't the case.

"Mostly about Richard and me—about the ways I feel pulled down and held back and how Richard has oppressed me from the very beginning and kept me from realizing my potential."

Now I felt instantly defensive on Richard's behalf.

"Honey, I know Richard likes to have you at home, and I know he appreciates all the volunteer work you do, but if you ever just sat down and told him you'd like to do something else, I feel certain he'd support you. He's always supported doing what you want. I figured you would have done it long before now."

"That's just what my doctor says," she said. "He says I've given too much for too long without asking for anything in return. He says it's time for me to say straight out what I want and make some demands of my own. He says people can't give me what I want and need unless they know what it is. We're going to make some changes around here."

I flashed on Cynthia at my wedding, holding her glass high and Richard rushing to see that it was refilled. I knew this wasn't what the doctor was talking about, but it seemed like an emblem of their life together. Since the very first, I had seldom seen Richard be anything but devoted where Cynthia was concerned.

Still, whether it was thanks to her therapist or just coincidence, that spring she enrolled at a local university.

"I'm going to start out with just one class and see how it goes," she wrote in a letter. "It's a psychology class. I've told Dr. Flek, and he says it's a tiny step in the right direction, like the Chinese proverb says. Just nine hundred ninety-nine miles to go! Anyway, if it works out, I'll take some summer school classes and then go full time in the fall. Dr. Flek says I should think in terms of a PhD. I don't know about that, but he says I'm smart enough. I told him about what happened that time at Thanksgiving, and he says someday instead of volunteering at a women's shelter I'll probably be the consulting psychologist. I'll be a professional then, even by Richard's unreasonably high standards. When I talk to Dr. Flek, it all seems possible, like it will all work out."

But it didn't work out, although she claimed it was through no fault of hers.

"You just can't be my age and sitting in a classroom along with teenagers," she wrote. "It's humiliating when they know the answers and I don't, and they're sitting there in their little short skirts and trading fraternity pins. I need affirmation right now. I don't need this."

I could imagine now-matronly Cynthia in her designer suits pulling up on campus in the Mercedes that had replaced her Volvo and tottering to class in her high heels. I knew several people who had gone back to school much later and been successful. I believed Cynthia could make a go of this, and I called her and told her so after I read her letter. I didn't need a crystal ball to see that down the road we would go through this again and that between now and then Richard would be the one who got blamed. I couldn't do much to help, but I didn't want to see their marriage get into real trouble.

"So you get a wrong answer once in a while," I said. "Didn't that ever happen to you when we were in college before? It sure happened to me."

"I just feel so old and out of it."

I decided to go for it. I might make her mad at me, but at least maybe she'd think about what I said, and by this time I no longer even really cared.

"Listen, Cyn, get yourself some blue jeans and get down off your high horse and get back to class and show them what you can do. You've wished ever since you and Richard got married that you could finish school. Now money isn't a problem and the girls are growing up and Richard is supporting your decision. You may not get another chance."

"I've actually already dropped out," she said. "The teacher was horrible, and I really let her have an earful before I walked out of her class. You should have seen the looks on the other students' faces."

She snickered then, obviously proud of the show she had put on.

"And besides, the girls are in so many activities, and I'm organizing an Easter brunch to raise money for a laparoscope for the women's unit at the hospital."

"What does Dr. Flek say about your dropping out?"

"He says I'm doing exactly the right thing by making a decision and acting on it. He said the old Cynthia would have been manipulated by Richard into staying in even if I had decided that wasn't what I wanted to do."

"I've never seen Richard manipulate you," I blurted out before I could think. "He's given you the life you wanted, and he's kept his promise to support you when you went back to college once your girls were in school. I don't know how you—or Dr. Flek—can say that." Then, knowing I had brought up a subject I really didn't want to deal with, I quickly added, "Are you still volunteering at the shelter?"

"Sometimes, but not very often anymore. Dr. Flek says I don't need to demonstrate to anyone that I'm a worthwhile person. He says a person doesn't need a lot of letters after her name to be a contributing member of society. My assignment for this week is to eliminate everything I do out of guilt or feelings of insufficiency. I've been volunteering in the library at Lorraine's school, but tomorrow I'm going to tell her teacher I'm not going to do that anymore, either. Dr. Flek says I'm a good mother and a good wife, and I don't have anything to prove to anybody. He says I'm much too talented to be shelving piles of books and cleaning up after grubby little kids while the librarian does nothing but sit behind the desk and check them out."

"Whatever you think is right for you," I said, biting my tongue against everything else I wanted to say and mentally apologizing to every librarian I had ever known.

She stayed in weekly therapy for a year and then switched to what Dr. Flek called "maintenance," where she went in once every three weeks.

"He says I'm a whole person now," she told me over the phone.

"I can make the right choices for myself and live with them. He says now that I have clarified my goals I can lean into my role as a community leader and make that the organizing principle of my life. I have confidence and I don't pussyfoot around anymore. I'm not shy about calling for more pillows at a hotel even if it's two in the morning or sending back my eggs if they're not done properly. When we go to brunch at the club I always ask for the eggs to be poached hard and they always come out runny. No more, Chef Billy!"

Whole or not, not long after that I started to suspect she was drinking too much. She'd always liked her Bloody Mary on Sunday mornings with her eggs and her glass of wine with dinner, but now when I called her at times not close to a meal, she was alternately giddy and morose.

"I think Richard's sleeping around," she slurred into the phone one morning. She had initiated the call. I calculated that if it was seven a.m. on the West Coast, it would be nine in Kansas City. I was trying to get out of the house for a breakfast meeting, but I reassured her and then dialed Richard's number as soon as we had hung up. He was miraculously between patients so I was able to talk to him right away.

"It's the malady du jour," he said when I had explained why I was calling. He sounded tired, despite its being morning, as if what I had said to him had worn him out. "First it was depression because her life was meaningless, so fine, she went to a therapist. Then it was the ever-present business about school, so she started back. Now she's not doing that, so it's something else. It's like she can't stand not being in crisis. So bingo, now she's drinking. She starts the morning with a slug of bourbon that she makes sure I see—somehow punishing me, I suppose. And when I get home, no matter if it's high noon or midnight, she's got a glass of red wine next to her. Believe me, you're not the only person to call and tell me."

I felt chastened.

"I'm sorry, Richard," I said. "It's just that if you didn't know, I thought someone should tell you. I don't like talking to you behind her back, but you know she's dear to me—you both are—and if there's anything we can do to help straighten things out, I want to help."

"You don't ever have to apologize, Mags. I know your worries come from a good place, but the fact is I've actually been talking to one of the shrinks at the hospital myself just to try and get a handle on what's happening to her—to us. It's like she doesn't want to work out her problems—she just wants to wallow in them and have people pay attention to her. I think that's probably at the root of everything, and I think I'm probably partly to blame. That crack I made the Thanksgiving you were here was unforgiveable, and I see that now. Don—that's my shrink—says he sees a lot of wives of professional men who feel like they're constantly overshadowed by their husbands, so I'm trying to make her feel important, and I supported her completely when she tried to take that class. I always said I would when both girls were in school. You've heard me say it."

"Could any of this be genetic—I mean, her mother was bipolar, right?"

"Yes, I think that's probably the answer to everything, but she refuses to be tested."

"I would have thought her doctor would have insisted on that as part of her treatment."

"He calls himself a doctor, but he isn't one. He's a master's-degree psychologist whose practice thrives on women who call themselves 'depressed.' The last thing he wants is for her to get completely well. She pays him a bundle of money to tell her what she wants to hear. He can't prescribe medication, of course, and I think a good regimen of lithium could be the ticket. The symptoms are classic. And you're right—with her mother's history, you'd think she'd be putting the pieces together herself and begging for help, but she just puts her head in the sand. She goes from wildly happy and productive to depressed and quiet, and when she gets down she blames me for everything, even suspects me of having affairs with everybody she knows."

I remembered her questioning me the one time I had gone running with Richard and told him about it.

"Jesus. Well, then, you know what I'm talking about. I just didn't know it went that far back."

"If there's anything I can do to help, you know I will," I said.

"Just cross your fingers. I think that's all anybody can do at this point."

As time went by the drama played on. Cynthia finally convinced herself, Richard, and her friends that she was indeed an alcoholic and went into a hospital for two weeks of rehabilitation. That was followed by a happy period during which she took a yoga class and returned to the women's shelter a couple of times a week. By that time email had entered our lives, and that gave her a means to send daily updates about what was happening in her life.

Despite the frantic pace of my own life—my children, my husband, and work—I told her almost nothing about what was happening with me. I went to Cannes with Peter, Jack was in pre-law at Berkeley. Freckled, red-haired Todd was playing the piano and dark-haired Mae took ballet, but when Cynthia asked how we all were, I usually just said, "Oh, fine." She never seemed to notice anything amiss and was happy enough to have the conversation turn back to herself.

That period was followed by another depression, and this time Richard got her to a psychiatrist by threatening to move out if she didn't go. That doctor prescribed the lithium that Richard had predicted she would, but Cynthia stopped taking it after only a few days, saying that it upset her stomach. She told me about all of this in a phone call.

"That's just crazy," I blurted out. She wasn't the only one who had grown more confident. "I've known people who took that drug, and they had to have the dosage adjusted several times before it was effective. You just have to live with an upset stomach until you get there. It won't take long."

But she was on to her next tirade.

"I think Richard's having an affair."

"Look, Cynthia . . ." I began.

I had heard all of this before. I was busy and annoyed. I was over my so-called friendship with her, but I knew what had happened to her mother, and I couldn't stand to abandon her.

"No, I mean it this time," she said. "I've gone to the national family practice meetings with him every year since we've been here, and last week he went without me for the first time. He didn't even tell me he was going until the day before he left. He knows how much I like all of the lunches and tours they arrange for the wives, and I have a cousin who lives in Chicago, so I could have seen her while we were there."

"Did he give you any reason?"

"Oh, yes, a very elaborate one. He said he got the reservation forms late and was just going to bunk in with one of his partners whose wife wasn't going, either."

"Then that probably explains it."

I was shuffling through a pile of file folders, fishing for some research notes while a reporter waited.

"It would, except when he got back he didn't want to have sex."

"Aren't those meetings usually just a week long?"

I thought of Peter and me and how sometimes our schedules only allowed for a couple of opportunities a month, but we didn't immediately accuse one another of infidelity.

"Jeez, Cyn, you are the only couple on the planet who have been married for as long as you have and still have so much sex. The rest of us don't worry about it if a week or two go by and we're not in the sack. Richard adores you. Surely that must count for something."

"As usual, you oversimplify everything," she said, and I could hear the chill I hated creeping into her voice. "The fact is, yes, sex is still a big part of our marriage and I'm sorry if it isn't like that for you."

I found the elusive folder and gave it to the reporter, who tip-toed out of my office and thoughtfully closed the door that had previously been open. I sank into my chair and closed my eyes. Cynthia had paused as if she expected some kind of retort, but I didn't give her one, and now she went on.

"It's like he put the brakes on. A year ago we were doing it at least a couple of times a week. In the last couple of months we've dropped off to a couple of times a month, and now suddenly nothing."

I was amazed Richard still wanted to have sex with her at all.

"I'm sorry, but unless you come up with more substantial evidence than that, I've just got to believe Richard was where he said he was and doing what he said he was."

"By 'substantial,' do you mean something like the red bikini panties I found in the pocket of his bathrobe?"

"Yes," I said. "Something like that."

⁂

"Richard has left me."

It was a cold, rainy Saturday morning. I had flown to LA to go to a movie premiere that evening with Peter. On television I had heard the night before that a foot of snow blanketed Kansas City. My first thought was that anybody who would even get out of bed under such conditions was nuts, let alone pack up and leave home.

I rolled over and looked at the clock. It was five in the morning, seven where Cynthia was. Peter pulled the covers over his head and groaned. By now he was used to her early morning and late-night calls, but they still annoyed him. I didn't tell him about the ones that came to the office during the day. In spite of everything, I felt ridiculously protective of her and wanted him to understand my need to be loyal. This time I could hear panic in her voice.

"Wait a minute," I said. I slid out of bed and padded barefoot down the hall to the study. I picked up the phone and heard Peter hang up the one in the bedroom.

"What do you mean he left you?"

There was no snow in Los Angeles, but it was chilly and damp. I settled into a leather armchair, pulled my knees up under my nightgown, and wrapped a sweater Peter had left there the night before around my shoulders.

"I mean packed a suitcase and told me it was over between us," she said. Her teeth were chattering. It sounded as if she were freezing rather than watching her life go up in flames.

"Did you have a fight?"

145

"You could say that. We were up all night talking."

"Well, what about? What did he say?"

I could hear her crying now—sobbing and blowing her nose.

"He said it was over. That he didn't think I was the same person he married and he just didn't feel it anymore."

"I'm sure this is temporary. All couples go through rough patches, and sometimes they need some time apart to sort things out," I told her, although I didn't really believe the platitudes I was handing out and hated myself for not having the courage to tell her the truth. I couldn't tell her that I also thought she had changed, that the friend I had counted on had abandoned me years ago and left in her place a look-alike so caught up in her own tangle of psychoses that even talking to her on the phone was like watching a person drowning. I couldn't tell her Peter's assessment that Richard was nuts to stay with her for as long as he had or my own feelings of resentment that our relationship had become so lopsided. I had come to dread hearing her voice on the telephone.

"No, it isn't temporary, Maggie. He had planned it for a while. He had even already rented an apartment. He took a few of his clothes and his medical books. He's sending one of the people from his office over to get the rest of his things Monday morning. He wants me to pack up whatever I want him to have. He says anything else I decide to keep is fine with him. He just wants his freedom."

I could tell she was waiting for me to say something supportive, but it wasn't easy.

"Nothing's settled for good, Cyn," I said. "A lot of people separate and eventually get back together. You've both been under a lot of stress lately. Give it some time. Maybe ask Dr. Flek to recommend a marriage counselor. Richard loves you, and you also have the girls in your corner. He's a good dad. He won't want to be away from them."

"There's someone else, of course. Probably the little bitch who went to the meeting with him."

"How do you know?"

"Because when people get divorces there's usually someone waiting in the wings. If there isn't, they aren't this eager to get out and they care a little bit about what they take with them. You can bet he's got a dolly waiting somewhere in a love nest."

I didn't say it to her, but the idea had crossed my mind, too, and if he did, I couldn't say I blamed him.

"But you don't know that for sure."

"If he does have her hidden away there," she said, as if she hadn't even heard me, "I swear to God I'll kill them both."

I didn't expect to like Richard's new wife, and I said as much to Peter while we were getting dressed to meet them at the restaurant where we were going to have dinner. Richard and I had already had our talk at Brady's a few days before and decided we'd all get together for dinner while they were in town. Peter and I were in the bathroom. I was putting on makeup, and he was shaving in the mirror over the other sink.

"This is weird," I said. "You don't often go out to dinner with your best friend's ex-husband's new wife."

"Well, for one thing, she's not really your best friend anymore," Peter said. "There's a certain level of give and take in a friendship, and that ship sailed a long time ago. All I see is you giving and her taking. All she ever gives anybody is trouble. She's some kind of albatross with whom you carry on this ridiculous charade. I don't know why you don't just tell her you agree with Richard that she's changed and you're not interested in pursuing a relationship with her anymore. The fact is you seldom see her, and every time she calls you get upset. I don't see what you have to lose."

"We go back too far. She was a good friend to me once. I just can't."

"I go back with a lot of people, too, but if they ever dumped the crap on me that she's dumped on you, it would be over. People fade out of each other's lives—it doesn't have to be a big confrontation if you don't want it to be. You don't answer the phone a few times, and she'll move on to some other poor sucker. And trust me, you'll feel relieved."

"That sounds easy enough, but I don't think there are any other poor suckers. I don't think she has anybody. I just can't do it."

"It's tough, honey," he said, folding down his collar and heading back to the bedroom. "But I have to tell you I'm looking a lot more forward to seeing Richard now that I know Cynthia won't be along."

༄

As the months had passed and events had unfolded, Cynthia had told me about Kimberly, but it was hard to discern what was true and what was cloaked in hatred and jealousy.

"He's going to marry the little slut," she had shrieked through the phone during one call. "So much for your theory about needing a little space."

When I asked questions, she answered them in a way that didn't give me any real information.

"How old is she?"

"Well, let's just say that when you and I were in college she was still playing with paper dolls."

"Have you seen her? What is she like?"

"In fact, yes I have. Chloe and I went to a movie one night and ran into them going in as we were coming out. She's a fucking nip."

I winced, hoping I hadn't heard what I thought I did, but I knew I had.

"A what?"

"A nip. A Jap. Or as you politically correct people would probably call her, a Japanese person."

"Jeez, Cyn, this isn't like you. I won't listen to you insult a whole country full of very fine people with such horrible language because you're mad at one of them."

She chose not to acknowledge my criticism.

"I think her mother is Japanese and her father was an American serviceman. You know what they say about yellow fever."

"Come on, Cyn. Really."

Again she ignored me.

"She's a doctor, too, of course. He met her when she was a resident on his service. I think she probably got into medical school under some equal opportunity quota. She can't be very bright and still want to be with Richard."

I swallowed the obvious. I didn't see that anything would be gained by my pointing out that she had wanted to be with Richard— indeed had done whatever it took to get him and keep him and wanted desperately to be with him at this very moment.

Peter and I got to the restaurant a few minutes early and were having a drink at the bar when Richard and Kimberly arrived. We saw them first. Richard was looking for us among a small crowd waiting for tables. She held on to his arm but not possessively. It was more like touching his sleeve, just to make sure they didn't get separated. While we walked toward them from the bar, I could see that she was small and beautiful. Her shiny black hair fell to her shoulders in a pageboy; her long bangs were swept behind one ear with a silver and turquoise barrette. When Richard pointed to us, she lit up with a smile that said she was genuinely happy to see us, as if we were already friends. She held out a hand to shake both of ours.

"Richard says you've been his friend for a long time," she said. "I hope you'll come to be mine, too."

Richard explained over a plate of lobster that he had met Kimberly, who preferred to be called Kim, at work, and he told us he had still been married at the time.

"Kim and I fell in love while I was still married to Cynthia," he said. "We've been friends for too long for me to lie to you about that. And I also know that you know what I've been through. All I can do is ask you to try and understand. I kept it together for as long as I could for the girls, but I just kept feeling like I deserved some happiness, too. It got very old, night after night, not knowing whether I was coming home to a hot meal and a happy wife or somebody who was drunk or somebody who met me at the door accusing me of ruining her life. I never meant to be unfaithful, and Kim never set out to break up a marriage. I moved out as soon as I knew what was happening. The idea of sneaking around behind somebody's back didn't appeal to either of us, and I knew I wanted to marry Kim as soon as I was free. As you can see for yourselves, she is a very special person."

Richard's plea was so tender that both Kim and I reached out to touch his hand. That made us all laugh and then we were fine. The ice had been broken, and we didn't mention Cynthia's name again for the rest of the evening.

❧

"So I hear you met Suzie Wong," Cynthia said.

I could tell by the ice in her voice that this wasn't the time to point out that the prostitute in the film had been Chinese. I had hoped she wouldn't find out about our meeting, that I wouldn't have to endure this call, but apparently Richard had told Chloe, Chloe had mentioned it to her mother, and now here we were.

"We had dinner with Richard and Kim while they were in town, yes."

"So you're calling her 'Kim' now. How very cozy. It must have seemed like old times—with one very big difference."

"That's not fair, Cynthia. If you remarry, I'll certainly want to meet your new husband. Richard's my friend, too."

"Still? After all he's done to me. Wow. That little slant-eye stole my husband away from me. Doesn't that count for something with you?"

"That's not all there was to it, Cyn," I said wearily. "I think you know that."

I knew I was treading on dangerous ground. I wanted to point out that it was she who had destroyed her marriage. Instead, I said, "You've said yourself many times that Richard kept you from pursuing your own dreams. Well, now you're free to do whatever you want. The two of you had a lot of problems, but now they're over and life goes on for both of you. You can make a whole new, fresh start."

"What did she have on?"

Apparently my little pep talk had been a waste of time.

"I don't know—a gray sweater and slacks, some silver jewelry, I think. What difference does it make?"

"I just want to know what she's buying on the money he makes.

I'm the one who suffered through medical school with him. Everything she has is by rights mine."

"That's not fair, either. You got a hell of a settlement, and she has a good job, so I imagine she buys her own things."

Cynthia's attorney had negotiated for her to keep the house while Richard was obligated to pay off the mortgage. He would support both girls through high school, pay for college, and provide each of them with a car and an allowance. Cynthia would keep the Mercedes, which was already paid for, and get monthly alimony forever unless she remarried.

"I'll never remarry," she had told me the day she read these details to me over the phone. "I'll find some young stud and move him in here, and Richard can pay for us to live together in his own house. We'll see how he likes that."

"That's not right, Cyn. And besides, when you meet somebody new and fall in love, Richard will be the last person on your mind."

"It's what he deserves after what he did to me," she said.

"He's taking good care of the girls."

"We're talking about me here."

"Okay, but he's taking good care of you, too. I know a lot of women whose lifestyles really changed after they got divorced, and not for the better. You're living in the same house and driving the same car and using the same credit cards. I don't see what more he could have done."

"He could have kept his dick in his pants when he met up with little Kimberly."

She put the accent heavily on the first syllable—KIM-berly— as if the name itself were something to ridicule. I could see that arguing was futile. I pleaded another call and hung up.

❧

In the first year after the divorce and Richard's subsequent marriage, Cynthia had given me a welcome reprieve from her telephone tongue-lashings. She felt I had betrayed her by meeting Kim and defending Richard, and our relationship had lapsed back into one of holiday cards and impersonal presents. It was hard for me to write back because now, in addition to not wanting to mention my work or anything interesting Peter and the children and I had done, I was self-conscious about having a husband at all.

Cynthia messaged that she had slept with two of her friends' husbands. It gave her a rush, she reported, to sit on the country club board of directors with a woman whose husband had just last week gone down on her while his wife was out of town. I didn't answer, but when she called on my birthday she said she and that particular man were having a serious affair, that they had done it on his living room floor while his wife was in the hospital having her gallbladder removed.

"How do you square that with what you've been through?" I asked her. "How can you do that to another woman?"

"I don't want to hear any of your sisterhood shit," she retorted. "If somebody did it to me, I can do it to somebody else. Nobody's husband is safe, not even yours."

I shook my head sadly when I put the phone back into its cradle.

"If you only knew what he thinks about you," I said aloud, "you'd know he is."

In one letter she reported that she had slept with the college boy who cut her grass and washed her car. I sent back a gift pack of condoms. AIDS was on all of our minds then, and as angry as she made me, I didn't want to lose her to such a horrible illness.

"Use these," I wrote on a "thinking of you" card. "Some of us love you and would like to keep you around for a while."

By return mail I got a note from her written on engraved ivory note paper that still said "Mrs. Richard C. Bartolucci." She thanked me for the "funny" gift and then added, "But who the hell cares?"

Whenever Cynthia did decide to call me, she seemed to have radar. If I was at home in San Francisco, she called me there. If I was at the apartment in LA, she found me there. If I went into the office on the weekend to catch up on work, she called me there. And her timing was impeccably bad, too. Her calls came just as I was leaving the house in the morning or going into a meeting at the paper or sitting down to dinner or falling asleep. She never left messages on my machine or with anybody else in the house. I just picked up the phone from time to time and there she was. I had a cell phone by that time, but I didn't tell her or give her the number.

The long periods when she didn't call at all seemed like holidays, but then one night Peter and I were stretched out in front of the fireplace drinking wine and watching a tape of the movie he was working on. Todd was spending the night with a friend and Mae had been asleep for hours. Peter slid his hand up under my sweater and pulled me to him. The phone rang.

"The little Jap's pregnant."

For a moment I didn't know who it was, and I didn't understand what she had said.

"I'm sorry, what?" I said into the phone.

"You heard me. I said the little Jap is pregnant. Maybe now he'll get his boy. I'll bet he's so happy his pecker is doing a dance."

In fact this was not news to me. Richard had called with the announcement the day Kim had gotten the word from her OB, but I didn't let on. I knew that he was every bit as happy as she suspected—although I couldn't vouch for what was going on in his pants.

"How did you find out?" I asked her.

"The girls had dinner with them tonight. Oh, God."

She was sobbing, and my heart went out to her. I reached out to touch Peter, who had withdrawn his hand with an audible sigh and gotten up for more wine when he figured out who was on the phone. Now he was back and making funny faces at the telephone receiver. I couldn't imagine what it would feel like to find out someone else was having his child. I felt the old tug, the old sympathy for poor, troubled Cynthia.

"Look, why don't you just move away from there?" I asked her. "Sell that house and come back out here. You know your dad and Caroline would love to have you and the kids closer, and the girls would love the beach. There's no reason to beat yourself up by being that close to a situation that makes you so unhappy."

"I can't do that and you know it. Chloe has started college here and Lorraine is going into high school soon. No, Richard screwed up their lives pretty badly, but he's not going to run us out of town. If I run into them, I'll just stare the slut down. I'm not the one who did something wrong."

I didn't hear from her again until the baby was born. This time her call came at one in the morning.

"It's a boy," she said, and then I heard her start to cry. "It's a fucking boy."

I looked at the clock.

"Did you just find out?"

"No. I found out yesterday, and I thought I could handle it, but I can't. The little slant-eye gave him the one thing I couldn't."

"It's over, Cynthia. They've been married for more than a year, and Richard's not your husband anymore. If they have a child, fine, that's their business. Your business is to get on with your life and not worry about them anymore. They say living well is the best revenge, and there's a lot of truth in that. Make your life so good that you don't care what he does. Now, tell me something else that's going on with you. Something good."

"What's going on with me is that he can't seem to stop ripping my heart out over and over again. This is going to devastate the girls."

I didn't think it would since Richard had reported in a call that the girls were crazy about Kim and looking forward to having a new baby in the family. He and Kim had decided not to know the child's gender ahead of time, so they asked the doctor not to tell them when he saw the results of the ultrasound. But what was a delightful surprise for them was a devastating shock for Cynthia.

"They love their mother, no question about that," he had told me, "but I think they see our place as an oasis of calm. They have to put up with a lot of the crap from her that I used to. They're too old for Kim to try and mother them, and she's not interested in replacing Cynthia anyway, so the three of them are just great friends. They're as excited about the baby as we are. In fact, they went to a baby shower some women at the hospital gave for Kim, but Cynthia doesn't know that."

Knowing these things, I had to be careful what I said and not give away what I wasn't supposed to know.

"I think you'll be surprised," I said. "They're both pretty grown-up, so it's not like a new baby brother is going to steal their toys."

"Why must you always side with Richard?"

"I'm not siding with anybody," I said, exasperated. "I'm telling you what I think is the truth, and part of it is that you've got to pull yourself together and stop obsessing over Richard. Obviously there are other men in the world who find you appealing. What ever happened to the guy you told me about from the country club?"

"That's been over for a long time. He dumped me, just like Richard did. He said I was too much woman for him, that I was making too many demands. But I got even. I sent his wife an anonymous letter saying he was having an affair with one of their neighbors. She's lost a lot of weight and looks awful and won't even speak to Doris. I love it."

"That's cruel, Cyn. That isn't you. You're better than this."

"I don't care, Maggie. Can't you understand that I don't care about much of anything? And if I can cause somebody else the same kind of pain I've gone through, it helps just a bit, like a drug that relieves the suffering just for a little while, just long enough that I can get to sleep or make it through a meal."

"I think once you have somebody really special in your life again you won't have these negative feelings anymore."

What I really thought she needed was good psychiatric counseling, but Richard had told me she had stopped seeing the one who prescribed the lithium, and I didn't want to suggest that she return to the infamous Dr. Flek, who had helped turn the troubled friend I had known into a loud-mouthed, self-absorbed steamroller.

"I don't want to get married," she said, "and there's always somebody willing to give me a little service, if you know what I mean."

"You mean sex?"

"Of course I mean sex, my little innocent. The men in this neighborhood are always horny. They drop by while their wives are out of town or late at night after a party and nobody's the wiser. Nobody's going to leave his wife over me, so nobody really gets hurt. They're all just zipless fucks."

"Doesn't it bother you how your lifestyle might affect Chloe and Lorraine? They love you, you know, and they look to you as an example."

She laughed huskily and her words began to run together.

"They know what I've been through. They'd cut me some slack."

"Are you drinking again, Cyn?"

"No, but I just found the most delicious sleeping pills in the back of the medicine cabinet. I think I can sleep now."

"Call me tomorrow and let me know how you are," I said. "I care about you, Cyn. Please don't wreck your life over this."

"I think that ship has sailed," she said, and then she laughed again and hung up without saying goodbye.

But she didn't call, and when I tried to reach her the next evening, Lorraine answered the phone and said her mother wasn't home. She had gone to a party at the club.

When I finally did hear from her several months had gone by. I was lying on the sofa reading a book. Peter was in Canada filming. Todd and Mae were watching a movie on television in another room.

"You'll never guess what I just found," she said.

She seldom said hello or identified herself anymore, as if the only calls I ever got were from her and no time had elapsed since we last spoke.

"Hi, Cyn. You're probably right. What did you find?"

"Richard's old pistol."

I sat up straight now and pulled the throw that had been over my legs up around my shoulders. I felt suddenly cold and apprehensive.

"How did you happen to find that?"

"I was cleaning out the bedroom closet. You know how you're always telling me to get on with my life. Well, I decided to get rid of some stuff that was Richard's, and I came across the locked box where he always kept the gun. He kept it high up on a shelf so there'd never be a chance of the girls finding it."

"Did you find anything else interesting?"

I was buying time to think what the right advice to give her would be.

"No, just some sweaters and old shoes and some medical journals."

"So why don't you call him and ask him to come over and pick them up?"

It seemed like the logical solution. All I could think of was getting the gun out of her hands before she hurt herself or someone else.

"You've got to be kidding," she said. "I cut his clothes to ribbons and burned them and the magazines in the fireplace. But the gun is mine. I'm an armed woman. I like that. It's like nobody can ever hurt me again."

"You know the statistics show that if you have a gun in the house, you're more likely to be shot with it than to shoot anyone else. It happens all the time. A burglar breaks in, you wave the gun, he takes it away from you, and boom! It's all over."

I kept my voice even and tried to coax her into promising me that she would call Richard immediately and have him come and get it. I felt like I was negotiating with a maniac, which now I realize I was.

"I don't plan to wave it around in front of a burglar, silly," she said. "I've got much better plans for this baby."

"And what might those be?" I was trying to stay calm.

"Oh, I'd probably never do it, but I do have a delicious fantasy about murdering Richard and Kim."

"Oh, my God! Just listen to yourself."

"Every woman dreams of killing the man who left her," she went on as matter-of-factly as if we were talking about the color of wallpaper or the price of cereal. "It keeps you going. And now that I know I have this gun, it's like any time I really wanted to do it, I actually could."

I had once lost someone I loved to another woman, but I had never for a moment wished him dead, and when he was, I had grieved.

"This is nuts, Cyn. Get rid of that gun and get yourself to a shrink and on medication before you do something you'll regret."

"Don't you want to hear my fantasy?"

"No, I don't."

"It goes like this: I go to their house some evening just after they get home from work. They'll be busy bringing the kid in from the sitter's and cooking dinner. They'll be drinking wine and tossing a salad and poaching chicken because they're too good to fry anything. Anyway, the back door won't be locked because it will still be early and probably light out. Maybe they'll be kissing when I come in. I'll shoot her first to make sure he sees it."

"Don't, Cyn, I can't listen to this anymore." But of course I did.

"Then I think I'll shoot him right in the dick, and when he folds over in pain, I'll go for his head. When they're both dead I'll go back home and call the police and say I'm a neighbor and I think I heard gunshots. Then they'll come and take the little nip kid and put him in some foster home, and I'll go on with my life, just like you're always telling me to do."

I felt sick.

"You need help, Cyn, I'm not kidding."

She laughed.

"Oh, you know I probably don't have the guts to do it, but it's nice to know I could if I wanted to. Meanwhile I'll just feast on the idea of Richard with his dick shot off and a hole in his head."

I wished Peter were home. I usually kept the content of Cynthia's more bizarre calls to myself since it irritated him that I even took the time to speak to her. Now I could have used his advice. If I called Richard and Kim, I might alarm them for nothing and sound like a nitwit myself. If I didn't call them and Cynthia made good on her plan, it would, in a way, be my fault that they hadn't been warned. I rang their number and Richard answered.

"I've got something to tell you," I said.

"You sound upset, Mags. Is everything all right?"

"It is with me, but I just got off the phone with Cynthia, and she told me that while she was cleaning a closet today she found your gun."

"Oh, Jesus," he groaned. "I forgot all about that thing when I moved out. Shows you how important it was to me."

"She says she has a fantasy of killing you and Kim—first her so you'll see it and then you."

I omitted the part about shooting off his penis, figuring that if the plan ever came to fruition, this would be the least of his worries.

"She really has gone around the bend, hasn't she? Well, it's not something I'm happy to hear, but I don't think she'd ever really do it. She harasses us all the time, but it's pretty harmless. She left some dead flowers on our doorstep once, and she ordered a bunch of pizzas and had them delivered here so we had to pay for them—stuff like that. But I don't think she's capable of murder. Even after everything that's happened, I don't think she'd do that."

"Well, at least you know," I said, more casually than I felt. "If anything should happen, I'd never forgive myself if I hadn't warned you."

"I'll get one of the girls to let me in when she's not home and I'll just slip in and get it. I'm not crazy about her having it anyway with them in the house. The chances of one of them being hurt are probably greater than her ever coming after us."

But a few days later he called me back.

"I had hoped to be able to set your mind—and mine—at ease, but I went over there this afternoon and looked in the closet where it used to be and in every closet and drawer in the place. The gun is gone. She's hidden it away someplace where I couldn't find it. All I can tell you is that she has a gun, and I don't have a clue where it is."

8

While all of Cynthia's drama had been playing out I had met Annie Hamilton, who turned out to be the best—and only, really—close woman friend I had made since Cynthia. I had lots of women friends, but Cynthia had been the only one I opened up to for so long, and when that went south, I decided the cost had been too dear to try it again. Besides, now that I was in my forties, I couldn't imagine bringing anybody new up to speed with the events of my life. I was too busy and tired to explain about the dairy farm and college and Ian and how I had met my husband and decided on names for my children.

Then I interviewed Annie for the job as assistant features editor when Carlos Wong, who seemed irreplaceable, left for a job with a features syndicate. She was only a few years younger than I was, but she had considerably less experience, just two years as a part-time beat reporter for a weekly neighborhood paper while she worked on her degree. She had been a flight attendant, she told me, but her dream had always been to be a journalist. She saved money while she worked and then used it to pay her way through journalism school. I thought momentarily of Cynthia and her reluctance to compete with students so much younger than she was, even if doing it would have given her what she had always thought would make her happy.

Just before Annie left the airline she met a man on one of her last flights, and after a whirlwind courtship that spanned several different cities, they had decided to marry. She had moved to San Francisco, where her husband, Jonathan, worked in the financial district and already owned a home. She had warned him that she was going back to school, and he was as excited as she was. He made enough money to support them until she was ready to pursue her new career, he told her, so she should enjoy the experience and not try to rush through to get out fast and get a job. But once graduated, she could hardly wait to get to work.

"I know you aren't legally able to ask me questions about my family life, so I'll just tell you straight out," she said. I loved this woman's spunk and fearlessness. "My husband and I are hoping to adopt a child, but if that dream comes true, we'll be hiring a nanny. I might take off a few weeks, but it wouldn't be any longer than that. I may be older than most beginners, but I promise you I have all the energy and drive of someone much younger."

She didn't have to tell me. She exuded enthusiasm. Typically I wouldn't have hired someone with so little experience, but she was bursting with story ideas and said working weekends wouldn't be a problem. Carlos checked her references, and I called her that same afternoon to offer her the job.

When we got to know each other better, I teased her that anyone could have guessed what her previous career had been. She had short dark blonde hair that she tucked behind her ears to show off her pearl earrings, and even on the worst days her makeup was perfect—charcoal eye shadow, a brush of pink across her cheekbones. She wore narrow skirts with hems that broke exactly at the back of her knee and coordinating jackets with the sleeves rolled up to expose a tiny watch and a single silver bangle. Her perfume smelled of orange blossoms and was light and clean. Her posture was perfect, and when she loaded a ream of paper into the copy machine, she bent her knees and lifted from the hips with her back straight as if when she raised back up her arms would be loaded with trays and she would be ready to serve us all lunch. When she spoke her voice was clear and pleasant, and she knew how to defuse tense situations between disgruntled reporters and overzealous copyeditors. I asked her once if her flight training had taught her to keep a perpetual smile on her face and if she had been required to spend several hours a day with a book balanced on her head.

Jonathan got on famously with Peter, and the four of us had even rented a condo in the mountains and taken the children skiing for a weekend. Most of the time, though, it was just the two of us, catching up with each other's lives while we drank coffee and went over potential story assignments, occasionally sending out for lunch or stopping for a drink after work just so we could talk. In just a few weeks she had my routines down and seemed to know what I needed just when I needed it. She also knew that I didn't like to be interrupted during meetings, so one day in 1998 I was surprised when she slipped into the afternoon budget meeting looking worried.

"You have a phone call, Maggie," she whispered.

"It can't wait?" I asked, frowning.

I knew the answer. She wouldn't have bothered me if it hadn't been serious.

"It's your dad," she said as she followed me out of the conference room. "I think something's wrong. It sounds like an emergency."

Now I started running toward my office and snatched up the phone on my desk from the other side.

"Daddy?"

I had never heard my father cry before.

"It's Mom, honey," he sobbed through the phone.

I froze. Only one thing could lead to a call like this.

"She's gone, baby."

For a fleeting moment I hoped ridiculously that he meant out to the grocery store or even that she had run away with a lover, but I knew better. Still, I needed more information.

"What do you mean?"

"It was an aneurysm. We were sitting at the kitchen table eating breakfast this morning. I was getting ready to fix some fences around on the back of the farm where it joins the Millers' property. She said she was going outside to work in the flower beds."

He was fully weeping now and could hardly speak, but he went on.

"All of a sudden she said she had a splitting headache and was going to take an aspirin. She stood up and collapsed. I called 911, and they took her to the hospital. The doctors operated. They said they'd try to save her, but they couldn't. She lived for a couple of hours, but she never regained consciousness."

I tried to speak. Around me figures moved through the newsroom in slow motion, and the ringing telephones and human voices became an overwhelming din. I thought for a moment I might pass out.

"Where are you, Daddy?" I said finally. My head was swimming, so I sat down in a chair.

"I'm still at the hospital, but I've called a mortuary and they're coming to pick up her . . . to pick her up. I called Bradley already, and we're meeting the funeral director tomorrow morning to make the plans. Could you come up here and help us with that, honey?"

"I'll be there this evening," I told him. "I'll be there as soon as I can."

I told Annie what had happened and took off. I stopped at home long enough to arrange for Maxine to stay over, call Peter in LA, and pack a suitcase. At the time I didn't even know what I was putting in, although later it turned out to be jeans, underwear, and the taupe suit.

"Are you going to be okay to drive?" Peter asked anxiously.

"I think so. I'll have to be. My dad really needs me."

"Look, why don't I get on a plane and drive up there with you?"

"You're really sweet to offer, but I'm leaving right now, and I'd like to be alone with Dad and Bradley tonight. I'll let you know when the funeral will be, probably in a couple of days. The kids will be here with Maxine until then so they can go to school. They can come up with you."

"You know I'm here for you, Maggie," he said. "I love you."

"I do know that," I said and thought fleetingly of Cynthia and every other divorced friend, and I thought of my dad losing his partner of nearly fifty years. "I can't tell you how much that means to me right now."

I drove north on the 101, across the Golden Gate Bridge and through the edge of scenic Marin County without seeing anything but the highway. I cried, finally, groping under my seat for the tissue box I kept there in case of fogged-up morning windows. I couldn't believe what had happened. Why my life-loving, ever-optimistic mother? I knew people who were bored by waking up in the morning and who spent their time complaining and making people around them miserable. My mother had brought joy to every life she touched in the form of homemade cookies, a phone call at just the right time, a long letter filled with snapshots and dried flowers.

Bradley had already arrived when I got to my parents' house—now just my dad's. He and Dad were huddled at the same kitchen table where my mother had collapsed just a few hours before. Mom's bright pink gardening gloves and a worn trowel lay on the counter beside the sink. A wheelbarrow filled with grass clippings and food scraps for her compost heap waited just outside the back door. Her favorite coffee mug with a cat's face on it that one of my children had given her for her birthday sat in the sink with dregs of coffee collected in the bottom.

I didn't ring the bell when I got there. Instead I went straight through to where they were and embraced them both at once. My once-robust, suntanned dad—now drawn and balding—looked suddenly very old. Bradley was over six feet tall and also had my mother's dusky red hair. After veterinary school he had joined a practice in Santa Rosa so he could continue to farm with Dad. He had been married for three years, but it ended when his bride, a fifth-grade teacher with whom he had gone to high school, announced she had played second fiddle to a pregnant horse for the last time. I couldn't really blame her, but the experience had left Bradley closed off and not much inclined to let another woman in. Currently he was dating an attorney, but both of them claimed they were only friends, neither one interested in marriage. When Kathy had to cancel a dinner date with Bradley to meet with a client, he didn't seem to care, and when a heifer in distress from too much green hay came between them, she always understood.

Dad poured a cup of coffee for me, and I sat down between them.

"She was sitting right where you are when it happened," Dad said to me. "I can't believe it. I just can't believe it. It can't be right. Look, her gloves and trowel are right there like she'll come downstairs in a minute and put them on and go outside like she planned."

I rubbed the back of his hand. Tears ran down his face, and he wiped at them with a paper napkin printed with tiny pink rosebuds.

That night the three of us stayed at home together. I slept in my old room, which, to the delight of Todd and Mae, Mom had always kept pretty much as it had been when I lived there. The only difference was that her mending and craft projects now covered the bed, and when they had overnight company it became the guest room—pennants, Beatles poster, frilly pink bedspread, and all. This time I found a pile of dresses she had almost presciently set aside for the Goodwill truck and a stack of seed catalogs she must have been considering for the garden where that very day she had been planning to prepare the soil.

All evening long the phone rang and neighbors dropped by with a procession of chocolate cakes, bowls of salad, and chicken casseroles. We put most of it away and ordered out for a pizza, which we ate with a bottle of the sauvignon blanc Mom always had in the refrigerator. Even though it was late spring, Bradley lit a fire in the living room fireplace, and when everyone else had gone home, the three of us sat in exhausted, stunned silence.

At ten the next morning we turned up at Cooper's Memorial Chapel. Call it whatever they wanted, it was still a funeral home where I didn't have any idea what to expect. My knowledge of funerals came from a mix of a couple I had been to as a child—where my memories consisted of seeing an old person I hardly knew lying in a satin-covered box and looking like a wax carving, then later eating a lot of deviled eggs and whooping it up outside with cousins while the grown-ups ignored us and stayed in—and *The American Way of Death*, which I had read for a sociology class in college. Somewhere among those scenarios lay the truth, I supposed. For sure I didn't know how to go about planning such an ordeal. Did this mean I was now one of the grown-ups—murmuring to one another in a softly lit room where bouquets gave off a sickeningly sweet aroma, pausing now and then to dab their eyes with tissues? No whooping outside anymore for me.

I didn't much care about what the coffin was made of or the color of the lining because I didn't think my mother would have, either, and in any event it was going to remain closed. If she had been here with us, we would have gone home later, poured a glass of wine, and made fun of the smarmy men in dark suits who had guided us through catalogs of flower arrangements and referred to her as "the deceased." How practical, she would have laughed, that one name fits all, a good profession for someone with a bad memory.

But she wasn't there with us. She was off in some other part of the complex where white tile and metal tables replaced the thick carpets and heavy wood furniture, having her body washed and drained of its fluids, ready to be put into the box that Dad, Bradley, and I were struggling to choose. Mom had always said she wanted a plain pine coffin like the pioneers would have used, but that wasn't available, and the funeral director—not Mr. Cooper but an assistant whose name was Howard Bond—hinted that families who really wanted to honor their loved ones opted for the mahogany and brass number, or at the very least the golden oak. When we chose the least expensive wood, a simple spray of her favorite white daisies, and a private graveside ceremony, he sniffed and turned us over to a man in charge of the grounds so we could select a plot and decide on a headstone. We disappointed him, too.

We held the graveside service the following afternoon. The only people present were Dad, Bradley, Kathy, Peter, Jack, Todd, Mae, and me. My dad had convinced my Aunt Judy, my mom's only sibling, not to spend the money to fly out from Chicago, but she had sent flowers and a donation to the public library where Mom had been a frequent patron. A Protestant minister who had never laid eyes on my mother went on for several minutes about what a marvelous woman she had been. I concentrated on the white trail being deposited by an airliner high above us and a group of cattle grazing on a distant hillside to keep from bursting into hysterical, inappropriate laughter. Back at the house a caterer served finger sandwiches and deviled eggs—on which I had insisted—to a crowd of people that included neighbors and my mother's many friends, an outpouring that moved me and would have delighted her. Women in black dresses and men in dark suits sipped wine and moved from Bradley to Dad to me, murmuring sympathetically and then disappearing into the sunlight, consciously giddy about getting back to their own lives, about simply being alive.

That night, our small party more than doubled by Peter and the children, we lit another fire, poured more wine, and munched on leftover sandwiches as we planned how we would go on through life without Mom.

"I've got to get back to LA tomorrow," Peter said regretfully. "It's the last thing I want to do, but every day I'm not there costs thousands of dollars and holds up production. We're behind schedule on this picture as it is. And Jack has to get back, too."

Jack had graduated from law school and joined a small LA firm. He lived in an apartment near the beach in Santa Monica.

"Why don't you come with us?" Peter asked me. "The kids have spring break next week anyway, and, Bradley, you're still coming down next week for the veterinary society meeting, aren't you?"

"I'm not really up for it right now," he said, nodding ruefully, "but I've been asked to give a paper that I think is important, so I feel like I need to be there."

We had recently given up the apartment in West LA and bought a home in Malibu. It was white and modern, with deco glass cubes for some of the windows, and patios and balconies off every room that overlooked the sea. The day we first walked through it I thought of Cynthia's house in La Jolla. They were really very similar. We had decorated with Asian rugs and eighteenth-century furniture to balance and soften the architecture and moved in the books and paintings we'd had at the apartment. The interior designer had had her doubts, but it had turned out just the way we wanted, an eclectic home that was distinctly ours and no one else's, and right now the idea of hibernating there for a few days sounded like an extremely good one. The managing editor had called to tell me to take as much time as I needed to recover from Mom's death, and I knew Annie could handle whatever came into the office until I got back. The funeral had happened so quickly that I really could have time to spend spring break with the kids and Peter at the house.

"What about you, Dad?" I couldn't indulge in my own healing if he had to endure his pain by himself. "Any chance of talking you into coming down for a few days? You could come when Bradley comes."

He shook his head, as I should have known he would.

"I'll have Bradley for a few days until he goes to the meeting," he said, "and I really don't mind being alone. Mom's things are here, our life is here. Besides, I still have a fence to fix, and Joe Miller has offered to help me with it. I'll be fine."

I wasn't sure about that, but he insisted and refused when I offered to stay on. We flew to Los Angeles the next afternoon and got home just in time for a sunset walk before dinner. At eleven o'clock that night the phone rang. I had gone to bed, exhausted, just after nine.

"Oh, good. I'm glad you're there," Cynthia blurted through the line.

I looked at the clock beside the bed. I wondered how she always managed to find me and what time it must be in Kansas City. I was glad Peter hadn't come in to bed yet, but I knew he had heard the phone and could probably guess who was calling me at this hour.

"What's up, Cynthia?" I asked.

"I'm coming out to visit my dad, and I thought if you were in LA, I'd come up for a few days. The girls are staying here. It'll just be me."

"When are you coming?" I asked, hoping her trip would not overlap with my stay.

"I'm flying to San Diego tomorrow, and I'll be in La Jolla through the weekend. I thought I'd drive up Sunday night and spend the first few days of next week at your place and then fly back."

I counted heads and bedrooms. If the kids doubled up in Todd's bunk beds, we'd have room for Bradley and her at the same time, and maybe having more people in the house would keep her from going morose on me and keep me from thinking constantly about the overwhelming disbelief I still felt at losing my mother. Still I wished she wouldn't come.

"That will work out, Cyn," I told her. "Bradley is going to be here at the same time for a conference, but we've got room. I just need to tell you that I may not be great company or the best hostess in the world. My mother died Monday. The funeral was yesterday, and I actually came down here to get away from everything and try to get my head back together."

I hoped maybe she would intuit that this would not be a good time to entertain a house guest, but that was not to be.

"Welcome to the club," she said. "Now you know how it feels. Okay, well then I'll see you Monday."

❧

I spent Friday and Saturday relaxing and gearing up for the days ahead. I walked on the beach and threw a Frisbee with my kids. I read and slept. Peter came home early when he could and made drinks for us at our patio bar. We held hands and listened to music and made love. Then just after we had picked Bradley up at the airport, Cynthia arrived. She drove a rented Mercedes convertible and wore designer clothes, but she was thin and gaunt and looked much older and worse than I had ever seen her. I would happily have traded her for the overweight, overbearing Cynthia she had been when I last saw her. Now she reminded me of a vulture.

"You've lost some serious weight," I said. When I hugged her in the driveway it was like I imagined putting my arms around an oversized tangle of paperclips or the skeleton dangling on a stand in my doctor's office would be.

"I have Richard to thank for that," she said. "When you can't force down any more than a piece of toast and a glass of water every day, dieting isn't hard at all."

It was impossible to put on a show of sympathy. I didn't think she remembered anymore that I had once come to her to get over a broken heart. She seemed to think she was the only woman who had ever gone through what she had, that even if other women lived through similar situations, their pain still couldn't possibly compare to hers.

"It has turned out for the best, though," she went on. "Men don't like fat cows. I certainly learned that the hard way. As you know, Richard likes them anorexic—and preferably with slanted eyes and yellow skin."

"None of that here, Cyn. I'm serious. We won't stand for any racist talk." Then, to avoid starting yet another fight before we even got through the door, I changed my tone and gave her a smile I didn't feel. "It's great to see you," I said. "Come on in."

That night went so well that I began to think I had been mistaken about her and that her visit might be good for me after all. Despite her initial remarks about her breakup with Richard and her racist comments about Kim, she seemed more like her old self than she had for years. She chopped a salad while I made spaghetti sauce, and once we were all settled at the table, she entertained my family with stories about our college days that I had completely forgotten. She reminded me of the time I turned our white blouses and underwear pink by washing them with a new pair of red socks and told them how we had heated chicken noodle soup in our popcorn popper. They roared with laughter, and I could tell she had won them over. Initially, when I had announced she was coming, Todd, now sixteen, had asked, "Isn't that the lady who threw the plate of food at her husband that time?" Mae, whose memories of that visit had vanished except for that one moment, grumbled, "Oh, great!"

"Your mother was the best friend a person could have," Cynthia told them now, sobering, "and she still is. I've been through some bad times, and she's always been there, either in person or at the other end of the phone line, talking me through whatever the crisis was at the moment."

I shot a look to Peter, who had gotten up for more wine and was just now pouring some for Cynthia. He winked and smiled at me from behind her, but I saw him shake his head ever so slightly. While she might have won my children's hearts, apparently she still hadn't won his.

⁂

"Your brother has turned into a hunk," Cynthia said the next morning.

Peter had gone to the studio early, Bradley had left for his meeting, and Mae and Todd were off to Disneyland with the family from next door. The two of us were finishing a pot of coffee on the patio as the sun rose higher and more bikini-clad college girls collected on the beach beyond my house.

"He's great," I said. I only realized later that I hadn't gotten the message she intended to send. "We weren't that close as kids. I was always the know-it-all older sister. But since we've grown up he's been a wonderful friend. I've been really glad we had each other this last week."

This time she was the one who missed the message. She hadn't mentioned my mother's death once since she had arrived, even though we had all been talking about it around her. She treated her impromptu visit as if it were something we had planned and looked forward to for months, as if nothing had happened that might keep me from enjoying her company as I would have twenty years or even two weeks ago.

"Is there anybody special in his life?" she asked now.

"He was married for a while, but it didn't work out. He dates a woman, but they say they're just friends. I think she must have been burned sometime in her past, too. I'd like to see him find someone he could really care for, but for now he seems happy with things the way they are. He has his practice, and of course he still farms with Dad."

That evening when everyone got home we built a bonfire on the beach and roasted hotdogs while we watched the sun go down. After it had dipped below the horizon I brought coffee down from the house and we laced it with brandy and drank it in the light of the fire. I noticed the whole time that Cynthia was hovering around Bradley. She wanted to carry his mug to him, and when she did she wedged her way in between him and Todd on the driftwood log where they sat.

We stayed on talking for another hour, but when the coffee was gone and the fire was dying I stood up and began to gather the cups back onto the tray.

"Ready to go in, honey?" Peter asked, hauling himself up beside me and dusting sand off the seat of his pants.

"Yep," I said. "Too cold for me."

The kids had already gone in, and from the family room windows I could see colorful moving images on the television set.

"I feel like a walk," Cynthia announced. "Anyone care to join me?" And then, without waiting to see who might take her up on her offer, she added, "What about you, Bradley?"

He smiled questioningly at me and shrugged his shoulders when I deliberately remained impassive. Whatever was about to happen wasn't going to be on my conscience.

"Well, sure. I guess so, why not?" he stammered.

They were gone for three hours. Peter and I guessed they had gone down the beach to a bar where they could have a drink and talk. Eventually we had gone on to bed and were both reading when we heard them come in. They were giggling and shushing each other as they came upstairs. We could hear them whispering as they tiptoed first into Cynthia's room, then back out into the hallway, then into Bradley's room. Then we heard the door click softly shut.

"They're both in Bradley's room!" I hissed to Peter.

"They're both adults. It's not our problem—or our business." He raised a cautioning eyebrow in my direction, then pulled his glasses from the top of his head and turned back to his book.

"Our children are sleeping across the hall from them!"

"Yes, and Bradley loves those kids. He won't do anything to hurt or embarrass them."

"Still, this is too icky. Cynthia and my own brother! Is that all this woman does?"

Soon we could hear faint, unmistakable sounds coming from Bradley's room. I was about to climb out of bed when Peter grabbed my arm and pulled me back.

"The kids are sound asleep, and there's nothing you can do, so why don't we just give them a little friendly competition?"

I couldn't help but laugh at his optimistic face, so I tumbled back into bed and he turned off his light.

In the morning I would not have known what happened the night before if I hadn't heard it for myself. When I got up, Bradley's door was open and his bed made. He was downstairs gulping coffee before heading downtown to his meeting, and Cynthia slept innocently in the room to which she had been assigned. When she finally came downstairs at ten she confessed to me immediately.

"I slept with Bradley last night," she said.

"No shit."

"You knew?"

"I think your secret is safe from the kids, but we heard you come upstairs and go into Bradley's room, that's all."

I didn't add that their lovemaking sounds had been a catalyst to Peter's and my delightfully spontaneous coupling.

"I think he might be the one."

"What do you mean 'the one'?" I asked, frowning. I handed her a cup of coffee and reached into the refrigerator for a plate of strawberries and sliced watermelon.

"I mean, I've screwed everything that moves since Richard left me. I guess I've been trying to prove that I'm still attractive to other men even if my own husband didn't want me. But last night I talked to Bradley like I haven't talked to a man in years."

"About what?" I heard my own voice raise a notch on the way to becoming shrill.

"About everything. You know, my childhood, my mother's death, my kids, what happened with Richard. We walked on the beach for a while, but mostly we just wrapped up in a blanket and talked. He told me a lot about himself, too, like about his wife and what went wrong there."

"Well, that's good, I guess," I said. "I mean, it's always good when you meet someone you feel like you can talk to about important things like that."

I was babbling, buying time. The truth was I was annoyed with both of them for letting this happen. It was completely inappropriate, especially in my house and considering the timing. What was Bradley thinking? I couldn't believe Cynthia had moved in on him while he was grieving and vulnerable, and I couldn't believe he took the bait, but I also didn't want him to be hurt. If one of them disappointed the other, I didn't want to be anywhere around. I guessed then, rightly as it turned out, that if their romance did go down in flames, I'd be caught in the middle. I envisioned another round of midnight phone calls once Cynthia was back in Kansas City, this time with me somehow to blame. I wished just once she would fall in love without my looking on.

"It's like we just clicked," she said. "I haven't felt that close to anyone since Richard—when it was good with him, I mean."

I tried to imagine Cynthia as my sister-in-law, the two of us cooking Christmas dinner in Dad's kitchen now that Mom would no longer be in charge, my brother in holiday photos that would include Chloe and Lorraine. But even though Cynthia was in a good mood now, I knew how easily she could turn dark, and if she ever sailed another loaded dinner plate at a man, I decided it had better not be my brother. For now, she was content to drop the subject and move on.

"So, what are the plans for today?" she asked.

"No plans," I said. "That's why I'm here. I'm taking a week off. My Day-Timer is sitting on the desk in my office in San Francisco, and I am officially unplugged."

"I guess what I mean is, are you planning a luncheon or cocktail party or anything while I'm here?"

"What?"

"You know, to introduce me to some of your friends."

"Not this time, Cynthia. I came here to relax. I'm perfectly happy to have you here, but I warned you on the phone that I wasn't really up to entertaining."

She made a pouty face and examined her manicured fingernails.

"Did I tell you I was back in therapy?" she said finally.

"Good," I said. I remembered her fantasy about killing Richard and Kim, and I was all for anyone who could talk her out of it. "Did you find somebody good?"

"Oh, I went back to Dr. Flek. I made such progress with him

before. The thing is, he has always said the trouble with me is I don't make my wishes known, so it's no wonder people have a hard time giving me what I need."

I waited for her to go on. I didn't see what this had to do with what we had been talking about.

"In Kansas City, when we have a house guest, we just naturally have a luncheon or a cocktail party. It's just expected. And I'd like to meet some of the people you know."

She waved her arm down the beach as if she expected me to produce Steven Spielberg or George Clooney, as if here we talked in our porch swings or gossiped over the backyard fence the way she did in the Midwest.

"It's different here, Cyn," I told her, and I saw her eyebrows shoot up. "Not better, just different. Everybody here—including us—guards their privacy. A lot of our neighbors are celebrities who want to be out of the spotlight when they're home. We're all busy, and when we have some free time we want to relax and spend it with our families. I wouldn't even know the people next door if they didn't have kids the ages of mine. Most of my friends are in San Francisco. And even then, they'd laugh their ears off if I suggested we have a ladies' lunch. Nobody has that kind of time. We enjoy getting together for lunch occasionally, but it's never anything we plan. One of us calls the other in the morning, and if we're both free, we run out for a salad. My friend Annie and I have a hard time getting away together, and she works in my office."

I saw the look that flashed across Cynthia's face and instantly regretted mentioning Annie's name. I didn't want to give her further reason to feel abandoned. I thought of a note I had once found in Mae's sweater pocket from a classmate asking her if they could be best friends. "Are you Ginger's best friend or mine?" asked the questioner in pencil on yellow lined notebook paper. Below, the writer had provided two boxes to facilitate Mae's answer: Ginger, me. The next day Mae had come home crying after trying to explain to Robin, who turned out to be the writer of the note, that she liked both girls equally and didn't see why they couldn't all be friends.

I sensed that despite everything that had happened over the years and despite her own active social life, Cynthia still would not take kindly to my having even one other friend. I knew I was treading on thin ice for another reason, too. I still remembered the conversation that had triggered the dinner-plate incident, and I didn't want Cynthia to get the idea I thought her days were unimportant because she didn't have a job and therefore had time to plan lunch parties while other people did not.

"It's just a different place. People don't do that kind of stuff as much here, that's all."

"Surely cocktails wouldn't be a problem?"

I considered what Peter would say if I told him we were inviting neighbors we barely knew in for cocktails so they could meet Cynthia.

"Okay," I said, sighing audibly although she didn't seem to notice. "Tomorrow I'll put together a lunch."

I begged off a studio tour with her and my children, even though I'd been planning to go along.

"I've been so many times, and if I'm going to serve lunch tomorrow, I have some work to do," I said.

What I didn't tell her was that my biggest chore would be to scare up a handful of women who would be free and willing to come. When they were gone, I dug in a kitchen drawer for my address book. I called Eileen from next door, Kay from the apartment complex where we'd lived, and Marissa, Peter's assistant at the studio. They made for an odd mix, but it would have to do.

Insofar as I had women friends in LA, they were it.

Peter laughed out loud when I told him about the lunch that evening. He got home just before Cynthia and the kids came back, so I had time to fill him in. He put his arm around my shoulders and pulled me with him as he went down the hall to our bedroom to change.

"I owe you one for nixing the cocktails," he said. When I told Cynthia people here protected their privacy, I had Peter in mind. His days were so busy and filled with all kinds of people that when he got home he wanted nothing more than solitude. "But I do not know why you put up with her crap. I'm really sorry you told her she could come this week. You and Bradley could both do with some time to recover, and all she cares about is herself. I've never known such a selfish bitch in my life."

"Thanks for letting Marissa have some extra time off at lunch tomorrow."

"She thinks it's a hoot. She said she wouldn't miss it for the world. She's looking forward to seeing you, but don't be surprised if she takes notes for the screenplay she's writing."

That night Cynthia and Bradley disappeared again after dinner. This time they took her rented Mercedes and said they might go to a movie. Peter watched a documentary on TV with the kids and I went to bed early again. Later, long after Peter had come in and gone to sleep, too, I heard Bradley and Cynthia come in and go directly to his room. This time their gasps and thumpings were more audible than the night before, but I had been asleep for hours and Peter was tired, too. We rolled into each other's arms, kissed, and went back to sleep.

In the morning, though, it was a different story. At five a.m., long before the alarm was set to go off, Peter pulled me to him and unfastened the buttons on my silk nightshirt. When the door flew open and Cynthia thundered in, I had flung it off and was astride my husband, going for broke and almost there. Both of us were naked. The sheets and comforter lay puddled on the floor at the end of the bed.

"We need to talk, Maggie," she said, and then, when it registered what she had walked in on, she said, "Oh, for the love of God," as if we were doing something disgusting and had annoyed her immensely in the bargain. "I'll be downstairs when you can get free."

She slammed the door behind her.

"Jesus fucking Christ!" Peter roared. I would be surprised if she didn't hear him. His erection had naturally wilted, and I slid back to my side of the bed and groped for the covers. "That woman is the most inconsiderate bitch I have ever known in my life. How soon can we get her out of here and back home to Dr. Flake?"

"Tonight. Her plane leaves at six. All I have to do is get through this lunch, and then we'll be home free."

When I got downstairs Cynthia was banging the doors of my cupboards and looking through drawers, crying and trying to put a cup of coffee together.

"What on earth is wrong now?" I asked her.

I was prepared to tell her I hadn't appreciated her early morning summons or her neglecting to knock before she walked into our bedroom, but her wild hair and mascara-stained cheeks stopped me. I had the feeling in the pit of my stomach that I always felt when Cynthia seemed on the verge of going around the bend.

"It's over between Bradley and me," she blurted out.

"Over?" I asked, incredulous. "I didn't know it ever started."

"I thought we had something special and important," she said. "But it was just a fling to him. It was a zipless fuck and nothing more. They're all alike. He's as shallow and sleazy as every other man I've ever known."

"Careful, Cynthia, this is my brother we're talking about," I told her, trying hard to hold my temper. "What the two of you did was totally inappropriate, and I'm annoyed with both of you, but he's still my brother."

I silently remembered the husbands and gardeners she had slept with mechanically for reasons she found easy enough to justify.

"I thought we might have a future together," she went on, crying so hard now that her shoulders shook. I took the coffee filters out of her hand and tore off a piece of paper towel for her dripping nose. "I asked him if he had some time off this summer. I thought he could come out to Kansas City or maybe we could go away together and really get to know each other. I was thinking maybe Jamaica or Cancun. He said he didn't want to lead me on. He said he'd had a great time with me here and he appreciated the talks we had. He even said I helped him clear up some things that had been on his mind, but he said his life is in Santa Rosa and he needs to get on with it."

"You have a life, too," I said sharply.

Any other time I would have put my arms around her and comforted her, but I was finally done. The friend I had loved was as good as dead, and once she left I didn't care if I ever saw her again.

"Oh, right!" she snapped.

"I'm serious, Cyn," I went on, softening my tone in an attempt to thwart her letting yet another one of her crises spoil the last day of our visit—or to cast my brother as the villain. "Someday when you least expect it you're going to meet the man you're looking for. You just can't be constantly on the prowl. Men hate that."

"I thought Bradley might be that man," she sniffed.

"Bradley marches to a different drummer," I said. "I have a

feeling that the first time he asked you to help him deliver a breach calf you might not think he was such a big deal."

She blew her nose and smiled half-heartedly.

"For right now," I told her, "I have a lunch to cook, and you need to get a cold washcloth on those eyes. We've got plenty of time. The guests won't be here until eleven thirty. I thought we'd start with a glass of wine on the patio and then have lunch in the dining room where it will be a little quieter and we can talk."

"I couldn't possibly come to a lunch now, Maggie," she said, her voice telling me she was amazed at my insensitivity. "Surely you realize that."

"What I realize is that I have literally overnight put together a lunch party in which I'm not the least bit interested in having to please you, and you'd jolly well better drag your butt down here for it."

I tried to disguise my anger by seeming to joke with her, but she erupted in tears and tore back to her bedroom, not coming back for the rest of the morning. I considered canceling the whole thing, but I couldn't very well imply to women I liked very much that I had only sought out their company to humor an out-of-town guest. I grilled some salmon that I had marinated in lemon juice and rosemary and made a salad of Bibb lettuce, grapefruit, and avocado. Then I set the table and tinkered with the daffodil centerpiece the florist had delivered the afternoon before. At eleven fifteen I knocked on her door.

"They'll be here in fifteen minutes, Cyn," I called out, but I didn't wait for a reply.

Eileen walked over at eleven thirty on the dot. Kay and Marissa arrived almost at the same time just moments later. I herded them outside and poured wine. Then I went upstairs to tell Cynthia it was time to come down.

"Everybody's here, Cynthia," I called through the door, "and Marissa and Kay have to get back to work, so we really need to eat right away."

I pushed open the door and looked in. After her intrusion on Peter and me, I didn't have any qualms about going uninvited into her room. She still wore the bathrobe she had on in the kitchen hours earlier, but she was back in bed. Her eyes were puffy and her hair still wild. When I opened the door, she turned away from me. I gave up and went downstairs.

"Unfortunately, Cynthia has a migraine and isn't going to be able to join us after all," I told them. "So let's go ahead inside and have lunch."

It actually went better than I had expected. We were all either in the movie business or married to men who were, and we all had careers of our own, so we had those things in common to begin with. Then the conversation took on a life of its own, moving to relationships and children and parents, and when they stood to leave an hour later, we all promised to do it again soon. As I walked with them to the front door, Cynthia walked down the stairs and past us dressed in a bathing suit, big straw hat—my big straw hat!—and sunglasses. She walked through the kitchen and out the door to the beach in plain sight without so much as a glance in our direction. She carried a book, a blanket, and a radio that was playing heavy metal music much too loudly. I threw up my hands in the direction of my guests.

"I haven't got a clue," I said.

෴

After they left, I stood for a long time at my kitchen window, watching Cynthia out on the beach. She rubbed sunscreen on her arms and legs and then settled down onto the blanket, pulling the hat over her face to keep out the glare. I stacked the dishes in the dish-washer and cleaned up the kitchen. In my memory I played over our life together. Peter was right. I should have disconnected years ago, but we had been through a lot together. I knew the details of her courtship and marriage to Richard as well as she did. We had lived one another's pregnancies and knew each other's kids. I knew who she had slept with, what her insecurities were. I knew the bright, warm, charming side that had captivated me the first day I met her at UCLA, and I knew the dark side that threw plates and burst into people's bedrooms and made outrageous demands on the advice of a quack who had made her more aggressive and selfish than she had been before she met him. I had loved her like a family member, but I realized now that our friendship was truly over. I stormed across the sand to where she lay basting.

"We need to talk, Cynthia," I said.

I don't think she had ever heard me use that tone of voice before. She sat up quickly and squinted at me, shading her eyes with her hand and looking at me with a puzzled expression as if she couldn't imagine what on earth about.

"It's too hot and public out here," I went on. "The guests are gone. I'd like it if you came inside."

I turned on my heel and walked back to the house without waiting to hear what she said. She picked up her belongings and followed me. Once we were inside I didn't even give her a chance to speak.

"How dare you!" I spat out at her.

"I guess this is about lunch," she said and rolled her eyes. My pubescent teenagers couldn't have done it any better.

"This is about lunch and a whole lot more," I said. "As it turned out, lunch was a lot of fun and I'm glad it happened. But your rude behavior was inexcusable. You knew I wasn't up to having guests, but you insisted, so okay, I invited some people over. You make high drama out of your perception that my brother has dumped you after a little fling under my roof with my children in the next room, and then you bail out on me before they arrive. I try to cover for you and tell them you have a migraine, and you trounce right past us on your way to the beach."

"I think I'm more upset about Bradley than you realize," she said. "I really thought we were falling in love."

"Horse shit!" I said.

Her eyes flew open in surprise. She had always been the swearer, I the writer looking for the most appropriate word. But this time I was so angry I didn't really care what I said, so I kept going.

"This has nothing to do with Bradley. You need to grow up and stop blaming every person you know for the problems you've made for yourself. We're big girls now. Sometimes we do things we don't feel like doing. When I came to Kansas City you hauled me all over hell and back to the country club and here and there, and I went, even though back then I felt like my life had ended with Ian's and I didn't give a flying fig about all of that phony bullshit."

"That's not fair," she shot back. "I was trying to entertain you to get your mind off your problems."

"Which is exactly what this lunch might have done for you today. All you had to do was sit up straight in a chair and swallow some food. As it is, the women who were here now probably think I'm a liar and you're neurotic as hell, which is exactly the truth."

"I don't need to be treated like this," she said. "You act like you didn't even want me to come."

"I didn't want you to come. I tried to let you know that in a subtle way when you called, but it went right over your head."

"So now you're saying I'm stupid."

"No, but you're the most insensitive and self-centered person I've ever known. You might stop and consider once in a while that you aren't the center of the universe, that maybe other people have problems and know pain, too, and they grit their teeth and get on with it."

"This is about your mother, then."

"Of course it's about my mother!" I was exasperated. "A week and a half ago she was alive. She wasn't even seventy yet, Cyn, and she was still youthful and full of energy. She was crazy about my dad and her family, and she loved her life. When I went home for the funeral there were projects scattered all over the house that she was in the middle of working on when she died. I had to plan her funeral and console my dad, and what I needed after that was to come down here and hunker down with my husband and my kids and my brother and just howl like a wounded animal. I haven't had the will to get out of bed in the mornings, let alone entertain a house guest and then give a party. Surely you of all people understand what I'm talking about."

The look I dreaded darkened her face.

"I certainly do know what you're talking about," she said, low and menacing, almost a growl, "and what I also know is that you had a mother for a whole lot longer than I did, so I don't have much fucking sympathy for you. You're just lucky to have had her for as long as you did."

"Get out of my house," I said.

She glared at me for a long moment, then turned and ran upstairs. Mae stuck her head around the corner from the family room where she had apparently been reading. She was smiling, but her eyes were wide with surprise.

"Way to go, Mom!" she said. "It's about time!"

❦

Cynthia packed her bags and drove off without saying goodbye several hours before her plane was due to leave. Bradley went straight to the airport from his afternoon meeting and flew back to San Francisco. Kathy picked him up at the airport and they had dinner together in the city before heading back to Santa Rosa. Late that night he called. They had had a long talk, he told us. He had asked her to marry him, and she had said yes.

9

Caroline Morgan stood under the awning over the entrance to the Neiman Marcus department store at Union Square, holding her long black coat closed against the December wind and waving at me anxiously when I got out of the cab as if she were afraid I might not recognize her. In her sixties now, she was as chic and elegant as I remembered from the couple of times I had met her all those years ago in La Jolla. She took my arm and steered me inside.

"So what brings you to San Francisco?" I asked when we were seated in the fourth-floor tearoom under the broad stained-glass dome.

"I'm here to visit some galleries and do some Christmas shopping," she said. "You remember the judge who married John and me and then later Cynthia and Richard? I come up every year about this time and spend a few days with him and his wife. We're old friends now, and I do love being up north during the holidays. I grew up in Michigan, and even though I love Southern California,

I still find it hard to get into the Christmas spirit when it's eighty-five degrees and I'm writing out my cards while I sit on the beach. A few days of rain and fog always manage to put me in the right frame of mind."

We laughed together, and a waiter came and took our orders for white wine.

"I know you must be very busy, and I appreciate your taking the time to see me," she said, shifting gears and suddenly serious. I could tell she was here to do business, and not pleasant business at that.

"I was delighted when you called, and it's nice to see you again," I said, "and besides, coming to this tearoom is always a pleasure. I don't often take time for a real lunch, so I especially appreciate it when someone lures me away from my desk."

"Of course I want to talk to you about Cynthia."

I hadn't heard from Cynthia since she had left my house in the spring, and I didn't want to. I had finally accepted that the person I had cared for so deeply was no longer there. Over the years that person had insidiously become as inaccessible to me as Ian and now my mother were. She turned up for elusive, charmed moments, and then she disappeared once again. If I had needed to talk to her or ask her an opinion, I couldn't be sure which one of her personalities might respond. I had long ago stopped sharing my thoughts with her and had just become the sponge that soaked up her tirades and spit out what she wanted to hear as smoothly as Dr. Flek did.

When I told Peter about what had happened the night she left, he said it was about time I stood up to her and stopped letting her suck me dry.

"I know you have a lot of history together," he said, anticipating my defense of her and holding out his hand like a traffic cop to halt what I'd say next, "but that relationship has been so one-sided for so long. I know it hurts, but the woman's a leech. When she's down, she expects the world to stop turning. When you're down, it's too bad. You're so much better off with her out of the picture."

"I know," I said quietly. "It's over. I don't want to see her again."

He had leaned across the breakfast bar where we were having a late cup of coffee and kissed me.

"And now that she's gone, maybe we can go upstairs and settle some unfinished business."

Since that afternoon, every time the phone rang and it wasn't Cynthia, I consciously felt a sense of relief. She was far away from me, so there would be no chance encounters at a theater or a restaurant where we'd have to pretend not to see each other or make tense, useless small talk and say how we really must get together for lunch one day soon. Once during that time one of the talk shows did a segment about friends divorcing one another, and I read about it in the TV critic's column with interest. I guess that's what happened to me. I had once loved Cynthia like a sister, but now I just wanted her to leave me alone. Initially I was less frank with her stepmother.

"You know I haven't seen her since last spring when she was out," I said.

Caroline shook her head.

"No, we haven't, either," she said. "She calls and writes, and we hear from the girls, but it's that visit that upset us so much."

She paused and folded her hands together in front of her lips as if she were praying for just the right words to convey what she had on her mind.

"We felt at that time that she might be a little bit—dangerous."

The word was difficult for her to say, but she had clearly decided it was the right one.

"Dangerous to whom?" I asked. I felt myself being drawn back into a maelstrom from which I had only recently escaped. "Surely not you and her father?"

"Oh, no," she said, laughing uncomfortably. "I don't mean that. I don't know if she's capable of hurting anyone else, but I think what worries me is that she might be dangerous to herself. I suppose that comes to mind because of what happened to her mother. It's just that she seems to be so moody and on-again, off-again. Do you know what I mean?"

The drinks arrived and we ordered the same club sandwich and coleslaw. I had come to realize that this lunch was not about consuming food, and I suddenly cared very little about what I was going to have to eat. When the waiter had gone again I said, "I know what you're saying, and to be perfectly honest it has crossed my mind, too."

"Beyond that, I'm a little concerned about Richard," she went on. "Their divorce went way beyond bitter. Even after all this time, it seems to consume her, like it's all she can think about. She talks about Richard like she wishes he were dead, and while I understand her anger, he is, after all, the children's father, and he's done a good job of taking care of them. Look at her, too. She kept the house and the car. Her lifestyle doesn't seem to have changed very much at all since they separated the way it does for a lot of women."

I thought about the gun and wondered how much I should tell her. On one hand it seemed the more people who had this information the less likely Cynthia would be to have a chance to hurt herself or anyone else. On the other, I could imagine her father's frustration and worry if he knew she was armed and unstable somewhere a couple of thousand miles away. But I told myself knowledge is power and dove in.

"I'm going to tell you something, Caroline," I said, "and you can decide whether or not to tell your husband."

I could see her tense up. Whatever was coming, she knew it wasn't good.

"Cynthia has a gun," I told her, and she gasped and put her hands over her mouth.

"Oh, God, no."

"It was an old pistol that Richard had forgotten about, and when he moved out, he left it behind. Cynthia called me up a while back and was making jokes about murdering Richard and Kim with it. I didn't know what to do then, either, so I called him and told him. He went back to the house and looked for it one day when he knew she'd be gone. He planned to take it, but she had moved it, and he couldn't find it anywhere. He says he doesn't think she's capable of murder, but I still thought he should know about it, and that's why I'm telling you. Her fantasies of killing Richard and Kim were probably just something people say when they're going through a bitter divorce, but I don't know what she might be willing to do to herself when she gets down—or to somebody else when she gets angry."

"There's a look she gets on her face . . . ," Caroline began.

"I know exactly the one you mean," I said, "and it scares me to death."

"John and I are flying out there for Christmas." She sighed. Clearly the trip wasn't one to which she was looking forward. "Maybe we can locate the gun and get rid of it then."

"I hate being the one to worry you and John."

"Better worried and taking action than finding out she's used the hateful thing on herself or somebody else."

The waiter brought our lunch, and for a few moments we nibbled in silence. When Caroline spoke again she changed the subject.

"You talk as though you've met Richard's wife."

"Yes, I have. They were in LA for a medical conference not long after they were married, and Peter and I had dinner with them. She's really a lovely woman."

I was as defensive now about Richard and Kim as I once had been when anyone criticized Cynthia, but I realized it wasn't necessary with Caroline.

"I'm sure she is," she said, smiling. "Nobody blames Richard for what happened. Heaven knows he tried hard enough to keep their marriage together. We both think he deserves to be happy, and from what the girls tell us, he seems to be. They adore Kim, and they've shown us pictures of their little brother, but of course we don't let on to Cynthia. I don't suppose you do, either."

"Oh, my God. No!" I exclaimed. "She knew I'd met her, and she thought I'd been disloyal, so I didn't ever mention Kim after that. Now I don't think I'll ever be talking to Cynthia again. Her time with me was such an unhappy experience that I haven't made any effort and I don't plan to. Much as I hate to say it to you, I've been content to just let it go."

"You've been a better friend than most people would be," Caroline said. "You don't have anything to apologize for."

With so much drama lying on the table among our drained glasses and half-eaten lunch it seemed ridiculous not to tell her the absolute truth about where my relationship with Cynthia had gone. I didn't want that to be a stumbling block when they saw her and tried to deal with her problems. I told her about Bradley and my mother's death and the ill-fated lunch party.

"Is there anything we can do while we're there to help patch things up?"

I shook my head sadly.

"I don't want them patched up, Caroline. For the past several years she has called me at all hours of the day and night to rant and rave about Richard getting married or Richard's wife having a baby or whatever happens to be on her mind at the moment. She calls Kim horrible, racist names that I also can't stand to hear. Then she treated me so badly when she was here and said such mean things to me. Instead of offering me any kind of comfort about my mother's death, she started in about her mother and said she couldn't feel sorry for anyone who had a mother as long as I had mine."

Caroline frowned and shook her head sympathetically.

"You'd think she'd understand better than anyone what you were going through."

"I want more than anything for her to get well and be happy. But to tell you the truth, having her out of my life is a huge relief."

When we left the restaurant later that afternoon we hugged as though we were the best friends Cynthia and I had once been. Saving Cynthia from herself had now become the bond that loving her had once been. Just after Christmas, however, Caroline called to say that while their visit to Kansas City had overall been a pleasant one, with Cynthia in good spirits, cooking and decorating the house and wrapping up extravagant gifts, they had been unsuccessful in locating the gun. In fact, one day while Cynthia was out, Caroline took advantage of her absence to search through her dresser drawers.

"She came back before I expected her to, and John didn't have a chance to warn me. She came up the stairs so quietly that I didn't hear her, and she caught me red-handed."

"What did she say?" I gasped.

"She said if I was trying to find the gun, I wasn't even warm and that she didn't much appreciate so-called friends who couldn't keep their mouths shut. I guess she figured out if I knew she had a gun, I must have heard it from you. We hadn't even mentioned your name up to that point."

"Oh, God! What did you do?"

"I told her I was simply looking for a bar of bath soap and didn't have any idea what she was talking about."

❧

Peter and I seldom mentioned Cynthia's name anymore. I wondered from time to time how she was and what she was doing, but my self-preservation instincts always kicked in. I wasn't willing to re-establish communication and risk the peace not having to deal with her had brought me. And I was too busy to spend much time thinking about her. Peter spent the summer filming in Scotland, and when I had some time off, the kids and I joined him there for a couple of weeks. When I got back, the managing editor called me into his office.

"We've got a slot open on the opinion page, and we'd like you to think about filling it," he said. "We need a woman's voice—somebody who can interpret what goes on politically in Washington and how it affects the average family here, who knows about balancing home and career, raising kids in a difficult society and that type of thing. You'd still have your same job, too, but there would be a pay increase. Could you let me know by the end of the week?"

I didn't need the time he offered me to think it over. I had kept a notebook of ideas for years in case an opportunity like this one ever came up.

"I can do it," I told him. "Annie's a gem. I can easily turn over some of my administrative responsibilities to her, assuming there could also be a raise for her, too."

"Done and done," he said and rose to shake my hand.

Now my days were longer, my weekends in LA more infrequent, but I loved the change in my routine, and it felt good to be writing regularly again. I worked on the planes that carried me to my husband or on the beach during the times I got to spend at our Malibu home. I wrote a column about Cynthia and me once when the subject was damaged friendships, but of course I didn't mention her by name, and she would have had no reason to read a San Francisco paper.

Then on a Sunday afternoon in September the phone rang, and the voice on the other end sounded like hers, but not quite.

"Aunt Maggie?"

"Chloe?"

"Surprise! I just got into LA and I don't know another soul here, so I thought I'd give you a call."

"It's wonderful to hear your voice," I told her, and I meant it. "Are you just out here for a visit?"

"No, I'm here to seek my fortune along with everyone else," she said, laughing. "I thought Dad would tell you I was coming. I'm starting the UCLA graduate filmmaking program, so I hope I can call Peter for advice sometimes."

I recalled now that Richard had told me she was applying, but we hadn't talked for a while, and I didn't know her dream had become a reality.

"That's great," I said. "And of course we'll help you any way we can. Where are you living?"

"I'm starting out in university housing, but I'm not crazy about living in a dormitory at this point in my life, so I'll probably move out as soon as I meet some potential roommates and figure out how to negotiate the freeways."

"Do you have a car?"

"Not yet. I flew out because classes start Monday. Dad and Kim are coming out to spend Thanksgiving with me and see my grand-parents in Riverside, so they're going to drive a car out for me then and fly back. In the meantime I'm on foot, which I know isn't very realistic in California."

She giggled, and when she did she sounded exactly like an early version of her mother before madness and jealousy and divorce snuffed out her joy and permanently silenced her laughter as far as I could tell.

"When can we see you?" I asked her.

"Whenever you want, but you'll have to come here until I have wheels."

"That's not a problem," I said. I looked at the clock and then at the strips of steak that were marinating in a bowl on the kitchen counter. "In fact, are you free for dinner tonight?"

She laughed again.

"Like I said, I don't have a car and you're the only people I know in this city, so yes, I guess you could say I'm free."

"I'll pick you up in an hour. Jack will be here, too. This will be fun."

Jack pulled in as I was backing out of the garage. He had been playing tennis and was still in his shorts and sneakers.

"I'm going to pick up Chloe Bartolucci," I called out my window. "Do you want to ride along?"

He slid into the passenger seat.

"What's she doing here?" he asked. "I still think of her as a little kid."

"She's going to graduate school in filmmaking."

Neither of us had seen Chloe since the fateful Thanksgiving, and pictures didn't do justice to her metamorphosis, so we both had a teenager in mind. But she had blossomed into a beauty who resembled both of her parents. She was tall and thin, and when she stepped out of the elevator at the dorm in a gauzy white dress and sandals, neither of us at first recognized her. She knew us, though, and ran toward me with her arms open.

"This is great!" she said as she hugged first me and then Jack. It was one of the few times I had ever seen him at a loss for words.

"Jesus," he said when she released him, a flush spreading across his face. "You grew up."

Later, over platefuls of fajitas and the margaritas that Jack mixed at our patio bar, Chloe told us her plans.

"My major in college was communications, and I've been working for the past couple of years at the ABC affiliate in Kansas City. I liked TV, but I'd like to produce something that wouldn't be so ephemeral, something lasting that takes a commitment. I applied to this program because it's one of the best in the country, and bingo, here I am."

Peter was listening intently.

"Do you have a special area of interest?" he asked her.

"Actually it's editing. I like working behind the scenes, taking what somebody else has shot and distilling it into its essence. I know LA is full of people who want to get into the movie business, but I'm not interested in acting. I hope that will eliminate some of the competition. I talked about it with one of my professors at UMKC, and he said I could make some good contacts in the UCLA program, and Dad said he'd help me pay. He was delighted that I was coming out here and going to the same school where he and Mom did. It means I won't see as much of him, but I'll be able to visit all of my grandparents occasionally, and he and Kim and Richie will have a reason to come out here more often."

"And your mother?" I asked. It had to come up sooner or later. "How does she feel about your being so far away from her?"

Previously she had been happy and optimistic, full of plans

and glad for an audience who wanted to hear about them. Now her face saddened noticeably.

"She's not happy at all. She wouldn't even drive me to the airport. Kim offered, but I didn't want a scene at the house, so I just took a cab. Mom feels like I'm abandoning her. She said if anything bad happens to her, it will be my fault."

"How could that possibly be?" I cried out. I was angry with Cynthia all over again.

"You know I lived at home all the time I was in college," Chloe said. "And more and more she came to depend on me."

"In what way?" I knew I was prying, but I had a sense that Caroline and John had seen only Cynthia's better side and that her outlook on life had not really improved.

"She doesn't like to go out much anymore," Chloe said. She had stopped eating and was twisting an orange woven napkin around her index finger and staring at it intently. I could tell she wanted to talk but didn't want to be more disloyal to her mother than she already felt she was. "She . . . she's almost reclusive."

"That doesn't sound like Cynthia," I said. "Both times when I came to visit she was working at the church or the country club or organizing some charity benefit. She was busy and gone all the time."

"After the divorce that all changed. Most of the charities just wanted her because of Dad being a doctor. When he and Mom got divorced they started calling Kim, but of course she has her own career and didn't have time to get involved with that kind of stuff."

"But what about her church activities?"

"She dropped out of the church after Dad left, too. She said she had just joined because he and my grandmother had nagged her to and she had never believed any of the hogwash—that's what she called it—they believed anyway. I think she also had some kind of argument with Father Hannigan. She figured out he was gay and said some really mean things about him. He stopped seeing her, and then the diocese moved him to another church on the other side of the city."

"But surely she's still involved at the country club. She loved that."

Chloe looked even more uncomfortable. She had twisted the napkin into a tight coil.

"Look," I said, "we don't have to talk about this. I didn't mean to pry, but I haven't been in touch with her since she was out here, and I just wondered how she was."

"It's okay. I know I'm among friends." She smiled weakly. "What happened is that she had an affair with one of the men who belonged to the club."

Across the table Todd and Mae looked up from their plates with widened eyes.

"When he told her it was over she told his wife she thought he was having an affair with someone else they knew. The wife made a big scene and ruined the other woman's reputation, which forced her husband to admit that he'd had the affair but with Mom. His wife left him, and the innocent woman and her husband split up because he didn't believe her when she told him it wasn't true. It was a big scandal, and when it was all over, the board of directors denied Mom's application to renew her membership."

"Wow. That's too bad." I didn't tell her I already knew this story, but I hadn't heard the part about Cynthia's being disinvited from the country club. "The Cynthia I used to know would never have done something like that. And I don't think she would have outed a gay priest, either."

"You have no idea," Chloe said. "She's done some other weird stuff, too. She still orders stuff and has it sent to Dad and Kim all the time. When Richie was born she called every department store in town and had all kinds of baby clothes and furniture delivered to them. They had to send it all back and explain that they didn't know anything about it. Before that she sent them commemorative plates and statues of Elvis. She had all these tabloids around the house with the mail-in coupons ripped out. And she had a string of boyfriends for a while—all married to her friends. She doesn't know that I knew about them. They came in late at night, stayed a couple of hours, and left. I could see their cars in the driveway from my bedroom window."

"I think the person I used to know probably still is deep inside, but her good qualities may have just gotten buried under a lot of disappointment and anger."

"I know, and I love her still. She's my mom. But sometimes she even gets violent. She slapped me a couple of times, always right after I had been out with Dad and Kim, and she had the locks changed and wouldn't give me a key to the house right before I left." Now the stories tumbled out of her. "I think Lorraine is going to move in with Dad and Kim until she finishes high school. Meanwhile, I'm going to follow my own dream and hope the price I pay isn't losing Mom altogether. I know that her mother committed suicide, and I talked to Dad about that. I wouldn't have left if I had thought it would lead to something like that. He convinced me that in her right mind she would want me to do exactly what I'm doing."

"I heard you say your dad is helping you out," Peter said now. "Does that mean you're supporting yourself?"

"I have a little savings from the job at the studio because I lived at home and didn't have many expenses, but basically yes. I'm going to start looking for a job as soon as I get settled and classes start. I guess I'll join all the other wannabes who wait tables and park cars."

"I was thinking more about an internship on our editing staff," he said. "You'd be able to make a little money while you learn the ropes and make some contacts. We could work around your class schedule."

"Oh, wow!" she said, then just as quickly added, "But I don't want to get a job just because you're a friend. I didn't come out here to take advantage of that. When I get a job in the business I want it to be because I'm the best person for the job."

Peter smiled.

"With an attitude like that, something tells me you will be," he said.

We sat talking at the table until nearly eleven. When it was time for Chloe to go, Jack volunteered to drive her back to the campus. Peter helped me clear the table and stack the dishes into the dishwasher.

"She's sure not anything like her mother," he said. "What a great kid."

"She's exactly like her mother used to be. That's what I've always tried to tell you. There was a time when Cynthia had some enthusiasm about life. It was just all gone by the time you met her. By the way, thanks for offering Chloe the job."

"Anybody who has had to put up with Cynthia and lived to tell about it deserves a break."

Once I figured out what was going on between Chloe and Jack, I wanted to be able to say I had seen it coming, that history had repeated itself in the lobby of a UCLA dormitory, that I had seen the sparks of passion fly and knew all along what would happen next. In fact, I had no such intuition, and given how Cynthia and Richard's relationship had turned out, I was glad I hadn't. The envy and admiration I had felt for their relationship in the beginning had turned to pure and simple dust along with their marriage. In view of the circumstances, I might have told Chloe and Jack to run for their lives in opposite directions while they still had a chance.

One reason I didn't catch on for so long was that my columns had expanded to three times a week, and a publisher had called to talk about the possibility of collecting some of them into a book. I put in long hours at the office and worked on the computer at home evenings and when I got to LA on weekends. Todd had inherited his older brother's love of basketball and joined the team, so I was once again spending Tuesday and Friday evenings watching his games in a bright, noisy gymnasium. Mae was going through puberty and needed my attention. During the winter months Peter came to us more often than we went to him.

"I don't know how much longer we can keep this up," he told me late on Christmas Eve as we lay in bed. He had come home for a three-week Hanukkah-Christmas celebration. Down the hall were my dad in one bedroom, Bradley and Kathy in another.

"We've been married all this time, and I still feel like we're dating. I once figured up that five months of living under the same roof at one time is our record."

"I do this on purpose," I told him, propping up on one arm and kissing him. "I don't want you to get bored. I have to keep you interested."

He kissed me back and rolled onto me, bringing evidence that lack of interest wasn't a problem. Later, while we were still lying close together, he brought the subject up again.

"You know I wouldn't ever ask you to give up your work any more than you'd ask me to give up mine," he said, "but I'm starting to realize that life doesn't go on forever. I'd like for us to have more time together. There isn't really much of my job that I can bring here or I would."

He had lost his own mother just a few months before and was still grieving. Obviously her death had caused him to think about some issues he hadn't wanted to consider before.

"Now that the column is a big success and you've got this book deal, what would you think about just doing that and giving up the features editor part of your position? Do you think they'd go for that at the paper? Would you?"

I had been thinking about just such an arrangement myself.

"I'd like to write full time, there's no question about that, and I think Annie would be a shoo-in for my job, but I think the brass would expect me to show up occasionally for meetings. I couldn't just drop out completely. And we'd need to consider the kids."

"It's not like we're taking them to someplace unfamiliar where they'd have to start all over. And I've already called the coach at the high school to see if there might be a spot on the team for Todd. We can convert one of the extra bedrooms into an office for you, and you could be in constant phone and email contact."

"I'm tempted," I said. "Just give me some time to think about the details."

Just before I dropped off to sleep he murmured, "I meant to tell you, Jack has been going out now and then with Chloe."

"You're kidding!" I said, sitting up in bed, instantly wide awake. "For how long?"

"Pretty much since she got here, I think. I didn't know anything about it for a long time, but it probably started that first day, when he took her home after she came to the house for dinner. I don't know if it's anything serious. He feels sorry for her like I do. Cynthia's kids haven't had the best time of it despite having a father who's a wealthy doctor and living in one of the best houses in town."

"How is she doing at work?"

"Great. Works hard, wants to learn. Everybody loves her. That's how I first found out Jack was seeing her. He picked her up after work one day and said they were going to dinner. I don't think either one of them has much time to date, but when they do, I gather they see only each other. After the cat was out of the bag, Chloe told me once about an afternoon they spent at Disneyland and another time about taking the boat over to Catalina."

On New Year's Eve Chloe and Jack arrived for dinner in the same car, and from the kitchen window I saw them stop for a long kiss before they came through the door. I knew about kisses like that, and they weren't exchanged between friends who were casually dating.

Before dinner I poured a glass of champagne for each of us, but before I could make a New Year's toast, Jack made one of his own.

"Here's a special toast to Chloe," he said, lifting his glass in her direction, and we all followed suit. "I'm crazy about her, and she's moving into my apartment this weekend."

10

Outside, a steady, cold rain pounded against the windows. Inside and upstairs in Jack's apartment, Mae and I scrubbed shelves and helped Chloe unpack her boxes. She had moved in during the winter break, but the cartons of her belongings that Richard and Kim had brought out in November had been stored in our garage until they could find room for them. I wondered secretly, too, if she wasn't a little skittish about making a total commitment to a man in the aftermath of what her parents' divorce had cost her mother. Maybe she thought having a few boxes of sweaters and photographs somewhere else would ensure her ability to cut and run without having to look back if the relationship went similarly sideways.

But on Valentine's Day Jack gave her a diamond ring and asked her to marry him and she said yes. Now he was in Washington, DC, for the weekend to take a deposition, and it was a perfect time for us to help Chloe clean up and rearrange while he was gone.

Chloe handed a gravy boat that Mae had just washed and dried up to where I was standing on a chair and putting little-used items on the top shelf.

"Mom's back in school," she said out of the blue.

"You've heard from her then?" I asked.

"I wrote a letter to tell her about the engagement. I can't stand to talk to her on the phone. I know that sounds horrible, but I guess you can understand. The last time I called her she went on about how first Dad had left her and now I had. Who needs it? I was upset for a whole week after that. It didn't help that I was trying to study for exams."

"But she did answer your letter."

"Yes. It was weird, though. She told me all about what she had been doing, all cheerful and chatty like people do in those form letters they send out at Christmas. At the very end she wrote that everyone who had ever broken her heart would be at my wedding and she couldn't bear to come, but she said she hoped I'd be very happy."

"So what did she say about school? I thought you told me she was reclusive and never went out."

She shrugged her shoulders.

"That's how she was when I left, but she says she's back in therapy with Dr. Flek and he has given her the support to pursue her dreams, even when her own family had failed her."

I shook my head.

"Good old Dr. Flake," I said. "That's what Peter calls him."

"I think he's right. Flek just asks her what she wants and then parrots back to her to go ahead and do it, and for that she pays him two hundred dollars an hour. Anyway, she still feels like she can't cope with going back to a college campus where everybody is a lot younger than she is, but she says she wants to make a contribution to society, so she's going to some technical college to become a paralegal."

"That's good," I said. "That's really good. She'd be working in an office and meeting people. This might be exactly what she needs."

"I sure hope so," Chloe said sadly. "She's wasting her life being constantly angry, turned in on herself and blaming everyone else for her situation."

Cynthia had not contacted me since our argument, although late in the previous holiday season I had wavered and sent her a card signed with no other message than our names. I hated the thought of her all alone in freezing Kansas City, especially when I found out from Chloe that Lorraine was going to use the winter break from school to go on a skiing vacation with Richard and Kim and help care for Richie.

I would have preferred to be planning the August wedding with the woman who had been my best friend, and I regretted having to mastermind the details without her. Richard and Kim were in Kansas City, Chloe was in class or at her job with Peter's studio sometimes well into the night, and Jack—the new guy in the law firm—was overbooked with legal cases. It fell to me to talk to the caterer and the florist and come up with ideas for the reception. I had made the deal I wanted with the paper and now spent most of my time in LA. I filed three columns a week and had signed a contract with a publisher for a collection. My helper was Mae, who was having the time of her life being at the hub of the excitement. Early on, Chloe had asked her to be one of the attendants, and now she pored over photographs of dresses and articles about what a bridesmaid was supposed to do.

"It's not like you're the first bride with divorced parents," I said to Chloe now, my annoyance at Cynthia's selfishness flaring up anew. "A lot of people have divorced parents who still show up on special occasions and act civilly toward one another. Jeez, she and your dad have been divorced for a long time. She really needs to let that go. Look at Jack's mom, for God's sake. She lives in Paris and he hasn't seen her for two years, but she's coming."

"I know," she said wistfully, "but I think Mom's made up her mind."

"Do you think it would help if I wrote to her?"

Opening that door was the last thing I wanted to do, but it was Chloe's feelings that mattered now, not mine. Like her, though, I wasn't willing to talk to Cynthia on the phone.

"Would you?" she asked, her eyes lighting up momentarily. "I don't think it would make a difference, but I want to give it every shot I can. It would be very nice to have both of my parents at my wedding, and maybe then Mom would see that everybody isn't against her and we haven't all abandoned her."

"Surely she must run into your dad and Kim occasionally," I said. "I know Kansas City is a big place, but they must go to some of the same restaurants and department stores."

"Lorraine told me that once she and Mom were waiting for their lunch to be served at an Italian place on the Plaza when Dad and Kim came in. Mom got up and went to the ladies' room and wouldn't come out. When the food came, Lorraine went in to get her, and she said she wouldn't come out until they left. Lorraine told her they had just ordered and it was going to be a while, so Mom told Lorraine to have their food wrapped to go. She left through the kitchen without ever going back to the table."

"It doesn't sound promising, but I'll try."

❧

"Leave it alone," Peter told me that night.

He had come into my office without my hearing him and saw what was up on my computer screen.

"I'm so glad to hear you're back in school," I had written, as if nothing had transpired between us to change our friendship. I wanted my letter to sound as casual as if I were answering one she might recently have sent to me. I would never have made the move on my own, but I kept reminding myself it was for the kids. "Now if I ever need some legal help, I'll know where to come."

"I can't leave it alone, Peter," I said as I deleted the part about using her services. I didn't really want to see her again, and she was the last person I would go to for professional legal advice. "She's Chloe's mother, and she has a responsibility—which she should regard as a privilege—to be at this wedding. A lot of divorced parents go to their children's weddings and manage to get through them without making a scene."

"They aren't Cynthia. The woman is a raving lunatic, and if she comes, I guarantee you she will spoil the whole day. Think back to the spectacle she made of herself at our wedding."

"Maybe she's better. She's back in school and she's seeing Dr. Flake again. I think the guy's a fraud, but at least she has someone to talk to."

He shook his head, unconvinced.

"Honey, that woman has ripped you and Richard and her own daughters to shreds. You've told me yourself how it has only been recently that you've been able to stop dreading answering the phone. She's mean, she's nasty, she's selfish. She's pathetic, and it's too bad that she has ruined her own life, but that's what happened. Nobody did it to her. It wasn't Richard and it wasn't her argument with you and it wasn't Chloe's moving out here. Plain and simple, she refuses to face facts and get on with her life. Imagine what it's going to be like if she does show up and disrupt the wedding. How are you going to feel then?"

"I think it's more likely that Chloe's wedding would be diminished if her mother doesn't come, and that's why I think I have to make every effort. Then if she doesn't come, Chloe knows we tried everything we could to get her here and she won't have to go through life feeling guilty about it."

"That's not what I mean. I'm sure Chloe wants her here—or thinks she does. But realize she didn't have the greatest childhood in the world growing up with Cynthia. I'm constantly amazed that Chloe has turned into the person she has. I keep looking for signs of Cynthia's neurosis, but they're just not there. Maybe the mental illness played itself out with her mother. I hope so. You know what Cynthia's mood swings are like, and she has been violent and physically abusive to Chloe on a few occasions. God only knows what's happening to Lorraine now that she's the only one left for Cynthia to use as a scapegoat."

"Chloe said Lorraine was thinking of moving in with Richard and Kim until she finishes school, but she didn't because Cynthia put the guilt trip on her."

"My point exactly. We've crossed this hurdle. It was hard for you to make the break, but you did it and Chloe seems to have, too. You finally stood up to her and put her in her place. She doesn't wake us up in the middle of the night anymore, she doesn't harass you. You heard Chloe tell us about the merchandise she sent to Richard's house. You don't want to get something like that started. Just be glad you're away from her and not in contact with her anymore."

"I've got to do this for Chloe."

"We're going to be Chloe's family now, and we can see the damage Cynthia could inflict on their special day. I am the groom's father, if you'll recall, and I don't want his wedding day ruined, and I know you don't, either. The best thing you can do for her is help Richard give her the wedding of her dreams and leave Cynthia out of it."

"I can't do that. You don't know how much I'd like to, but I can't in good conscience deliberately exclude a mother from her daughter's wedding."

"But you said Chloe already asked her and she said no. You're not excluding her. She's excluding herself."

"I have to make this one last try, but that's all it is—a last try."

"Do what you think you have to do, but if she comes, I think you'll be sorry."

He threw his hands up into the air and left. I turned back to the computer.

"I know Chloe has already asked you to come out here and be a part of the wedding, and you've said no," I wrote under my breezy beginning. "I'm writing to make one more plea. She loves you and wants you here, and so do the rest of us." I deleted that part. Chloe was the only one who wanted her here, and I didn't want to raise any hopes that I might be willing to resume our friendship. "I understand that running into Richard might be unpleasant for you, but it wouldn't be impossible. I've been to many weddings where divorced parents managed to celebrate with their children without its being too uncomfortable. I think Richard will be staying with his parents in Riverside, so once the ceremony and reception are over, you won't have to see him again."

I purposely left out any mention of Kim. I wanted to stay as neutral and to the point as I possibly could.

"Naturally you are welcome to stay with us, and we can pick you up at the airport," I continued and then deleted it immediately. It was something I would have said at one time, but I wasn't going to say it now. Old habits die hard. "I'm sending along one of the invitations and a photograph of Chloe's dress. I know you'll think they are both as beautiful as we do. She really wants for you to be involved."

Almost immediately Cynthia wrote back, clearly not wanting to talk to me, either.

"As usual, you have focused on what is important to you and completely missed the point about why I can't possibly come to Chloe's wedding. The pain of seeing Richard and his *WIFE* would be much too great for me to bear. Despite the close friendship we once shared, you still don't seem to realize what I suffered because of him. Now that Chloe has left me, too, it would be equally difficult to see her and pretend that things were the same between us.

"You also seem to have conveniently forgotten what I went through because of Bradley. Chloe tells me he is married now, and I assume he and his wife will be at the wedding, too. Adding in your husband, Richard's parents, and my own father and stepmother, how many people would that make who would be whispering about me and laughing behind my back? I'm starting to get my life back together now, and I can't risk the setback such an encounter would surely cause.

"Incidentally, I very much resent my name being listed on the invitation as one of the hosts of the wedding. Can you imagine the embarrassment of seeing 'Dr. and Mrs. Richard Bartolucci and Mrs. Cynthia Bartolucci' when I pulled it out of the envelope? Whatever were you thinking?

"I do, however, appreciate your planning my daughter's wedding. With your busy career and your expanding family, you must have very little time."

When Peter got home I was sitting on a step by the mailbox in dazed silence with the letter in my hand. He sat down next to me and glanced through it quickly.

"What a bitch!" he said. "I'm sorry for Chloe, but I'm relieved she's not coming. You're working way too hard and Richard is paying way too much money to have her ruin everything. If she did come, she'd find a way to turn the spotlight on herself and wreck the whole day."

"It's so ironic," I said when he handed the letter back to me and I looked at it again. "Do you remember how much time I spent on the phone with Richard and Kim trying to word the invitation so nobody would be offended?"

Richard and Kim were footing the bill for the wedding, so I tried to consult them every time an important decision needed to be made. I had come to the telephone for that call with three different etiquette sources that I had checked out of the library. We were afraid to leave Cynthia off and afraid to put her on. Apparently we had made the wrong choice, although I suspected that if we had omitted her name, that would have made her mad, too.

"Well, we both got what we wanted," Peter said, leaning over and kissing me on the cheek, then standing up to go inside. "You know you did your best to get her here, and I know she's not coming. Now on the day of the wedding we can all relax and enjoy ourselves."

The night before the ceremony we hosted the rehearsal dinner at our house. It had been a frantic week that made me smile as I looked back on Peter's innocent prediction about our being able to relax. Five days before the wedding I had to be in New York to meet with an editor who was helping me collect my columns for the book. Jack was embroiled in the closing arguments of a case he was handling. Chloe wasn't taking summer classes so she could work full time with Peter at the studio, where they were in post-production and working against a tight deadline.

People were coming into town from everywhere. Bradley and Kathy were driving down with Dad, and Jack's mother, Claire, was flying in from Paris. Richard, Kim, Lorraine, and Richie, who had flown in the day before and spent the night in Riverside, were driving in with Richard's parents. Cynthia's parents were driving up from La Jolla, and somehow we all expected to converge at a synagogue in Westwood at the same moment.

Miraculously, it happened. Fifteen minutes after the appointed time the rehearsal began. First Connie, a friend of Chloe's from the studio, then Mae, then a grown-up Lorraine I hardly recognized walked down the aisle, followed by Chloe on Richard's arm. Jack and Todd, along with Larry—Jack's best friend since high school—and Paul, a colleague from the law firm, waited in front. I sat between Peter and Kim, sobbing into a tissue, whether out of emotion or exhaustion, as seriously as if we were watching the real thing and both Chloe and Jack were my own children.

Later, though, we did relax. While we were at the rehearsal the caterers had been at work in my kitchen, and when we got home with a crowd of guests in tow, the place had been magically transformed. The caterer's assistant had set up extra tables and decorated them in the purple and mauve wedding colors. Champagne chilled in buckets next to a table where glasses waited on white linen for the toast that was sure to come. On the coffee table in the living room was a tray of canapes—shrimp salad in endive boats, deviled eggs garnished with caviar, and tiny tartlets filled with baked cheese. In the kitchen the caterer, Jean-Paul, carved generous slabs of roast beef onto a platter. A large dish filled with caprese salad waited on the counter, and some Thai chicken warmed in a chafing dish.

"Everything looks great," I told him. "Thank you so much. Do you need me for anything?"

Initially I had thought about cooking the whole spread myself, but Richard and Peter had talked me into having it catered, and looking now at the feast spread before me, I was glad they had.

"The hardest part of my job is keeping people out of their own kitchens," he said with a sniff. "Please just go out there and enjoy your guests. You might also ask the bride's father to open the champagne. Dinner will be served in about twenty minutes."

They had set up extra tables so that along with our dining room table we were able to accommodate everyone who had come. I had only seen Claire a couple of other times before she left the country when she occasionally came by to pick up Jack. She still looked glamorous with her oversized sunglasses that protected the big eyes that Jack had luckily inherited, and she still made movies. I had seen her in one on television just a few nights before. At this moment, however, she was fading from the exhaustion of the trip and while making a valiant effort, obviously needed sleep. Richie had eaten earlier and was now tucked into a toddler bed in the study. Kim had offered to hire a sitter, but Chloe was adamant.

"He's my brother, and I want him here for everything," she said. "He probably won't remember much about it, but when he grows up he'll see the pictures and know he was a part of my wedding and my family."

Cynthia's systematic driving away of her husband and children only seemed to strengthen their determination as survivors to close ranks and get it right. When I came back out from the kitchen, Kim had an arm protectively around Chloe, who was wiping away tears. She shot me a look telling me that something had happened, but

I didn't have a chance right then to ask what it was since Richard was pouring champagne. The brief sad moment quickly gave way to a much happier one.

Later, when we were seated and the servers were bringing our plates I had a moment of longing for Cynthia so intense that it brought tears to my eyes. There was a time when if one of our children had been doing something as special as getting married, we would have shared every detail. But now everyone dear to her congregated in my living room and dining room—her father and his wife, the man who had been her husband, her two daughters, and me, her one-time best friend—all of us celebrating a moment that by rights should have been hers. I wondered again why she couldn't set aside her poisonous negative feelings for just a couple of days. Here I sat at the same table with my husband's ex-wife, and despite her fatigue from the flight we laughed and talked as if we were old friends. Certainly Cynthia's situation was different—Peter was already divorced from Claire when we met and there was no reason for hostility between us—but this was Chloe's wedding. If an event of this magnitude didn't snap her mother out of her selfishness and misery, I couldn't imagine what would.

When we had finished dinner and our guests were lingering over dessert and coffee, I slipped into the kitchen to check on the caterers. Kim followed me, and from the window we could see them stacking baking pans and cartons of dishes into their van. She took advantage of the moment for a short, whispered conversation.

"This must seem very strange to all of you not to have Cynthia here," she said. "It would be like a family reunion for her, except that she chose not to come. That's really too bad."

"You're more generous than Cynthia deserves," I told her. "The person Cynthia has turned into just spreads venom wherever she goes. She has nearly destroyed her daughters, and you of all people know what she did to Richard. I'm glad you're here, I really am."

"There's more," she said, and she made a face as if she were in pain. I could see she knew I wasn't going to like whatever it was she was going to tell me.

"When we got here tonight a mail truck followed us into the driveway. Since you were inside Richard signed for the packages. There were three of them, big boxes, all addressed to Chloe. While you were working with the caterer I went into the study to put Richie down, and she and Richard and Jack carried in the boxes. Since it wasn't time for dinner yet she decided to open them. She suspected they might be from her mother, and they were."

She paused and took a breath. I motioned with my hands for her to hurry up and tell me the rest.

"Inside each of them were household items that a newly married couple might use, but they were all secondhand, some of them even spotted and stained. You can come in and see later. I don't want to make a big deal out of it to the others, especially John and Caroline. They worry so much, and they want to believe that Cynthia is doing okay. Anyway, there are gray dish towels and sheets that have stains on them. There are two beat-up old saucepans and what looks like an entire set of dishes that are cracked and chipped. Either she has boxed up some of her old things or she did her shopping at a very bad garage sale."

"I can't imagine what she was thinking. And what timing—to have them delivered here the evening before the wedding."

Kim pulled an envelope out of her pocket in her dress and handed it to me.

"Oh, she knew what she was doing. In a kind of sick, warped way, I guess this explains it," she said.

The note paper still said "Mrs. Richard C. Bartolucci" at the top. Below she had written, "I saw no reason to invest in nice linens or silver since this marriage has little chance of lasting. A man who tells you how much he loves you when you are young and pretty doesn't always stick around when you get older and a younger model comes along. Nevertheless, I am sending along some items you might find useful for the duration. Then when he cheats on you, you can walk out and leave it all behind for him to deal with."

I folded the note and handed it back to Kim.

"This is not the woman I used to know, I swear," I said. I flashed on the time she had walked through the rain to bring me soup, but just as quickly I remembered her fantasies about what she'd like to do to Richard and Kim, and I shivered involuntarily.

"I know," Kim said. "Richard says the same things. I think we just have to downplay this and put the focus on the really beautiful gifts people have sent. We've got to make tomorrow the happiest day of Chloe's life."

I nodded and we squeezed each other's hands like conspirators. Then the caterers came back in to finish cleaning the kitchen and Kim and I returned to the few remaining guests in the dining room. I put on a smile for their benefit, but I couldn't get Cynthia's inappropriate gifts out of my mind. My heart went out to Chloe, who just that morning had expressed the hope that maybe her mother was planning a surprise appearance. It seemed Cynthia wasn't happy with her own self-destruction. She wanted to take everybody she knew and loved down right along with her when she crashed and burned.

Later that night, when everyone else had gone, Chloe showed me the "gifts" her mother had sent as if to purposely make a complete mockery out of her marriage and ruin her wedding day. I fingered dented measuring spoons, mismatched pillowcases, a rusty flour sifter, frayed washcloths.

"Your mother is deeply troubled," I told her, taking her into my arms. I thought of the irony. Cynthia should be filling this role, but instead it was from her that Chloe most needed to be protected. "Try to forgive her and put this out of your mind. We'll send all of this stuff to a thrift store where maybe someone will be able to use it. Meanwhile, we've had a magical night, and you and Jack are going to have a wonderful life together. And don't forget that every single person who was here tonight loves you and Jack so much."

The next day no one would have guessed how much pain Cynthia, even absent, had caused the night before. Peter had arranged for us to hold the reception at a beachfront venue in Santa Monica, and Mae, Kim, Lorraine, and I spent the afternoon hanging decorations and laying out purple and mauve napkins with "Chloe and Jack, August 20, 2000" printed on them. Richard, Peter, and Todd had taken Jack and the other groomsmen out for an early game of tennis followed by a breakfast that passed for a bachelor party. Then at four o'clock we all converged at the synagogue, this time dressed up, nervous and sober in keeping with the seriousness of the day.

I had stayed with Chloe and her bridesmaids in the office where they had been dressing for as long as I could, but when I heard the music begin I slid into the seat next to Peter's. Todd would escort Claire in as the rightful mother of the groom, leaving me free to enjoy watching my careful planning play out. I took Peter's hand, and he raised mine to his lips and kissed it. He was wearing a tuxedo, and he had recently shaved off the beard he had worn for so many years. I thought to myself that it was almost as if I were having an affair with a new man, and then just as quickly

I thought how grateful I was that he was the same husband I had always had, that our love and respect for each other had only grown stronger and never diminished, that Todd and Mae had never had to share their time between two bitter households.

Across the aisle Richie squirmed in Richard's mother's arms, and she patted his bottom and rocked him back and forth without caring that the rose-colored linen dress for which she had spent nearly a month shopping was dissolving into a wrinkled mess. In my row beyond Peter were Bradley and Kathy and then Dad. When Claire was seated in front of us she turned around to take both of our hands, her eyes brimming with tears. Our sons and the other groomsmen had taken their places in front with the rabbi, and they were all looking expectantly toward the back of the room.

"There is so much warmth and love in this room," I whispered to Peter. "I can't believe Cynthia isn't here." I looked back over my shoulder, thinking, as Chloe had, that she might have tiptoed into the room and taken a seat, unnoticed, in an inconspicuous back corner. But she hadn't, and Peter, knowing exactly what I was doing, said, "Give it a rest, honey. This day is way too important to have her ruin it."

And then the wedding march began, and we all stood and turned to see Chloe, smiling and beautiful, clinging to her father's arm and seeing only Jack up ahead.

11

In the fall, with the wedding behind me, I went to San Francisco for two weeks. For months I had been filing my columns remotely and only turning up occasionally for staff meetings, but now the book was well underway and a syndicate had picked up the column. Because of this there was a mountain of mail awaiting my attention—offers of speaking engagements, requests for information, some fan letters from readers who agreed with something I had said in a column, and a few most unflattering ones from those who did not. Annie called me at the end of September and begged me to come up.

"I can pack everything up and send it down if you absolutely can't make it up here," she said, "but you've got a pile of stuff to handle." Then she laughed. "Besides, I miss you, and I want to see the wedding pictures."

She and Jonathan hadn't been able to come to the wedding, but they had an excellent reason for declining. They had just that week adopted the baby for whom they had been wishing and waiting for so long. Their agency had been monitoring the progress of an unmarried African American woman who had made the choice to give her child a better life, and when he was born he was theirs. In the pictures Annie sent, his bright brown eyes and cocoa-colored skin made him look like he should be on the cover of a magazine rather than tucked into the bassinette beside Annie and Jonathan's bed.

"Let me talk to Peter tonight, and I'll call you back tomorrow. He's off on location, so I'll have to wait until he gets back to stay with the kids, but then I don't think I'll have any problem working it out. It's time I got seriously back to work again."

Since the wedding I had been concentrating on my two younger children. It wasn't that I had ignored them exactly, but during the months between Jack and Chloe's Valentine's Day engagement and their August wedding we had all been preoccupied. Even when I took an evening off from my computer to watch a movie with my family I had a bridal magazine or the yellow pages in my lap. Now Todd was getting ready to graduate from high school and Mae was practicing for her driver's test. I needed to put on the brakes and slow my life down. I wanted to enjoy them before they left the nest, too, and I was planning weddings for them.

Chloe and Jack had gone backpacking through Mexico for their honeymoon.

"Where did we go wrong?" Peter asked me the morning after the wedding. We were standing in the driveway where we had waved them off. "Don't they know about resorts and room service?"

When they returned Chloe flew to Kansas City by herself to visit Cynthia. She took the wedding album and a copy of the video we had had made of the ceremony and reception. When she got back, Jack was in court, so I picked her up at LAX. She hugged me when she saw me as if she hadn't seen me for years.

"That bad, huh?" I asked.

She nodded and made a sad face.

"I ended up spending most of the time with Dad and Kim. Mom kept telling me how busy she was like she was trying to prove to me that she was doing just fine, even if I had left her in the lurch. I wanted to take her out for dinner one night, but she said she just couldn't fit me in. One day I bought lunch at a deli and surprised her at the school where she's taking classes, and she got all mad and embarrassed. The worst was showing her the wedding pictures."

"I can imagine," I said. "You were damned if you took them and damned if you didn't. If you hadn't taken them, she would have thought you were deliberately trying to cut her out of the loop."

"Exactly. And she got really upset over the pictures of Richie. You know how she is. She was calling Kim all kinds of racist names and saying she should have been the one in the pictures. I reminded her that both you and I tried to get her to come, and now she's saying you're a hypocrite and trying to hurt her, too."

"You're kidding!" I said.

"No, you won't believe this. I showed her the video, which was probably a mistake, but anyway I didn't want her to think I was keeping anything from her. There's that minute or so where the videographer was actually taping Lorraine and Mae trying to eat their cake with their gloves still on, but you and Dad are in the background. He's hugging you, and he gives you a kiss on the cheek and tells you he loves you. Do you remember where I mean?"

I did. We still watched the video almost every day and saw things each time we hadn't noticed before.

"You can't really hear him, but you can read his lips if you're watching closely enough. To tell the truth, I think the pictures of Dad were all she cared about seeing. Everything else seemed pretty incidental."

"That's one of my favorite parts of the video," I said. "Your dad is one of my oldest friends, and it was quite a day for both of us when our children married each other."

"I know that, and so does everybody else, but Mom decided that the two of you are carrying on behind Kim's back."

"Oh, my God!" I said. I couldn't help laughing at the ludicrousness of what she had said. "Doesn't she realize that your father lives two thousand miles away and that except for this wedding I only ever see him once or twice a year or so when he comes out here to go to a medical conference or visit you and your grandparents? And doesn't she stop to think that if we were kissing each other out of passion, we probably wouldn't do it in a roomful of people? And with a video camera pointed at us to boot?"

I remembered the time, years ago, when Cynthia had thought Richard was coming on to me because we had gone jogging together, but I didn't mention it to Chloe.

"You know I'm not trying to hurt your feelings, right?" she said. "I'm only telling you all of this so you can see how far gone she is. I'm glad Jack didn't go with me. She didn't have anything good to say about him, either. She reminds me of that old lady in *Great Expectations* who storms around in her wedding gown telling the little girl not to trust men."

We had left the airport and were driving up the Pacific Coast Highway toward our house, where Jack was going to meet her for dinner before they went home. The lowering sun made a brilliant path on the ocean water that seemed to lead right to my car. It was a picture I never tired of seeing.

"How is Lorraine doing with all of that?" I asked.

"Not good, really, although she tries hard. Dad got her a job for the summer as a receptionist for another doctor he knows, and she's started her junior year of college. She just keeps out of the house as much as possible. She babysits Richie and stays over with Dad and Kim whenever she can. I talked to her about coming out here and going to school, but Mom is putting the same guilt trip on her that she tried to use on me. Lorraine feels pressured because she's the last one at home, and she worries that if she leaves, Mom might spin completely out of control."

"Well, Lorraine has your dad there. He won't let anything bad happen."

"I hope you're right," she said. "It's sad, but I feel like I don't even know my mother anymore."

"I know, honey. I feel exactly the same way."

Peter and I, a continent apart, looked at our separate calendars and found a time when I could be away.

"I'd like a few days with you when I get back before you take off," he'd said. "A feller gets mighty lonely up here in the wilds of Canada without his woman."

"Same here. And by the way, Todd and Mae are both standing right here. Would you like to say hello?"

A week after he returned I flew to San Francisco. It was five in the evening when I landed and too late to get anything done at the office, so I took a cab directly from the airport to our house. Despite missing Peter and the kids almost from the moment my plane left the ground in LA, it felt good to be back. I opened the doors and windows to air the place out. We had a housekeeper who came in regularly to clean and keep things in order, but the rooms still smelled musty and had a feeling of not having been lived in for a while. I turned on some music and poured a glass of wine, a little giddy with the prospect of having time alone to read and sleep, catch up on my work, soak in the tub, and do pretty much as I pleased. Then the phone rang.

"You're here!" Annie squealed.

I forgot about wanting to be alone and looked at my watch.

"Are you leaving work now?" I asked.

"Yes. Is the bar open?"

"You bet it is!" I sang into the phone.

I could hardly wait to see her. I never thought I'd use the phrase "best friend" again, but Annie had gradually filled that role in my life. I was grateful to have a woman with whom I could talk about whatever was on my mind. With Annie I could also talk shop, a subject that had frequently made our husbands' eyes glaze over when we got together socially. Often our conversations translated, almost verbatim, into my columns. Now she was standing in my front door with a cardboard box full of letters and FedEx packets.

"No rest for the wicked!" she sang out. "There's more in the car."

Then she hugged me.

"God, it's good to see you. The paper is a nuthouse, in case you've forgotten. And it's worse without someone to commiserate with."

I poured wine for her and we traded photographs—my wedding pictures for those of her son, Bryan. She was especially interested in seeing the wedding video, pushing pause occasionally to ask questions about who people were and how they were related to Chloe and Jack. Relaxed on my sofa, we put our feet up on the coffee table and hooted with laughter—at the look on Lorraine's face as she caught her sister's bouquet, at Todd dancing awkwardly with the girl from next door.

"So which one is Cynthia?"

"She didn't come to the wedding."

"She didn't come to her own daughter's wedding?"

"She's mad at all of us. Chloe and I both wrote to ask her, but she wouldn't budge. I guess she thinks she's punishing us, and it did hurt Chloe, but I think in the end Cynthia is the one who probably suffered most. At least we didn't have to worry about her spoiling the whole thing."

I pointed to two figures on the television screen.

"That's her ex-husband with his wife, Kim. I've told you about them. He left Cynthia to marry Kim, but she drove him to it. Nobody could blame him. It's really a sad story. When we were in college they were crazy about each other."

When we got to the scene where Richard kissed me I told her the story Chloe had told me.

"It sounds like she might be seriously ill," Annie said, frowning. "Has anybody tried to get her some help?"

"You have no idea. She's been in therapy on and off for the past several years, but the guy she goes to doesn't seem to make much progress. She calls him Dr. Flek, but he isn't a real doctor—medical or otherwise. Peter calls him Dr. Flake. Apparently he collects a big fee for telling her everything she wants to hear and that everything she does is great."

"Is she on any kind of medication?"

"Not the last I heard. She always resisted it when Richard suggested seeing an actual psychiatrist. Her mother was bipolar, and so many of her symptoms point to that. If she could get on the proper medication, she might be able to have a happy, productive life. All I know now is what Chloe tells me, and it's all so upsetting to her. I try not to pry, and to tell you the truth, I don't really want to know. We've been out of touch since we had the argument a couple of years back, and I like it that way. Now I just listen when

Chloe needs to talk."

"Is she dangerous?"

"I used to think so. I don't know anymore. I do know that she has a gun—or did. She once told me her fantasies about killing Richard and Kim, but that was a long time ago. They weren't very pretty. I told Richard and he went back to the house once while she was gone, but he couldn't find the gun. Then her parents went to visit her. I told her stepmother about the gun, and she looked for it, too, and couldn't find it. I hope that means she's gotten rid of the damn thing."

"All the same, that's pretty scary. Normal people don't sit around thinking about killing someone."

"Richard told me she's left them alone for the past several months. She used to harass them—you know, call them at all hours, have stuff delivered to their house, that kind of thing. I hope she has finally accepted that he isn't her husband anymore, but I still worry that she might hurt herself. Chloe went to see her when she and Jack got back from their honeymoon, and from what she tells me it sounds like Cynthia is consumed by hate. When Lorraine moves out, I'm afraid she might get despondent and try to do herself in. Ironically, her mother committed suicide, which I think may be at the heart of all the problems Cynthia has ever had. She never was really happy, even in the best of times, but she was a good friend for a while. We were really close when we were younger."

"You never know about people," Annie said. "It's sad. The waste of a life, really."

"It all makes me appreciate having a sane, normal friend like you even more," I told her.

"Sane? Normal? Who are we talking about here?" she said.

We laughed, and then I pushed "play." On the screen Jack

peeled a pink satin garter down Chloe's leg and threw it into a forest of waving tuxedoed arms.

I woke up well before the alarm went off and had just gotten out of the shower and put on a warm chenille bathrobe. I shuffled in a pair of heavy athletic socks out to the kitchen and started the coffee. Then I went out to the front step for the newspaper. I flipped on the television set and tuned in to a national news program. It was only six o'clock and I had a couple of hours before I was due at an editorial meeting downtown. When the phone rang I thought instinctively of Cynthia's early morning calls. How many of them had I answered in this very kitchen at just about this hour? This time it was Chloe, and she sounded upset.

I could hear my pulse thudding in my ears.

"What is it, honey? What's happened?"

In the split second before she spoke I visualized every member of my family dead in a car crash, my house burned to the ground, Peter in a hospital somewhere. When she told me the problem was once again Cynthia, I felt shamelessly relieved.

"She went berserk at that school she goes to," she said. "From what Dad said, some attorney she knew from when she belonged to the country club had come to lecture on legal ethics, and she decided he was talking down to her, despite the fact that she was in a classroom full of people at the time and he probably didn't even notice her. Anyway, she stood up and started yelling things at him, how he was an inconsiderate, condescending bastard. She said she knew his wife and he'd be nothing but shit if it hadn't been for her working to put him through law school. Then she asked him if he was still sleeping with his secretary and how ethical he thought that was and when he planned to leave his wife and ruin her life."

She sniffed and blew her nose. When she spoke again, she sounded as if she had suddenly come down with a bad cold.

"Anyway, the teacher apparently ran out of the room and got a security guard, and they ended up calling the police. They took her to the police station, but nobody filed any charges, so she got to go home. Lorraine had to go down there and pick her up."

"When did you find all of this out?"

"Late last night. Lorraine called. She was a mess, as you can imagine. She called from Dad's house. She said Mom had had a lot to drink and gone to sleep. Dad drove Lorraine to the school to pick up Mom's car. He wanted her to spend the night with them, but she was afraid Mom would wake up and be all alone and scared."

My heart went out to Lorraine. Nobody at twenty-one years old deserved this kind of pressure and responsibility. I wanted to shake Cynthia.

"What's going to happen now?" I asked.

"Lorraine said the security people told Mom to stay away from the school, so I guess there goes her plan to be a paralegal."

"I'm so sorry about that," I said. "I was hoping that might have been her chance to put a life together for herself and stop dwelling on the past."

"I know," she said shakily. "I hoped so, too, but now we're back at square one."

"Is there anything I can do? I've got a few more days' work to finish up here, but if you really need me, I can be on a plane today."

"No. I'll keep you posted if anything else happens. I just wanted to talk to you about it. There's nothing you can do. I don't think there's anything any of us can do."

⁓

"Cynthia's been committed to the psych ward at Samaritan," Richard said flatly through the telephone.

For once I had gotten a crisis call from one of the Bartoluccis during normal waking hours. It was late in the afternoon on a gray, wet Monday, the first day of November. I was working at the computer in my office in LA, trying to finish a column about Thanksgiving for the syndicate that was due the next day. A cold cup of coffee and a half-eaten candy bar left over from trick-or-treaters the night before that had been my lunch sat on the desk beside my keyboard. In the kitchen I could hear Peter rummaging in the refrigerator for something to eat. He had gotten in from another trip to Canada early that morning and had slept most of the day. He stuck his head through the office door and frowned his question.

"Richard," I mouthed.

Not realizing the gravity of the call, he went back to his foraging, and I said to Richard, "What happened?"

He sounded tired and exasperated, as he often did when our conversation concerned his ex-wife. The difference when he called to tell me something about his real life with Kim and Richie and Lorraine was remarkable. Then he sounded full of energy and excited to be talking to me.

"Well, you heard that she got kicked out of the school where she was studying to be a paralegal, didn't you?"

"Yes, Chloe called me when it happened, but that was several weeks ago. I was hoping no news was good news."

"Not in this case. Lorraine said after that Cynthia wouldn't leave the house for anything. Lorraine has had to buy groceries and do all the errands on top of school and her part-time job. She said there were days when Cynthia didn't even get dressed or come out of her bedroom. So after a while she just went back to her normal routine. She said she made breakfast for Cynthia every morning and dinner in the evening, but other than that Cynthia didn't seem interested in much interaction. Then today, out of nowhere, she got all dressed up and came to my office."

This was not what I had expected to hear. The sense of dread I had experienced had to do with wondering if Cynthia had done something to hurt Lorraine. Next to that anything else would truly be good news.

"To your office?" I asked. "Why?"

"My theory is that she saw what chaos her theatrics could cause, and she decided to have an encore. She came into my waiting room this morning when it was full of people and started shouting accusations and saying I had ruined her life. As usual, she blamed Kim, and then she buttonholed one of my pregnant patients and told her not to count on her husband's being around when the child got to high school. My receptionist told me she tried to take Cynthia's arm just so she could get her out of the waiting room, but she broke loose and started hitting her. Ellie pushed back in self-defense, and Cynthia lost her balance and fell and knocked over a plant. I heard all the commotion and came out from the examining room where I was working with a patient. By that time Cynthia was screaming and crying, doubled up in the fetal position and howling like a banshee. It was humiliating, all right. From the looks on the faces of my patients, I think some of them were trying to decide if I was really the kind of person they wanted to be their doctor. I guess she accomplished her mission. Pretty counterproductive, since I'm the one still paying for her goddamn house."

"What happened then?"

"I was able to confine her to my office while my nurse called 911. Meanwhile, I called Flek and told him to get down here and deal with his patient. I regret that she ever got tangled up with that guy. Her big priority back then was that her shrink not be part of our social circle, but if I'd known then what I know now, I would have held out for somebody I could trust, friend or not. If we'd had an actual psychiatrist on board, the outcome might have been a lot different."

I could hear his regretful sigh across the miles.

"But she believes in him and he's all we've got for a mental-health professional, if you want to call him that. I just want to be done with the whole thing."

"I can understand that," I said.

"I know I probably sound like a cold son of a bitch, and I wouldn't say this to anyone else but you. It isn't like I didn't try to hang in there with her as long as I could to help her get straightened out. But when it was over, it was over. You know what I mean? I thought that's what divorce meant. That person is no longer your wife and nothing she does can hurt you anymore. The thing that makes me maddest of all is what she has done to the girls. Lorraine is beside herself. I think she's going to need some counseling to get through all of this, but you can be sure I'll shop around more carefully this time before I send her to anybody."

"So Cynthia's at the hospital now?"

"Yeah, Flek talked to the emergency room people, and they admitted her to the psych ward. But even now I'm not finished with it. I consult over there, so everybody knows me. Honest to God, it's like it never ends."

"How is Kim doing with all of this?"

"I called her right after it happened. She's great, like she always is. She drove right over to the house and helped Lorraine pack some of her things. We're going to have her stay with us at least for the duration. I'd like to make it permanent. It makes me nervous to have her living with such a nut case, and you know I never did find that gun. I'm going to go over there while she's in the hospital and have another look."

"Have you talked to Chloe?"

"No, that's one of the reasons I'm calling. I hate to tell her this stuff over the phone and then not be there to support her. I think she needs to hear it from someone who can offer her some comfort."

"And that would be me?"

"Would you mind?"

"Of course not. I think you're right. I'll call Jack and ask him to bring her over here for dinner."

"Thanks. I owe you. Now for the second favor."

"Anything. Shoot."

"Kim and I have been talking about this ever since I got home this evening, and we want to spend some time with both of the girls. This is hard for them, and I hate it that we're spread out all over the country. Chloe already told us a couple of weeks ago that she and Jack wouldn't have enough time off at Thanksgiving to fly back here. So we're thinking of bringing Lorraine and all of us coming out there. The problem is my parents will be in Hawaii while they have some work done on their house, so we'll need to book a hotel. Do you know of any near Jack and Chloe?"

"No, I don't. The only place I know of that isn't booked for the holiday weekend is our house. My dad and Bradley have some new calves they can't leave for the whole long weekend, so the guest room is yours and Lorraine can have Jack's old room. It will be so much fun to have you. This time we won't be in the middle of a wedding, so we can just have a good visit. Hopefully you and Kim can forget about what's going on back in Kansas City."

"You're the best, Maggie. You always have been. Okay, then how about this? I'll take everyone out for Thanksgiving dinner so you don't end up cooking for the whole crowd. Pick a place you like and make reservations for all of us."

"I like this plan a lot," I said, laughing. "You've got yourself a deal."

☙

The ten of us ate Thanksgiving dinner on the patio overlooking the ocean at Mar Pacifica, just up the beach from our house.

"I think we wouldn't be eating on the patio in Kansas City," Kim said, and we all laughed. She lifted her wineglass in my direction. "Thanks to Maggie and Peter for having us all in their home to stay and for picking such a great place to have dinner."

I toasted back, gesturing to the roast turkey and pumpkin ravioli that lay half-eaten on my plate.

"Thank you for getting me out of the kitchen," I said. "May I never cook another Thanksgiving turkey again."

Peter rolled his eyes.

"She's wretched when she's spoiled," he said, squeezing my knee under the table. "Absolutely insufferable."

It was an easy day, a lazy day. We drank too much and laughed a lot. Richard sat between his daughters and across from Peter and me at the table. When dinner was over the kids went back to the house, and Richard, Kim, Peter, and I stayed behind for a cognac.

Richard lifted his glass.

"To many more Thanksgivings together," he said.

"It's a tradition," I said. "Now that we're all sort of related, we should do it every year."

"Of course I can't help but remember the year I wore my Thanksgiving dinner on the front of my shirt," he said wryly.

"No more of that," I said, winking at Kim. "Your wife doesn't seem to be the plate-throwing type."

"She's wonderful," Richard said, kissing his wife impulsively on the top of her head. "I can't imagine what my life would be like if I hadn't met her."

⁂

Back at the house I eased wedges of pumpkin pie, my only contribution to the day's feast, onto plates, and Todd topped each one of them with a curl of whipped cream. Kim poured cups of coffee and loaded them onto a tray to carry into the living room. The sun had gone down, and the house was suddenly chilly. Peter built a fire in the fireplace, and Chloe lit the candles on the mantelpiece. I watched them from the kitchen door, but in the gathering dusk they didn't notice me.

This is what it's all about, I thought. *My family, my dear friends, all of us together.* Earlier in the day Dad had called, and Bradley and Kathy had gotten on the extension together to wish us a happy holiday. Except for missing my mother, I couldn't remember a better Thanksgiving ever.

"Cynthia, Cynthia, Cynthia," I whispered. "This is what you gave away. This is what your anger has cost you."

I thought about the first Thanksgiving I had known her before she and Richard had even met. Back then the happy days of our budding friendship, as delicate and hopeful as a new love affair, had far outweighed the ones when her mother's jealousy and ultimate suicide got her down. Now I imagined her back in Kansas City, eating a hospital dinner alone from a tray on which the cup would be paper or plastic and none of the utensils would have sharp edges.

When had it happened? When does water become coffee? When do milk and eggs turn to ice cream? Was her fate sealed the day she found her mother dead and blamed it on herself or was it really tied up with Richard and a fear of losing him so deadly it drove him away? Or was it purely chemical, an organic swill with no diagnosis, a misfiring in her brain that maybe now could be cured with medication?

"Honey?" Peter called. "Our forks are poised, and I don't think we can hold out much longer, but we're doing our best to wait for you."

I grabbed a paper towel and blew my nose.

"Here I am," I said as I sailed through the door.

For the next several minutes we were quiet, the only audible sounds the clatter of forks on plates and an occasional murmur of appreciation. When we had finished, Chloe turned to Jack and smiled at him, arching her eyebrows in question.

"Do you think it's time?" she asked him.

"Sure, go ahead."

She cleared her throat dramatically, as if she were about to make an important speech, which in fact was what it turned out to be.

"Earlier today someone said that now we are all one big family and we should plan to make Thanksgiving dinner together a tradition," she said. "Today there were ten of us. Jack and I want to tell you that next year there will be eleven."

Her voice cracked, and Jack folded her in his arms. I looked at Peter, then Kim, then Richard in disbelief. Todd got more to the point.

"Do you mean you're . . . ," he asked, pointing to Chloe's midsection, too embarrassed to say more.

"She's trying to tell you we're expecting a baby, nitwit," Jack said, grabbing his brother in a headlock and ruffling his hair with his knuckles, laughing.

"When?" I asked.

"I'm only two months," Chloe said. "So it's going to be a long wait. But we thought today would be the perfect time to tell everybody since both of our families are together." Then she smiled sadly. "Well, except for our moms."

We all hugged each other happily and asked them all the usual questions—how did she feel, had they had picked out names—but later in the kitchen I felt obligated to ask Chloe some practical questions. She had helped me carry the dishes back out, so we had a few minutes alone to talk. I took the stack of plates out of her hands and set them down on the counter. Then I took her face in my hands.

"How do you feel about all of this, honey?" I asked her. "It's so sudden."

"Thanks, Maggie," she said. "I know what you're saying and I appreciate your concern, I really do. This is sooner than we had planned to start a family, and we talked about the options, but all we kept coming back to was how excited we were about having a baby. I'll be finished with school before it's born, and we can afford good child care, and we have a lot of support from our families—especially you and Peter. Mostly I want to do it right, to have a child and not screw it up like I feel my mother did with my sister and me, and Jack wants it as much as I do. I think we'll be fine."

I pulled her into my arms.

"I'm sure you will be, and I'm really excited, too."

❦

It was late Saturday night, and Chloe and Jack had taken Lorraine, Todd, and Mae to their apartment to make pizza. Kim was upstairs reading Richie to sleep, and Richard, Peter, and I were sipping Grand Marnier in front of the fireplace, trying to make the evening last since their plane would leave early the next morning.

"You two have been incredible friends," Richard said, swirling the amber liquid in his glass and concentrating on it instead of looking at us. "I want to ask your advice about something."

Peter and I looked at each other and then back at him.

"I don't know what our advice is worth," Peter said, "but we're always happy to listen."

"I want Lorraine to come out here and stay."

I interrupted before he could go any further.

"Really! But what about school?"

"I think a fresh start would be worth the few credits that might not transfer. And with living with Cynthia and taking care of her, it's not like she's having a great campus experience. She'll have her final exams before Christmas, and then I'd like to see her transfer to UCLA."

"Could she get in that soon?" Peter asked. "I think the deadline for applications for the winter semester has already passed. You need to ask Chloe about that. She'd know."

Richard smiled slowly.

"One of the few benefits of being a contributing, card-carrying alum," he said. "I called a friend of mine on the board of regents and explained that I was having a bit of a family emergency and needed to enroll my daughter this winter. He said he thought they could work something out."

"Have you talked to Lorraine about this yet?" I asked.

"It's a touchy subject with her," he said, frowning. "She loves it out here. She'd love to be near her sister, especially now with a baby on the way. And she's interested in business. UCLA has a good business school."

"So why is it touchy?" I asked him. "It sounds like a great idea. It's a good opportunity for her, and it would get her away from the mess with Cynthia."

"That's the problem," he said. "She feels guilty about leaving her mother. I tried talking to her a little bit on the plane out here, and she said it sounded like a great idea if only she didn't have to care for Cynthia."

"But Cynthia's in the hospital."

"All the more reason for Lorraine to feel guilty. Cynthia makes lists every day of clothes and magazines and whatever else she wants, and Lorraine takes it when she goes to see her, even though Cynthia is often in a foul mood and just asks her to leave once she has what she wanted. But Lorraine knows her mother won't be in there forever, and she feels like she should be at home when Cynthia is released."

"That's too much for a kid," I said.

"My point exactly, and Kim agrees. We want her to come out here and start to lead her own life. We'll miss her, but with both of the girls out here and my parents getting older, we'll just plan to come out more often. Especially now that we're going to be grand-parents. Jesus, does that sound strange. Anyway, my argument is going to be that I'll hire a full-time nurse or caretaker or compan-ion or whatever it takes when Cynthia comes home. I don't mind spending the money. It's the emotional turmoil my whole family is constantly in that drives me nuts."

"That's generous of you," I said, "and it should persuade Lor-raine. She can always call and email. They could stay in close touch."

"Now comes the other problem. Enrollment is no problem, but housing is. The dorms are full-up, and I really don't want to put her into an apartment by herself right away. I think she's going to need some moral support. I thought the perfect solution would be for her to stay the winter semester with Chloe and Jack, come home for the summer and then move into a dorm in the fall. I was going to talk to Chloe about it while we were here, but now that she's pregnant, I think she and Jack need the time alone together. They haven't been married very long, and they need to concentrate on each other between now and when the baby comes. I think having someone else—even a family member—live with them would be too much pressure to put on them. I don't want to make the situation better for one of my daughters at the expense of the other. So I'm open for suggestions. I'd like to have all the details covered when I bring this up again with Lorraine. Do you know anybody whose kid is looking for a roommate or who rents out rooms?"

I looked at Peter. He nodded and smiled.

"How about our guest room?" I asked. "She'd be in a home that's already familiar and comfortable for her. She'd get to see lots of Chloe and Jack and be around when the baby's born. And we'd encourage her to keep in touch with her mother, but if she was ever down and needed to talk, she'd be with people who love her and understand her situation. It's perfect! All she needs is a car to get back and forth from the campus and she's all set."

"You're kidding," he said. "That would solve everything, but it's a lot to ask. And you two have done so much for us already. I didn't bring this up to suggest that you . . ."

"We love your kids, you know that," I said before he could finish.

"Well, I'd certainly pay you whatever I'd pay for an apartment or a room in the dorm."

"We'll iron out the details later," I told him. "Now your job is to convince Lorraine."

❧

In the small hours of the morning Peter and I still lay awake talking.

"We're going to regret not sleeping when we have to get up in a few hours and go to the airport," I said, burrowing more deeply under the covers and snuggling into his back.

"There's a lot to think about," he told me. "But I think it will all work out fine. It's not like we're taking in a stranger here, and she'll certainly be better off away from Cynthia. God, how does that woman manage to poison everything she touches?"

"Every time I talk to Richard or Chloe, I think about how much I appreciate what we have," I told him. "Our life is so simple compared to theirs. It seems like we're always coming and going and catching planes and talking across oceans, but at least nobody's suicidal, nobody's running amok. We're in love, our kids don't have to wonder which personality we're going to have on when they come home from school."

"We're very lucky," he said, turning toward me and kissing me. "And I'm glad we can do something to help out. I know how important that family is to you—and now me, too."

"In a way it's like I'm appropriating her whole family. Richard is one of my best friends, Chloe is my daughter-in-law, and now Lorraine is going to come and live in my house. It's crazy the way it has all turned out. Sometimes I think how much fun it would have been if Cynthia could have stayed well and she and Richard had stayed together and now we'd all be looking forward to having our first grandchild together."

"Life is a little crazy that way," Peter said. "If they had stayed happily married, they would have had a life in Kansas City and we'd have had our life here, and the two of you might have drifted apart and never seen each other again anyway. Chloe and Jack might never have gotten together, and we wouldn't know Kim. You never know."

"Well, whatever else happens, I'm grateful for you," I told him, and we kissed deeply.

He pushed my nightgown up around my waist and parted my legs gently with his hand.

"Just how grateful are you?" he asked playfully.

I forgot about Cynthia and Richard and fell in love with my husband all over again.

12

I pulled the list of cities off the fax machine and looked instinctively for Kansas City, and when it wasn't there, I felt an unreasonable sense of relief. My book was coming out in April, and the publisher was sending me on a two-week reading tour that would start in Los Angeles and go to Seattle, Denver, Salt Lake City, Dallas, Chicago, Miami, and New York. I'd end up back in San Francisco for a big publication party the paper was hosting. It was ridiculous, at one of the most exciting times in my life—certainly in my career—that my first thought was of Cynthia, but there it was. If I was reading in Kansas City and didn't call her, she would see it as a snub. If I told her about it, she would say I was once again waving my career in her face. Now it was a problem I didn't even have to consider.

Lorraine came into the office. It was a Tuesday afternoon, and she had finished with her classes for the day. Like her sister, there was no mistaking that she was Richard and Cynthia's child, but her thick dark hair was short and a mass of curls, and she was an inch or so shorter than Chloe and the tiniest bit heavier but attractive—sturdy and athletic. She wore contact lenses to school and round wire-rimmed glasses most of the time at home. Now she carried a letter that the postman had just left. She opened the envelope and read to herself for a minute, frowning.

"It's from Mom," she said. "It's the first time she's written since I've been here."

Lorraine had moved in with us the week after Christmas and had written her mother weekly, but now it was late March and here was the first reply. When she had tried to call the hospital, the nurses had said Cynthia couldn't have calls, although Richard had told me privately that this was not the case. She was simply punishing Lorraine for leaving her.

"Well, good," I said, trying to be cheerful but feeling the familiar clutch in the vicinity of my stomach. "It's about time. What's new with her?"

"She's out of the hospital. She says that's why she didn't write before—they wouldn't let her have a pen and paper. But I know that's bullshit. Dad said she was uncooperative and that's why they kept her as long as they did. He said one of the nurses there told him it seemed like Mom didn't want to get well, like she enjoyed the attention she was getting. Anyway, she's out now and back home. She says she has a caretaker, a woman named Marian, who looks after her, but she says it would be a lot more pleasant for her and a lot less expensive for Dad if I just moved back there."

She looked out the window toward the ocean, puffed up her cheeks, and then let the air out slowly in a gesture of frustration.

"I don't know what I should do," she said finally.

"I do," I said. "Come here and sit down. Let's talk."

I gestured toward the sofa that was near my desk and that pulled out to accommodate an extra sleeper when we had a houseful of overnight guests. I sat down at the other end and pulled my knees up under my chin, a comfortable, familiar position I had assumed countless times in better days with Cynthia.

"Maya Angelou once wrote, 'When people show you who they are, believe them.' Well, honey, she has shown you over and over who she is, and she has shown me, too. I was a loyal friend while she walked all over me, and you know how she treated me. She seems not to want real professional help or really to get well and be the person she has the potential to be. But the person I knew when we were younger would want you to be the very best person you can, to make a life for yourself and follow your own star. That's what she was doing. It went wrong somewhere along the way, but that's where she was headed. Yes, always remember that she's your mom, but never let guilt get in the way of your dreams. As for your dad, he and Kim make enough money to pay for you to be here and your mom to have a caretaker. You and Chloe and Richie are at the center of their lives, but he told me having you here allows him to sleep nights. Your mom broke all of our hearts, but now we all have to do the best we can for ourselves and each other and get on with our own lives."

She started to cry then, and I held her while she got it out, then handed her a tissue so she could dry her eyes, blow her nose, and get on with the letter. She read for a few more seconds in silence.

"Oh, well, this is good," she said in a more upbeat tone.

"Mmm?" I said. I wanted to know what was going on, but I didn't want to pry. I had gone back to the computer and was calling up the file I planned to work on.

"She has a job."

"You're kidding!" I said. "I thought she just got out of the hospital."

"She did. She says Flek arranged this job for her before she was released so she'd have something to look forward to. He thinks having a job is what she needs for her self-esteem, so he got her on as a receptionist at the women's clinic where she used to work as a volunteer. It's better now, she says, because she's getting paid for what she does."

I frowned into the computer screen.

"I wonder about that," I said.

"What do you mean? I think it sounds great. She always wanted to work at the clinic."

"She always wanted to be a psychologist," I said. "There's a big difference. I'm not sure I think it's the best thing for her to be that physically close to her dream but separated from it so far emotionally and educationally."

I could sense Lorraine tensing up. For a few moments she had believed everything was going to be all right with her mother, and now I had put doubt into her mind once again.

"But then," I added quickly, "I'm not her doctor, and I'm sure he's doing what he thinks is best for her."

Fortunately she could not hear the quotation marks I had put around "doctor" in my mind.

"Yeah, I think so. Thanks, Maggie," she said, and she disappeared up the stairs and into her room.

That night I called Richard and Kim's house in Kansas City. Kim answered the phone. Richard had a critical patient, so he would be at the hospital most of the night.

"Lorraine got a letter from Cynthia today," I told her. "She says her mother is out of the hospital. I just wanted to check in with you and make sure everything's okay back there."

"Not really, I'm afraid," Kim said, and I heard in her voice the weariness I had so often heard in her husband's. "She's out, yes, and back home, and the caretaker is in place, but she's no better than she was when she went in. Richard says she can turn it on and off like a faucet. In the beginning she was abusive and belligerent. She wouldn't eat, and she wouldn't follow the rules. Nurses on the staff out there were on the phone to Richard two or three times a day, just like the two of them were still married. He thinks she was just trying to get attention. Once she realized that nobody was going to be manipulated by her behavior—that Richard and I were going to stay married and Chloe wasn't going to run to her side, and especially after Lorraine left—she must have decided it wasn't worth it, and she wanted out of that place fast. Flek told Richard it was like a miracle had happened. One day she's refusing meals and threatening to kill herself, the next she's signed up for the flower-arranging class and offering to help shampoo another patient's hair. I don't think she really put anything over on the nurse and she certainly didn't fool Richard, but the Flake bought it hook, line, and sinker, and a few weeks later she was out and pronounced well."

"That's just scary," I said.

"You bet it is," Kim shot back. "There's never any knowing what kind of state she'll be in. She uses her mental health to manipulate everyone around her. Sometimes I think a good slap is all the medicine she needs."

I laughed out loud.

"That doesn't sound like you," I said.

"I know," she answered, "and you know I don't mean it. But it does get old and wear us down. She yanks all of us—you, the girls, Richard and me—around like we're on leashes. It would be nice someday to have a life that doesn't always involve having to consider what's best for Cynthia."

"I know what you mean," I said. "I'm out here with her daughters, and I see how much pain she causes them. Chloe wants to share her pregnancy with her mother, but she's afraid to. Lorraine is eaten up with guilt for leaving her. There have been times when I didn't think a good kick in the rear was such a bad idea myself."

❦

I stuck my tongue out at the receiver before I hung it up. The call had been from the publicist who was arranging the book tour.

"Anything wrong, honey?" Peter asked.

We were still having breakfast, but it was mid-morning in New York, where at this very moment an office full of people were making plans to fling me around the country in just a matter of weeks.

"No, not really," I said. "I'm just beginning to feel like a commodity, like I'm a can of peas they're trying to sell instead of a columnist who's written a book. They have me scheduled for photo opportunities with writers and editors from the newspapers in the cities where I'll be, and some of the TV appearances and radio shows and signings are back-to-back. It'll be fun, but it'll also be exhausting. And when I go back to a different hotel in a different city every single night for two weeks, I'll be all by myself with nobody to hash it all over with. I wish you were going with me."

"So do I. And if we didn't start filming just a week before you leave, I'd try to rearrange my schedule and do it."

I kissed his cheek as I got up from the kitchen table and headed back to the coffee pot.

"You'd hate it anyway," I said. "You're a good sport, but listening to me read the same excerpts and answer the same questions every day for two solid weeks might even bore me to death."

"It's too bad one of the kids couldn't go with you."

"I've already thought about that, too. I'd love to take Mae and spend the time with her, but she's got too much going on at school. Todd's got basketball practice, Jack and Chloe are hard at work, and Lorraine's in classes. That doesn't leave anybody."

"What about Annie?"

"I doubt if she'd want to be away from the baby for that long."

"You'll never know until you ask. The worst thing that can happen is that she says no."

"That would be fun. Of everybody I just mentioned she'd find it the least dreary."

"Then call her. If the publishers won't pay her expenses, we will. I'd like to know you had somebody with you to make this trip less of a drag. Two weeks away from home is a real bummer when you're by yourself. I know."

I called the publisher's office first. They said they had already budgeted for an assistant, and if I had someone I wanted to bring along to fill that role, that would be fine with them. They never intended, a cheery voice at the other end of the line assured me, to send me all over the country to turn up at universities and TV stations and bookstores on my own.

Then I called Annie.

"God, that sounds like so much fun," she said. "I'd love to do it."

"What about Bryan? Can the nanny cover?"

"That's the only catch. She has her own family at home, but my mom has been talking about coming to see us. I might not be able to be away the whole two weeks, but I could probably manage one."

"That would be great," I said. "The publisher has somebody they can send along for the second week. By then you and I will have the bugs worked out."

"Let me call Mom. If she says yes, we're on."

Within minutes, the phone rang. It was Annie.

"Let's go!" she sang through the phone. "My mom will stay with Bryan for a week. I don't feel good about leaving him for any longer than that, but I could go with you for that long and then fly back here from Dallas the Sunday you leave for Chicago."

"This is perfect," I said. "It's the first time I've started to look forward to the trip. Now it's beginning to sound like fun."

"If Mom is out of the hospital and has a job, I guess it's time for me to tell her about the baby," Chloe said. She had given Peter a lift home from the studio because his car was in the shop and stayed for a cup of herbal tea. It was warm enough that we took it outside and drank it on the patio. She was obviously pregnant now, and she wore black leggings and a flowing maternity smock. Watching her blossom was bittersweet for me. She was the picture of Cynthia. Her dark hair had grown quite long and today hung free. She wore sunglasses and smiled up at the late-afternoon sun.

"You're telling me you haven't told her yet?" I said, my voice going from placid to shrill in the space of those few words.

I could already imagine all of the potential repercussions. Cynthia would think her daughter was hiding something from her or that Richard and her children were plotting something against her with me implicated, as well. With Cynthia, it was impossible to tell which scenario might play out, but the chances were it wouldn't be pretty.

"There hasn't been a good time, Maggie. I wanted to tell her myself, either in person or by phone. I didn't want her to read it in a letter or hear it from somebody else. She wouldn't take my calls at the hospital, even though Dad said she was allowed. So now that I know she's out, I'm going to try to work up the nerve to call her."

"Maybe she'll surprise you and just be happy," I said, although I didn't believe those words myself. "You know she's been in the hospital and having intensive therapy for a few months."

"Right. And now she's back with Dr. Flek. We all know what that means. She's probably crazier than she ever was."

"Chloe!" I felt obligated to express surprise even though I couldn't have agreed with her more and couldn't stifle a laugh. Cynthia's years with the so-called therapist had served only to take her further and further in a downward spiral.

"You know what I mean. I just want her to get well, and I don't think he's the one to help her do it. Dad doesn't think so, either, but there isn't anything any of us can do to change things."

"They say faith in your doctor is half the battle," I told her.

"Well, she certainly has that."

༼

"I've got the best news!"

It was a week before Annie and I were scheduled to leave for the book tour, and the publicist was on the line from New York. "We've had a last-minute addition to your itinerary—Kansas City."

"How is that good news?" I barked. "I don't want to go to Kansas City. I have some bad memories from there. I'd really rather skip it."

The woman at the other end of the line couldn't possibly know how her announcement had caused my stomach to sink, and beyond that it just sounded like a lot more work.

"But here's the thing," she said, her enthusiasm obviously

deflated. "By a wonderful coincidence the Midwest Editors and Publishers Association is having their annual meeting the weekend of the fourteenth. It's a big conference and everybody there will be in a position to promote your book. Their lunchtime speaker had to bow out because of illness in the family, so I was able to schedule you in. You'll pick up a very generous speaker's fee, and someone from the Palmer Bookstore will pick you up immediately afterward so you can sign books for two hours later in the afternoon. Their store is in Country Club Plaza. That's a really posh shopping center in a nice area . . ."

"I've been there," I said dully, the memory of eating ice cream and listening to Cynthia's accusations as clear and painful as if it had been yesterday. "I know where it is. I went there when I was visiting a friend once."

"Great!" the voice said. "Then you know what a break this is for you. We'll book you on a flight from Dallas to Kansas City Saturday morning and then to Chicago on Sunday afternoon. You'll still be there in plenty of time for the event that evening. Do you want me to see if I can get a guest pass to the lunch for your Kansas City friend?"

"No. My friend doesn't live there anymore, but I might have Annie with me, so I'd need one for her."

I had told the white lie just so the situation wouldn't get more complicated than it already was and I wouldn't have to go into a long story with a publicist I didn't even know, but I smiled sadly after I hung up the phone. What I would give to say yes and bring Cynthia, but in the end what I had said was for the most part true.

That night over dinner I told Peter what had happened, and he said, "Why don't you just tell them you don't want to add on another city? They don't own you, you know. You do have the right to just say no."

"I've thought about it. I really have. I could still call and cancel.

But it is good exposure for the book, and the publicist is right. It's a great opportunity to speak to the newspaper and magazine people. But it's more than that, too. I can't let Cynthia spoil a whole city for me. Kansas City is a great place, and Richard and Kim are there. If I go this time and don't see her, I'll be free of this feeling of dread every time I hear anything about the place. Kim's right. Cynthia manipulates all of us like puppets. But if I go this time, maybe I'll be free of all the bad feelings."

I dialed Annie's number at home.

"I know you've got reservations to fly back to San Francisco from Dallas when I leave for Chicago on Saturday," I said, "but there's a new plan. The publicity department has just added Kansas City. I'm going to speak at a lunch meeting and then go directly to the bookstore. It's a good opportunity, but you know how I feel about going to where Cynthia is. I actually thought about how relieved I was that Kansas City wasn't on the original itinerary, but now it is."

"Are you going to tell Cynthia you're coming?" she asked.

"No. It's a no-win situation. We haven't been in touch for a long time, and I really don't want to see her. Of all the places I'm going, that's the place I'd most appreciate having you along. Any chance you could extend just for one more day?"

"I'd like to. Let me see what I can do," she said and then minutes later called to say her mother was happy to have more time with Bryan.

Next I called Richard's number. He wasn't at home, but Kim answered and I told her I'd be coming.

"This is great, Maggie!" she said. "Richard and I will pick you up at the bookstore and bring you back here for the evening. In fact, why don't you and Annie plan to spend the night with us? We'll make dinner and we can have a good visit. I know you're going to be worn out."

"That sounds wonderful," I said gratefully. "I'll be so glad to see you. You know I have some trepidation about coming to Kansas City at all. It's been a long time since I've been there, and the whole idea just conjures up bad feelings."

"Are you going to try and see Cynthia while you're here?"

"No. I hope she doesn't even hear that I'm going to be in town. There won't be any publicity about the talk because it's a closed meeting, and the bookstore doesn't have much time to advertise. I'll just fly in, make the appearances, see you and Richard, and slip out again."

"Sounds good," she said. "I can't wait to see you. We'll have a great time."

I did my first appearance on Monday evening at a bookstore in Los Angeles before Annie and I flew out Tuesday morning for Seattle. My whole family, which I now took to include Chloe and Lorraine, came to the reading and told me afterward what a hit I had been. Jack reminded me to read a bit more slowly, and Mae said I should wear bigger earrings that wouldn't get lost in my hair. Peter said every man I met would fall in love with me and he was sorry now that he hadn't planned to come along.

The next morning I said goodbye to Peter at home before he left for the studio.

"I don't like this," he said, pulling me close to him.

"You're a fine one to talk! I'm going to be gone for two weeks. Sometimes you're away for months at a time."

"Not because I want to be," he said. "I wish I could at least drive you to the airport."

"We've been through this," I said. "There's probably already a crowd of people at the studio wondering where you are, and Chloe doesn't have a class until this afternoon. She's going to drop Jack off at the office and then pick me up. It works out perfectly."

After he was gone I saw the kids off to school and then finished packing. Chloe drove me to LAX and dropped me at the curb.

"Promise me that you'll tell your mother about the baby soon," I said as I hugged her goodbye across the center console. "If you don't, I think it will drive a wedge even further between the two of you, and maybe hearing such good news will actually help her recovery."

"I hope so," she said. "I'm actually going to call her tonight. I promise."

"But please don't tell her I'm going to be in Kansas City," I added as an afterthought. "I don't plan to see her, and I don't want any drama while I'm there."

The rest of the week went by in a blur. In Seattle I addressed a literary organization, in Denver I turned up at two different bookstores, and in Salt Lake City I spoke to a lecture hall filled with journalism majors. In Dallas it was another bookstore. The books sold well, and I signed my name more times than I could count. Each evening there were cocktails and dinners with professors or owners of bookstores or newspaper editors. The people in New York had done their work well. I carried their faxed itinerary in my handbag and consulted it repeatedly. In some cases they had allowed us only an hour between each event, two hours to get ready for dinner.

Most nights Annie and I were delivered back at our hotel just in time to collapse into bed and get ready to do it all again the next day. Except for a few hours spent riding in airplanes, the time alone for good talks had not materialized. Still, I didn't know how I would have managed without her. She carried books and watched after my coat and bag while I was otherwise occupied. She made sure there was a glass of water on the podium and the microphone worked properly. She reminded me to put on lipstick and whispered into my ear when I had forgotten someone's name. Back at the hotel, just as we dropped off to sleep, she would laugh with me about someone at a reading who had been obnoxious or asked a question I had already answered. She made sure each of the grueling days ended on a high note. I had always told her I could tell she had been a flight attendant; now I told her she had missed her calling as a personal assistant to a star, looking after and fussing over what the Hollywood publicity people call "the talent."

Then, on Friday night in Dallas, we finally had a chance to relax. I had signed books at a bookstore all afternoon, and then we had gone to a cocktail party at the home of a newspaper publisher. I consulted my bundle of faxes to be certain, but it was true. When the party was over at seven thirty, nothing else was planned. We were free.

Back in our hotel room, still dressed up for the party, we consulted a telephone book giddily. Then we took a cab to an Italian restaurant and immediately ordered a bottle of wine that we told each other we had certainly earned.

"It's been a week!" Annie said, her glass raised in my direction. "Author! Author!"

I laughed and clinked my glass against hers.

"It would have been a hell of a week without you," I said. "I'm really going to miss you next week."

"It was nothing. The publisher would just have sent someone else," she said in mock humility.

"I can't imagine operating under this pressure and on this schedule with a stranger," I said. "I wish you were going to be with me for the rest of the tour. But at least now I know the ropes. Whoever they send won't think I'm an amateur!"

"I wish I could come, too," she said. "It's going to be hard to go back to the real world after hanging out with a celebrity and all the parties and fun, but I'm also looking forward to getting back home to Jonathan and Bryan."

I nodded sympathetically.

As if reading my mind, she said, "I guess you know how that is. Having a husband and a child really changes your life. When I was flying, I didn't see how my life could get much better. It was hard work, but I was in a different city every night, dating interesting men. But when I met Jonathan, nothing else mattered. I just wanted to marry him and come home to him every night for the rest of my life."

"And now you have Bryan."

"That's the best part of all," she said, smiling. "I don't think I ever told you that we tried for a long time to have a baby of our own. When I first met you it was still too painful to talk about. Just before I got the job at the paper we had gone through some tests and found out that we couldn't, and the problem was with me. I cried and cried the day the results came back, but after we got Bryan, I thought how could it be any better? How could I love a child more than I love him just because a different set of eggs and sperm had bumped into each other?"

"I'm really happy for you," I said. "My family's not what I expected, either. I sometimes forget who is an actual product of my loins and who isn't. I've had Jack since he was seven, and I love

Cynthia's girls as much as if they were my own."

"It's like every day is special," she said. "When I wake up I wonder what new thing he'll do. Or I try to imagine the future, what he'll be like when he's ten or twelve or sixteen. We're thinking of applying for a second baby, but it takes a long time, and if Bryan's the only child I ever have, I'll still count myself so incredibly lucky. In fact, I guess you and I are both pretty lucky. Good families, good jobs. And I count among my good fortune having you as my friend."

"Ditto," I said. "It's hard to get to know somebody new at our age and with everybody so busy. Sometimes I think it's like if you didn't make your women friends in high school or college or the early years of your career, you're sure not going to make them now. At some point it takes too much effort to tell someone new your story."

The waiter brought our salads and we started to eat.

"I guess our meeting was just meant to be," Annie said as she buttered a bread stick. "Whatever—I couldn't be happier at the way everything has turned out."

We clinked our glasses together again, and then smiled in anticipation as the waiter arrived with our plates of pasta.

13

April in the Midwest can be unpredictable, Kim had told me when I called to say I was coming. It could be rainy and cold, or an early spring might just as easily produce blue skies, daffodils, and lilacs. On a few occasions it had snowed this late. On others they had record-breaking heatwaves. It was chilly in Dallas, so I zipped the lining into my trench coat and left it there during the flight just in case.

Our landing reminded me of the one so many years before, when I had been coming to Cynthia for comfort and the brilliant colors had been such a source of surprise. This time the greens were fresh and yellow, some trees scantily clad in buds and nothing more. Dogwood, bright pink redbud, and brilliant yellow forsythia bloomed everywhere.

The last time I had landed at this airport, Cynthia had greeted me, and seeing her, I had felt the healing I sought begin almost immediately, not anticipating the tense and unhappy days that lay ahead. This time a young woman with straight black hair pulled into a clip at the back of her neck held up a sign that said "Maggie Patterson." The interlude of peace and quiet that Annie and I had celebrated with our dinner and wine the night before was over and I was "on" again, as if someone had flipped a switch that set me to smiling, talking, and shaking people's hands, which I did now.

"We don't have much time," the woman said tersely, as if it were my fault that the plane was a half-hour late. "It's a good drive into the city, and the luncheon starts in half an hour. I hope you don't have much luggage."

She hustled on ahead of us toward the baggage claim, obviously hoping we would match her pace and catch up to her. I looked at Annie and winked.

"Ah, celebrity!" I said.

When I look back now and try to piece together the parts of the mad, horrible puzzle that made up that afternoon, I find it ironic that the talk I gave to the newspaper editors and publishers after our polite lunch of chicken salads and iced tea was on the subject of security. Not the kind of electronic metal-detector protection that might have saved us all from what was about to happen, but about choosing topics for columns and the ethical dilemma in bypassing a subject that might threaten a writer's safety or that of her family.

When the lunch was over, the car that had been promised in the fax was waiting outside. Annie and I climbed in and the driver loaded up our luggage, which we would unload again and pile at the back of the bookstore until we left to go home with Richard and Kim when the signing was over at five.

As we pulled up in front of the store, I remembered again the day Cynthia, Chloe, and I had sat outside eating ice cream. The area was filled with fountains built from Spanish tiles, and I couldn't remember which one we had sat by when she had quizzed me about my relationship with Richard. There was no ice cream store in sight.

A poster in the window displayed a copy of my book jacket and a picture of me. It advertised that the signing would begin at three, but already it was quarter after, and through the window I could see that a small crowd had gathered inside. Richard sat on a bench at the front of the store. They hadn't been able to find a sitter, it turned out, so Kim had stayed at home with Richie.

I left Annie to supervise the luggage, waved to Richard as I was hustled past him, and handed off my coat to an anxious-looking man wearing a brown cardigan sweater and half-glasses who could have been sent from central casting to play the part of a bookstore owner. He smiled nervously and steered me by my elbow to a table piled with books even while he was saying hello.

I signed books for the next hour almost without looking up. Most of the customers were women who told me something I had written touched them or they thought it came so close to their own opinion that they felt like they had written it themselves, comments for which I was grateful. They bought copies for their daughters and sisters, which I signed as personally as if the recipient had been the one who waited and stood through the line. At one point Annie brought me a cup of coffee and a saucer of biscotti from a counter the bookstore provided for its shoppers. I gulped the coffee, but later—much later—the biscotti still remained uneaten, evidence that just a few hours before, my life had been normal and today had been as ordinary as any other day. What strange things we remember.

The crowd thinned out and dwindled to nothing just after four.

"We're expecting a surge around four-thirty, when the shops and department stores in this area close," the man in the cardigan told me, less nervous and more talkative now. "Several people told me they planned to stop by when they got off work."

"In that case, would you mind if I took a short break?" I asked him. "I'd just like to get some air and maybe freshen up a bit—ten minutes maybe."

"Sure," he said hesitantly. "But what if someone comes in to buy the book while you're gone?"

Annie had overheard our conversation and came to my rescue, as usual. She had refilled her coffee cup and was talking to one of the people who had bought the book.

"I'll fill in," she said. "If anybody comes in, I'll pin them down so they can't leave before you get back."

"Thanks," I said, smiling gratefully. "I promise not to be long."

I used the restroom, put on some lipstick, and went out a side door. I didn't remember the area well enough to go very far, but that didn't matter. What I wanted was air and not to smile or talk or write my name for just a few minutes. I turned left and walked to the corner, where I turned left again. At the next corner I waited for a stoplight. Then I crossed the street and climbed up a knoll on the opposite side to sit on a bench outside what looked like an upscale apartment complex. I closed my eyes and breathed in the spring air. It reminded me of home, and I missed Peter and promised myself I'd call him as soon as I got to Richard's house. I glanced at my watch to see what time it would be right now in California.

More time had passed than I thought since I left the bookstore, so I walked briskly back, crossing the street on a light that was already green and turning the corner just in time to see a dark-haired woman in pants and a sweater open one of the glass doors and go inside.

"Cynthia!" I said aloud, and then immediately told myself not to be ridiculous. The bookstore hadn't had enough advance time to do much advertising, and even if they did, if Cynthia hadn't seen fit to come to her own daughter's wedding, she certainly wouldn't waste her time on a book signing, especially not one that honored me. It was just that she was entrenched forever in my subconscious, like an old lover you often think you see in a crowd but it turns out to be someone else every time.

I saw it all, from start to finish, and in the time since it happened I have played it back over and over in my mind as if it were my favorite memory instead of the one that each time brings with it overwhelming disbelief and terror, the recollection of an afternoon that changed and damaged my life and those of some of the people I loved best in the world forever, the genesis of nightmares that now will never go away. Over and over I try to figure out what I could have done to change the events that turned on the circumstances of a few moments in time. If I hadn't so desperately needed a break and wanted those few moments to myself, or if I had just gone to the bathroom and come right back out, how differently what happened that afternoon might have turned out.

Or if I had thought faster or moved more quickly when I saw the woman pull a pistol out of her handbag and fire. I had come in the door behind her. Why couldn't I have stopped her? Why didn't I have the presence of mind to knock her down or bat the gun out of her hand? Couldn't I have startled her or caught her attention to make her lose sight of her mission or fire in some random direction so that the bullet would have lodged in a bookshelf or a fat volume of Shakespeare's plays that would first become police evidence and then, much later, the prize possession of an eccentric collector who would tell his grandchildren the story of how the book had saved a person's life?

But none of those things happened. What did happen was that the woman called out my name in a high, shrill voice and then fired, hitting the person she thought was me. Instead it was Annie, who had been busy restocking the table with books for the arrival of the late crowd we had anticipated. I saw her as I came in the door, bent over a box that had been stashed under the table, about to come up with an armload of books. I saw the look on her face change from curiosity at hearing someone call out my name, to terror, to pain. I saw her head disintegrate as the bullet found its mark as surely as if her assailant had been practicing on a target constructed to resemble her body in exactly that position every day for the past several years.

It all happened as if in slow motion. Annie rising up with the books, the owner ducking behind the counter, a few customers taking cover behind bookshelves. One ran by me, screaming, and out the door. By now there was no question in my mind.

"Cynthia!" I screamed.

She whirled in my direction, her face a mask of horror as she realized her mistake and now fixed on me as her target.

"You've got it all, haven't you, but not anymore!"

Then she raised the gun, pointed it at me, and fired.

The bullet whizzed past me so close that I could hear its buzzing sound and feel the breeze it made before it bored a small, neat hole in the glass door and came to rest, we learned later, in the driver-side door of an empty car parked against the curb outside. After the second failure she gave up on me, pointing the gun instead at her own temple and preparing to shoot. But a customer who had been hiding behind one of the shelves had the presence of mind to throw a book that hit her arm hard enough that the gun clattered to the floor. She glared at him like a petulant child and then she began to sob, her shoulders shaking, her whole body seeming to shrink before my eyes.

"It wasn't enough that you had a husband and children and a career and a book published, was it?" she said through clenched teeth. The owner had recovered enough to come out from behind the counter and pick up the gun in case Cynthia should change her mind. "No, you had to have my family, too, didn't you? You were at the wedding where I should have been, and now Chloe's literally a member of your family. But even that wasn't enough. You weren't happy until you had Lorraine, too. And yes, I saw the video you tried to hide from me. I saw you kissing my husband. I knew what was going on between the two of you from the time you went running together. Or said you were running. God only knows where you slipped off to and what you did. You wanted everything I had. Well, you got it all, but you can't have my grandchild. When Chloe has that baby, it's mine."

She was almost screaming at me now, and tears ran down her face. Fluid from her nose dripped untended onto her lips and down her chin.

At that point real time started again. Two policemen, who had been flagged down by the shopper who fled, charged into the store with their weapons drawn, admonishing everyone to stay where they were and not to leave until they could be questioned. They handcuffed Cynthia and called for a backup unit that eventually took her away. An ambulance arrived wailing its siren and left in silence, its tragic cargo beyond the hope that a quick trip to an emergency room and a team of trained neurosurgeons might have offered. The second car arrived, and as the officer led Cynthia out the door she came face to face with Richard.

"Blame him," she cried out. "It's his fault. I should have shot him, too."

৵৲

None of us slept that night. It was hours before we were free to leave the bookstore. Everyone present had to be questioned, especially Richard and me, and it took a while to tell our long, complicated story. Then we drove together to their house, both of us too dazed to even remember how we got there. Richard had called to tell Kim what had happened, but he hadn't had time to give her all the details. The moment we stepped inside the house I could tell that she had gone to special pains to make the evening a special one. Candles on the dining room table that had blazed earlier had been extinguished, but carefully arranged fresh flowers were everywhere. Richie lost interest in the toy fire engine he had been playing with in his pajamas and ran across the room in smiles, his arms reaching up for his daddy. At last I burst into tears.

"Tell me everything," Kim said. "What exactly happened? And how?"

Richard took his wife into his arms and began to sob, too.

"Oh, Jesus, honey," he said.

Neither of us could speak enough to get the story out, so for a while we just stood there, Richard and me crying, Richie looking at his mother in question, Kim still largely in the dark.

"You already know most of it," he told her finally. "Annie's dead, and it was Cynthia who shot her."

"How did Cynthia even know Annie? And why would she want to kill her?"

"She thought it was me," I said flatly.

"Oh my God! But I still don't understand," Kim said. "Did Annie look like you? None of this makes sense."

"Annie didn't look anything like me," I said, digging a tissue out of my handbag and blowing my nose. "But she was in the wrong place at the wrong time, where Cynthia thought I would be. The police said she was so obsessed with the idea that I would be sitting at that table that she just thought it was me. They said there was no doubt she had rehearsed the thing over and over in her mind, and her scheme didn't allow for any variables. She was an amateur. She planned to just walk in and shoot, and that's what she did."

I looked now at the dining table set for four people—a place ready for Annie to eat, Annie's luggage at this moment in the trunk of Richard's car, a guest room down the hall freshened in anticipation of her arrival. In San Francisco, Jonathan, who by now would have gotten the call from the police, had no doubt been looking forward to his wife's homecoming, maybe buying flowers or gassing up the car for the drive to the airport the next day. Her mother would be wrapping up a pleasurable week with her grandson and might have been secretly wishing her daughter would stay away for a little longer. Little Bryan, the light of Annie's life, would grow up without her, would never remember her at all. Jonathan would remarry, and the family would decide it would be the best thing all the way around if the child called this new wife "Mom."

Once again everything seemed to be moving in slow motion. Eventually Kim hustled Richie off to bed. We put some of the mushroom risotto she had made onto our plates, its creamy perfection long since turned to paste, poured wine, and clung together on the living room sofa like refugees. We ate little, preferring instead the anesthetizing effects of the alcohol.

"I can give you a sedative tonight if you want," Richard told me, but I shook my head.

"Thanks a lot, but I want to face this head-on. I don't want to wake up in a muddle and remember that something is wrong but I can't figure out what."

"I've got to call the girls," Richard said.

"Be very careful with Chloe," I reminded him, smiling sadly. "We have our grandchild to consider."

"I hope they haven't already seen this story on television."

"I want to call Peter, too," I said. "And then I have to call Jonathan."

Ultimately we sat up dozing all night, none of us willing to be away from the others.

⁂

Peter arrived on an early flight the next morning and picked up a rental car. The police had called several times the night before with more questions, and we were too exhausted to drive out to the airport. Besides, Richard and Kim's house was by that time surrounded by reporters and photographers carrying cameras and notebooks and microphones. I couldn't blame them—they were just doing their jobs. Years ago I might have been doing the same thing, but I couldn't stand to talk to them, either, and the police had already held a briefing and told them all there was to know.

"What about your movie?" I had asked Peter the night before when I called.

"The movie be damned," he said. "They can shoot without me or wait until I get back. Right now I don't really care. I just want to be where you are. I knew something like this was going to happen someday. It could have been you, Maggie. That's all I keep think-

276

ing. It could have been you. It was supposed to be you."

When he arrived, we were all still on the sofa, dressed exactly as we had been the night before. Like Jacqueline Kennedy in her pink suit, the last thing on any of our minds had been changing clothes. I had been watching for his car out the window. When I saw him turn into the driveway I ran to the door with Richard right behind me.

"How are the kids?" we asked Peter in unison.

"They're all at our house," he said. "Chloe and Jack will stay there until we can get back. Naturally Chloe and Lorraine are upset, but they have each other, and Chloe knows her first priority has to be the baby."

"When you go back, I'm going with you for a few days," Richard said, and Kim nodded her head vigorously.

"The girls need you now," she said. "I'll handle your patients and try to keep Richie out of the spotlight as much as possible."

For a few hours we all tried to rest, although sleep was still out of the question. Peter and I lay naked under the sheets in the upstairs guest room. Sex was out of the question, too, but we needed to be as close together as we could get. Finally I was able to speak the words that had been on my mind since the moment it all happened.

"Annie's death is my fault," I whispered.

"Don't do this to yourself, Maggie," he said. "Cynthia is crazy. We've known that for a long time, and this finally proves it once and for all. I hoped it wouldn't come to this, but I've never believed she was playing with a full deck."

"It was supposed to be me. All I can think of is Annie's face. It's like I saw the moment when she realized she was dying. I saw her future disappear behind her eyes. She had just told me the night before how happy she was. And now, thanks to me, it's all over."

"Our perspectives are a little different on this one," he said, pulling me still closer to him. "You feel guilty because it wasn't you, but all I can think of is that it might have been you. I might have been flying out here to claim a body instead of coming to be with my wife."

"But that's the point. Jonathan *is* flying out here to claim a body. I called him last night, and he seemed pretty much in shock. He may not even remember the call, but he'll remember that if it hadn't been for me, his wife would still be alive."

Kim tapped on the door.

"Maggie? Your publicist is on the phone. It's on TV in New York, and she says she has to know what to do about the rest of the tour."

"What tact," Peter said. "Really? Do they expect you to actually show up in Chicago and sign books after what's happened?"

I climbed out of bed and wrapped a robe around me.

"I've got to talk to her. They've been really wonderful, but the tour is over."

I talked to the publicist, and together we composed a message to be sent to the people who had planned to host me for the rest of the trip. She wanted to say "postponed," but I insisted on "canceled." Five children in California needed me right now, and my immediate job would be not to let the joy of my grandchild's new life be overshadowed by the evil of one that had gone so tragically wrong. Cynthia had destroyed every life she touched. Despite her threats in the bookstore, I swore to myself that today her damage came to an end. If I had my way, she'd never lay a hand on the baby we all so eagerly awaited.

The police came by with more questions and told us they would call us if they had any further questions. After they left we went downtown to wait for Jonathan's arrival at the city morgue to identify his wife's body and arrange for the sad trip back home. He was dazed, stunned; and facing him was the hardest thing I have ever had to do in my life.

"I know you were her friend, Maggie," he said robotically. "I know it wasn't your fault."

After that we gave the police our number in California and they offered to drive us to the airport when we were ready to leave, but Kim wanted to go, to be with us for as long as she could.

We had booked three seats together on an evening flight. By midnight we would be home.

Epilogue

Cynthia's trial date kept being postponed into the following year, but then it was over in just two weeks. Of course the jury found her guilty. Besides me, the owner of the bookstore, another clerk, and five patrons all testified that they had seen Cynthia murder Annie in cold blood, at first believing that she had killed me, and then that she had turned to me and fired again. Based on her record of mental illness and a thorough examination by a court-appointed psychiatrist, her recent hospitalization, and the testimony of "Dr." Simon Flek, however, the verdict was amended to read "by reason of insanity." A month later the judge sentenced her to thirty years in prison with whatever portion of that time deemed necessary by prison psychiatrists to be spent in a high-security mental facility. Her court-appointed attorney released a statement to the press in which he said doctors had full confidence that his client could be rehabilitated.

Originally Cynthia had called a high-priced criminal attorney from her country club days who then called Richard to say he understood that he would be responsible for the fee.

"You've got to be kidding," Richard said. "She's not my wife." Then he hung up the phone without saying goodbye.

It turned out the gun everyone had been trying to find for so many years had been hidden beneath the spare tire in the trunk of Cynthia's Mercedes all along, which explained why it never turned up when Richard and then Caroline searched every possible hiding place in the house. Apparently she had hidden it there at the very beginning, when she had hatched her scheme to murder Richard and Kim. It was only when I became the object of her hatred and revenge that she must have taken it out, loaded it, and headed for where she knew I would be.

The bookstore owner testified that for years he had taken posters of upcoming events to the women's shelter where Cynthia was still the receptionist, which explained how she had known I would be in town. He remembered that he had handed the one about my reading to her and asked her to hang it in the community room.

"We like to do everything we can for those women," he said. "We give them a discount on the books. We want to let them know somebody cares."

John Morgan suffered a mild stroke when he heard the news about what his only child had done, but by the time of the trial he was recovered enough to fly to Kansas City and attend. I saw him the day I was there, and during the lunch recess we had a few minutes outside in the corridor to talk. He looked older than his years and ashen. He walked with a cane and his speech was slightly slurred. He leaned heavily on Caroline, who, unsmiling, never left his side except to give me a hug.

"That damn gun," she said, as she held me close to her.

Months earlier Chloe had given birth to an eight-pound baby

girl named Rachel Anne—a nice blend of Catholic and Jewish, she and Jack explained, and a tribute to the woman who had died so needlessly and in my place.

Richard testified about his marriage and Cynthia's gradual disintegration to the point where he felt he had to leave to save his own sanity. I talked about how Cynthia and I had been such close friends until her anger and jealousy had driven us apart forever. We both brought letters she had sent to us, and Richard produced return receipts for the baby furniture, flowers, and food that over the years had appeared unsolicited at his door. He had saved them in case he ever needed them at an occasion like this one, but he never really believed he'd have to use them. They were introduced as evidence, exhibits A and B and on and on. It was excruciating to hear all of the testimony against someone we had once both loved, and when it was my turn I could feel her cold eyes going right through me on the stand.

Still, while the jury didn't have much choice but to find her guilty in some way, I could tell from the looks on their faces that some of them thought she was a woman wronged, that Richard was a tyrannical husband and I a faithless friend, that maybe we brought it on ourselves and if we had kept up our part of the bargain, this wouldn't have happened at all.

I ended up wearing one of my best suits—tan with a salmon-colored blouse—for the one day I was in the courtroom. I needed all the courage I could muster, and I thought by that time I had been through so much and matured enough that I wouldn't let the taint of such an occasion spoil the outfit for me. I was wrong, of course, but eventually it fit Mae perfectly and she didn't have the bad feelings about it that I now had. She wore it for her first job interview—and she got the job. Cynthia wore a charcoal pinstripe pantsuit, which I thought was an odd choice since it made her look a little like a member of the mob.

I sat on an aisle, where I could easily get up and out when I was called to the stand, and when the court recessed for the day I was still sitting there, gathering up my jacket and handbag, when the officers led her out. Peter and Richard sat beside me, but they were talking to each other, turned the other direction. No cameras were allowed inside, either, and so no one, not my husband or my friend or the others milling around in the courtroom, saw her turn to me as she passed and mouth the words "I'll get you yet."

For the benefit of the people who now mattered, Cynthia had already begun the good-girl act, had started to play the victim. For the next few years she would attend counseling and study at the prison library, virtually guaranteeing her release before her sentence was completed.

The sales of my book skyrocketed after the murder made national news. Previously it had been selling in a nice, steady trickle, mostly to women who had read my column in their local newspapers. Now bookstores couldn't keep it in stock. The publisher called for a second printing, and my agent sold both foreign and paperback rights. I got a hefty advance to write another book, despite my pledge never to write a word about Cynthia or Annie, never to talk about either of them or describe what had happened that day in the bookstore. I've kept that promise until now, but I spend a lot of time alone, and I had to tell my side of this story to somebody.

Our house in Los Angeles, Jonathan's in San Francisco, and Richard and Kim's in Kansas City, even Chloe and Jack's apartment building, were besieged by tabloid reporters. They climbed trees to see into windows and tried to bribe my children's friends with hundred-dollar bills to bring them a letter, a photograph, a quote—anything they could print that concerned me or Cynthia or one of Cynthia's children. No one complied, and eventually they gave up, although one day in the supermarket I saw my face on a cover under a tabloid headline that read "Author's Girlfriend Slain in Lesbian Love Triangle."

Before she was convicted, Cynthia sold the rights to her story to a television network, with the understanding that the profits would go to the women's shelter and not to her daughters. Simon Flek also got in on the action, and client confidentiality be damned. He said he knew Cynthia better than anyone, and the network offered him six figures to be their technical consultant on the project should it ever come to fruition. So far, thankfully, no such film has been made. In the courtroom he said that Cynthia had simply been through more than one woman should have to bear.

Cynthia served eighteen of the thirty years to which she had been sentenced, and during that time, true to our promises to one another, the rest of us put our lives with her behind us and moved on. Jack eventually became full partner at his law firm, and after Chloe finished graduate school the studio hired her full-time as an editor. I am so proud of her. Sometimes I go to the movies she has worked on just to watch her name roll by in the credits. They had two more children—a boy, Ryan, and a girl, Delaney. After college Rachel Anne announced that she was going to join the Peace Corps. She spent two years in Paraguay and liked it so much that she signed up for two more, and that's where she is now. Ryan is in college, majoring in computer science. The bipolar disorder that took Cynthia's mother's life and wrecked her own skipped her daughters and then landed squarely on Delaney, but she is a fighter. Once she was diagnosed she began the medication that has enabled her to function successfully. Knowing what happened to her grandmother and her great-grandmother, she is determined that the same things won't happen to her. On the occasions when the dark side threatens to overwhelm her, she heads to my house and walks or sits on the beach for hours. She says the roar of the waves drowns out the noise in her head. She's a senior in high school now.

Lorraine was, indeed, cut out to be a businesswoman. She got an MBA and soon landed a banking job in San Francisco. We had been on the verge of selling our house there, so we were delighted to keep it and have her live in it full time. She had dated very little in high school and college and preferred to go out with groups of friends rather than with one special person. Peter and I worried that maybe Cynthia's toxicity toward men really had scared her away from relationships, but that turned out not to be the case at all. Two years after she moved north she asked if she could bring someone special for our family Thanksgiving. She arrived with Clemmie, an artist who had emigrated from Zimbabwe. They had met when Clemmie came to the bank to hang some of her paintings in the lobby. She wore a bright yellow and orange traditional dress and head wrap to honor our celebration and turned out to have a big heart and a sense of humor that kept us laughing that whole weekend. She soon moved into the house with Lorraine, and when same-sex marriage became legal, we had yet another family wedding.

Richard and Kim bought a condo at Marina del Rey so they could come out more often and spend more time with the girls and their families. Richie followed his parents into medicine, and when he had finished his residency joined them in their practice. He married a violinist with the Kansas City Symphony who also teaches at the University of Missouri campus there.

Another promise we all kept to each other was to maintain the tradition of combining our two families every Thanksgiving. Our group has grown considerably since that first one, and it's hard now to tell where the Bartoluccis end and the Goldbergs begin. We're not all there every year, but we do the best we can.

My Mae became a corporate event planner, a choice she says dates back to her helping to plan Chloe's wedding. She hasn't married, but she has lived with Roger, who works in online marketing, for more than ten years, and we count him as one of our own. Todd sells real estate and is married to Daniela, a woman he met in Mexico while he was on a romantic weekend with another girl-friend—not exactly a meet cute, but it seems to have turned out the way it was supposed to. Now Daniela works with him as his office manager, and their two boys, Frankie and Javier, are in high school.

I saw Jonathan once when I walked into a restaurant in San Francisco to meet a friend. He was sitting in a booth with a woman I guessed to be his wife. Bryan was there, too, now sporting corn-rows and wearing a purple and gold San Francisco State sweatshirt, along with two much younger girls who had blonde hair like their mother. The woman was messing with Bryan's hair and he was laughing and batting her hand away. This, then, was "Mom."

Jonathan didn't notice me, and once I registered what I was seeing I turned immediately around and fled before he could. Seeing me could only have brought him pain, and I don't think I could have held it together to even say hello.

I lost Peter when he was sixty-three. We had gone to Lake Tahoe for a rare skiing weekend alone. He was a much better skier than I was, but he was usually content to stay with me on the blue intermediate runs. When I told him I was finished for the day, he said he was going to do a couple of black-diamond mogul trails before he stopped. I went to the bar in the lodge and bought a cup of mulled wine. When I saw the ski patrol coming slowly down the mountain with their precious bundle wrapped in the sled behind them, I thought what a shame that someone had been injured on the very last run of the day.

"It was probably a heart attack," the coroner told me later. "We see that all the time up here." Like that made it acceptable that the husband I had adored for so long was suddenly and with no warning just . . . gone.

My children constantly urge me to sell the beach house and move to a smaller place that would be easier to manage, and Richard and Kim call me every time a unit at their condo complex goes on the market. Todd is forever emailing me listings that he thinks would be perfect for me.

"Mom!" he says in exasperation, "why do you want to rattle around all alone out there in that great big house?"

But these walls hold too many memories for me to leave, and like Delaney, I take solace on the beach where Peter and I used to take our walks and watch the sunset. When everyone is together this is still where we have our celebrations.

People ask me if I think I'll marry again. What a stupid, insensitive question, even though I know they mean well. No one can possibly know the answer to that question. I don't ever say "never," but at this point I can't imagine anyone taking Peter's place. He was an extraordinary man, and we had an extraordinary marriage. It would be hard not to measure everyone I met against him. Someone else asked me if I thought I would get a dog, like that would mitigate my loss and make everything right again. People don't know what to say—I understand that—but sometimes I wish they would just pat my arm and stay quiet.

I gave up the column not long after Cynthia's conviction. I

couldn't stand the idea of people reading what I had to say just because my picture had been in the paper so often that I had become some kind of freak, like the bearded woman at the circus used to be. I guess you could say Cynthia took that away from me, too, but the fact is that I had always wanted to write fiction, and now that I had a publisher, it seemed like the right time to give it a try. I've written three novels so far—all published under a pseudonym. I don't want people to read them just because they're curious, either.

The day Cynthia was released—about a month ago now—I saw her on a news program getting into a car with Flek outside of the prison. I wouldn't have recognized her if her name hadn't been splayed across my television screen. She had aged dramatically, and the once-luxurious mane of dark hair was mostly gray and badly cut. She was thin and gaunt, and she wore a pair of blue jeans, a white T-shirt, and black tennis shoes. Her face had hardened, and when a reporter put a microphone in front of her and asked what her plans were, she glared at him, shook her head, and pushed it away. Flek, however, was obviously happy for the opportunity to be in front of the cameras once again. I had not been in the courtroom when he testified, so I had never seen him before. He was tall and thin and bearded—very good-looking actually. It was easy to see how he had lured in all of the people he had harmed.

"My patient has been fully rehabilitated," he said. "At last she will be able to put all of this behind her and start over again. Maybe now she will finally be able to live the life she truly deserves."

Book Club Questions

1. As the novel opens and Maggie is deciding what to wear to Cynthia's trial, she observes that we always remember what we were wearing at significant moments in our lives. Does your experience support that idea? Can you recall what you were wearing at momentous times in your life? Do you think in this situation it made any difference?

2. Even though they have completely different backgrounds and personalities, Cynthia and Maggie quickly become fast friends when they are roommates in college. How do you account for this? Have you ever made such a friend in this way?

3. Maggie's friendship with Annie is different from her relationship with Cynthia. Why do you think this is the case? What did Maggie get from Annie that she couldn't get from Cynthia? How do these two friendships illuminate different parts of Maggie's character?

4. Cynthia clearly has a mental disorder that she refuses to have professionally diagnosed and treated. Would she have been a different person if her mother had not taken her own life? What role could her father have played in her development? What aspects of Cynthia's upbringing seem to have the most impact on her later in life?

5. Maggie remains Cynthia's friend long after Cynthia has begun to treat her badly. How do you account for her tenacity? Does Maggie's background play a role in the way she behaves? Is she co-dependent or in any other way complicit in the toxicity of the relationship? When would you have given up on Cynthia?

6. Why does Richard stay with Cynthia as long as he does? Do you think he was right to leave? Was there anything more he could have done to convince her to get professional help and save the marriage?

7. The story spans a period of time in which many technological advancements were made. Could any of those that were developed after Cynthia went to prison—cell phones, the Internet, Facebook, Instagram, Twitter, GPS, Life360 and the like—have changed the outcome of this novel?

8. Did you figure out who Cynthia's victim would be before the scene at the bookstore? If not, did you have someone else in mind? How did you arrive at your conclusion?

9. When Cynthia fired the gun, she called out that the expected grandchild would be hers, and at her trial, she mouthed to Maggie that she wasn't finished punishing her for "stealing" her family. Now that she has been released from prison, is Maggie safe? Are other members of her family? Do you think Cynthia has been rehabilitated?

10. Does anyone in your life suffer from a mental issue that threatens to ruin their own lives and the lives of those around them? If so, what might you do to help?

Acknowledgments

This book owes its existence to several people who turned up in my life exactly when I needed them to. After I had been away from the San Diego Writing Women for more than a decade, Sharon Whitley Larsen invited me back for Zoom meetings during the pandemic. At one of those gatherings of some of the most helpful, encouraging women on the planet, Georgeanne Irvine suggested that I contact Mascot Books. That led me to Lauren Magnussen, the production editor/fairy godmother who has shepherded the project from Day One to its finish, waving her magic wand when necessary to make what I wanted to say more elegant. She introduced me to Dayna Jackson, a rare editor who knows numbers as well as words and saved me from myself many times over. Luisa Fuentes listened to my ideas and combined them with her artistic talent to design a cover that is truly the face of the story I had to tell. To my delight, Jess Cohn at Mascot selected my book for the launch of the Subplot imprint. I don't know the names of many of the people who worked to bring this novel into print, but I am no less thankful for their efforts.

I appreciate all of the people who have told me stories and taught me the many ways untreated mental illness can present itself and ruin lives. They know who they are. Also, Lesley Frederikson, my talented and indispensible personal editor who makes everything I write better, and Carmen Zermeño, trusted first reader, who challenges me with questions that keep me accurate and honest. My husband, Phil Allen, makes our home such a joyful, peaceful, and fun place to be that creativity is inevitable.

For the gift of having all of these people in my life I am beyond grateful.

About the Author

Photo by Phil Allen

Glenda Winders is an award-winning fiction writer, editor, and journalist, whose work has appeared in major magazines and newspapers nationwide. Her first novel, *The Nine Assignments*, was published in 2016. She lives with her husband in Columbus, Indiana.